A CRIME IN HOLLAND &
THE GRAND BANKS CAFÉ

When a French professor visiting the Dutch town of Delfzijl is accused of murder, Detective Chief Inspector Maigret is sent to investigate. The community seem happy to blame an unknown outsider, but there are culprits closer to home, including the dissatisfied daughter of a local farmer, the sister-in-law of the deceased, and a notorious crook. And in *The Grand Banks Café*, Maigret investigates the murder of a captain soon after his ship returns from three months of fishing off the Newfoundland coast. The ship's wireless operator has been arrested for the murder — but the sailors all blame the Evil Eye. . .

GEORGES SIMENON

♦

A CRIME IN HOLLAND
&
THE GRAND BANKS CAFÉ

Complete and Unabridged

ULVERSCROFT
Leicester

A Crime in Holland first published in French as *Un Crime en Hollande* by Fayard in 1931

This translation first published in Great Britain in 2014

The Grand Banks Café first published in French as *Au Rendez-Vous des Terre-Neuvas* by Fayard in 1931

This translation first published in Great Britain in 2014

This Ulverscroft Edition published 2019
by arrangement with
Penguin Random House UK
London

A catalogue record for this book is available from the British Library.

ISBN 978–1–4448–4334–7

Published by
F. A. Thorpe (Publishing)
Anstey, Leicestershire

Set by Words & Graphics Ltd.
Anstey, Leicestershire
Printed and bound in Great Britain by
T. J. International Ltd., Padstow, Cornwall

This book is printed on acid-free paper

Contents

A Crime in Holland

Translated by SIÂN REYNOLDS

1

The Girl with the Cow

When Detective Chief Inspector Maigret arrived in Delfzijl, one afternoon in May, he had only the sketchiest notions about the case taking him to this small town located in the northernmost corner of Holland.

A certain Jean Duclos, professor at the University of Nancy in eastern France, was on a lecture tour of the northern countries. At Delfzijl, he was the guest of a teacher at the Naval College, Conrad Popinga. But Popinga had been murdered, and while no one was formally charging the French professor, he was being requested not to leave the town and to remain answerable to the Dutch authorities.

And that was all, or almost. Jean Duclos had contacted the University of Nancy, which had asked Police Headquarters in Paris to send someone to Delfzijl to investigate.

The task had fallen to Maigret. It was more unofficial than official, and he had made it less official still by omitting to alert his Dutch colleagues on his arrival.

On the initiative of Jean Duclos, he had received a rather confused report, followed by a list of people more or less closely involved in the case.

This was the list which he consulted, shortly

before arriving at Delfzijl station:

Conrad Popinga (the victim), aged 42, former long-haul captain, latterly a lecturer at the Delfzijl Naval College. Married. No children. Had spoken English and German fluently and French quite well.

Liesbeth Popinga, his wife, daughter of a high school headmaster in Amsterdam. A very cultured woman. Excellent knowledge of French.

Any Van Elst, Liesbeth Popinga's younger sister, visiting Delfzijl for a few weeks. Recently completed her doctorate in law. Aged 25. Understands French a little but speaks it badly.

The Wienands family: they live in the villa next door to the Popingas. Carl Wienands teaches mathematics at the Naval College. Wife and two children. No knowledge of French.

Beetje Liewens, aged 18, daughter of a farmer specializing in breeding pedigree cattle for export. Has stayed twice in Paris. Speaks perfect French.

Not very eloquent. Names that suggested nothing, at least to Maigret as he arrived from Paris, after spending a night and a half the following day on the train.

Delfzijl disconcerted him as soon as he reached it. At first light, he had travelled through the traditional Holland of tulips, and then through Amsterdam, which he already knew. The

4

Drenthe, a heath-covered wasteland crisscrossed with canals, its horizons, stretching thirty kilometres into the distance, had surprised him.

Here was a landscape that had little in common with picture-postcard Holland, and was a hundred times more Nordic in character than he had imagined.

Just a little town: ten to fifteen streets at most, paved with handsome red bricks, laid down as regularly as tiles on a kitchen floor. Low-rise houses, also built of brick, and copiously decorated with woodwork, in bright cheerful colours.

It looked like a toy town. All the more so since around this toy town ran a dyke, encircling it completely. Some of the stretches of water within the dyke could be closed off when the sea ran high, by means of heavy gates like those of a lock.

Beyond lay the mouth of the Ems. The North Sea. A long strip of silver water. Cargo vessels unloading under the cranes on a quayside. Canals and an infinity of sailing vessels the size of barges and just as heavy, but built to withstand ocean swells.

The sun was shining. The station master wore a smart orange cap, with which he unaffectedly greeted the unknown traveller.

Opposite the station, a café. Maigret went inside and hardly dared sit down. Not only was it as highly polished as a bourgeois dining room, it had the same intimate feeling.

A single table, with all the daily papers set out on brass rods. The proprietor, who was drinking beer with two customers, stood up to welcome the newcomer.

'Do you speak French?' Maigret asked.

A negative gesture. Slight embarrassment.

'Can you give me a beer . . . *bier?*'

Once he was seated, he took the slip of paper from his pocket. The last name on the list was the one that his eyes lighted on. He showed it, pronouncing the name two or three times.

'Liewens.'

The three men began conferring together. Then one of them, a big fellow wearing a sailor's cap, got up and beckoned to Maigret to follow him. Since the inspector had no Dutch currency yet, and offered to pay with a hundred-franc note, he was told repeatedly:

'*Morgen! Morgen!*'

Tomorrow would do! He could just come back.

It was homely. There was something very simple, naive even, about it. Without a word, his guide led Maigret through the streets of the little town. On their left was a shed full of ancient anchors, rigging, chains, buoys and compasses, spilling out on to the pavement. Further along, a sail-maker was working in his doorway.

And the window of the confectioner's shop displayed a bewildering choice of chocolates and elaborate sweetmeats.

'No speak English?'

Maigret shook his head.

'*Deutsch?*'

Same reply, and the man resigned himself to silence. At the end of one street, they were already in the countryside: green fields, a canal in which floating logs from Scandinavia took up almost the whole width, ready to be hauled through Holland.

At some distance appeared a large roof of varnished tiles.

'Liewens . . . *Dag, mijnheer!*'

And Maigret went on, alone, after vainly trying to thank this man who, without knowing him from Adam, had walked with him for a quarter of an hour to do him a favour.

The sky was clear, the air of astonishing limpidity. The inspector walked past a timber yard where planks of oak, mahogany and teak were stacked in piles as tall as houses.

A boat was moored alongside. Some children were playing. Then came a kilometre with no outstanding features. Floating tree trunks covered the surface of the canal, all the way. White fences surrounded fields dotted with magnificent cows.

Another clash between reality and his preconceived ideas. The word 'farm' for Maigret conjured up a thatched roof, a dunghill, a bustle of barnyard fowls.

And he found himself facing a fine newly built structure, surrounded by a garden full of flowers. Moored in the canal in front of the house was an elegant mahogany skiff. And propped against the gate, a lady's bicycle, gleaming with nickel.

He looked in vain for a bell. He called, without getting any reply. A dog came and rubbed against his legs.

To the left of the house ran a long low building

with regularly spaced windows but no curtains, which could have been an ordinary shed but for the quality of the materials and especially its bright fresh paintwork.

A sound of lowing came from that direction, and Maigret went on, round the flowerbeds, to find himself in front of a wide open door.

The building was a cowshed, but a cowshed as immaculate as a dwelling. Red brick everywhere, giving a warm, almost sumptuous luminosity to the atmosphere. Runnels for water to run off. A mechanical system for distributing feed to the mangers, and a pulley behind each stall, whose purpose Maigret discovered only later: to lift up the tails of the cows during milking so that the milk wouldn't be contaminated.

The interior was in semi-darkness. The cattle were all outside, except for one cow lying on its side in the first stall.

And a girl in her late teens was approaching the visitor, speaking to him at first in Dutch.

'Mademoiselle Liewens?'

'Yes. You're French?'

As she spoke, she kept her eyes on the cow. She had an ironic smile which Maigret did not at first understand.

Here again, his preconceived ideas were turning out to be wrong. Beetje Liewens was wearing black rubber boots, which gave her the look of a stable-girl. Her green silk dress was almost entirely covered up by a white overall.

A rosy face, too rosy perhaps. A healthy, happy smile, but one lacking any subtlety. Large china-blue eyes. Red-gold hair.

She had to search to find her first words in French, which she spoke with a strong accent. But she quickly reacquainted herself with the language.

'Did you want to speak to my father?'

'To you.'

She almost pouted.

'Excuse me, please. My father has gone to Groningen. He won't be back until later. The two farmhands are on the canal, unloading coal. The maidservant is out shopping. And this cow has picked this moment to start calving! We weren't expecting it. And I'm all on my own.'

She was leaning against a winch, which she had prepared in case the birth needed assistance. She was smiling broadly.

It was sunny outside. Her boots shone as if polished. She had plump pink hands with well-kept nails.

'It's about Conrad Popinga that I . . . '

But she gave a start. The cow had tried to stand up with a painful movement and had fallen back again.

'Look out! Can you give me a hand?'

She picked up the rubber gloves lying ready for duty.

★   ★   ★

And that was how Maigret began his investigation by helping bring a pure-bred Friesian calf into the world, in the company of a girl whose confident movements revealed her physical training.

9

Half an hour later, with the newborn calf already nuzzling its mother's udder, Maigret was stooping alongside Beetje, soaping his hands up to the elbow under a brass tap.

'Is it the first time you've done anything like this?' she asked with a smile.

'Yes, the first time . . . '

She was eighteen years old. When she took off her white overall, the silk dress moulded her generous curves, which, perhaps because of the sunny day, looked extremely fetching.

'We can talk over a cup of tea. Come into the house.'

The maidservant was back. The parlour was austere and rather dark, but spoke of refined comfort. The small panes in the windows were of a scarcely perceptible rose tint, which Maigret had never before encountered.

Shelves full of books. Many works on cattle breeding and veterinary science. On the walls hung farming diplomas and gold medals won at international exhibitions.

In the middle of all that, the latest publications by Claudel, André Gide and Paul Valéry . . .

Beetje's smile was flirtatious.

'Would you like to see my room?'

She was watching for his reaction. No bed, but a divan covered with a blue velvet spread. Walls papered with Jouy prints. Some dark-stained book shelves with more books and a doll bought in Paris, clad in a frou-frou dress.

One might almost have called it a boudoir, and yet there was a rather solid, serious and down-to-earth feel about it.

'Like a room in Paris, don't you think?'

'I'd like you to tell me what happened last week.'

Beetje's face clouded, but not over much, not enough to suggest that she was taking the events too tragically.

Otherwise, would she have given him that beaming smile of pride as she showed him her room?

'Let's go and have our tea.'

And they sat down facing each other, in front of a teapot covered with a sort of crinoline tea cosy to keep it warm.

Beetje had to search for the right words. She did more than that. She fetched a French dictionary, and sometimes broke off for quite a long time to find the exact word.

A boat with a large grey sail was gliding along the canal, propelled by a pole for want of wind. It manoeuvred its way through the tree trunks in mid-stream.

'You haven't been to the Popingas' house yet?'

'I arrived an hour ago, and all I've had time to do is help you to deliver the calf.'

'Yes . . . Conrad was so nice, a really lovely man . . . He went all over the world as second lieutenant and then first . . . Is that what you say in French? Then once he had his master's certificate, he got married, and because of his wife he took a job at the Naval College. That wasn't so exciting. He used to have a little sailing boat too. But Madame Popinga is afraid of the water. He had to sell it. He just had a rowing boat on the canal after that. You saw mine? Well, almost the same kind! In the evenings, he tutored pupils. He worked very hard.'

'What was he like?'

At first she didn't understand the question. She ended up going to fetch a photograph of a strapping, youngish man, with cropped hair, rosy cheeks and light-coloured eyes, who seemed to radiate bonhomie and good health.

'That's Conrad. You wouldn't think he was forty, would you? His wife is older . . . About forty-five. You haven't seen her? And very different . . . For instance, here everyone's Protestant of course . . . I go to the Dutch Reformed Church, which has more modern views. But Liesbeth Popinga goes to the Reformed Church of the Netherlands, which is stricter . . . more, what's the word? Conserving?'

'Conservative.'

'Yes. And she is the chairwoman of all the local charities . . . '

'You don't like her?'

'Oh yes . . . but it's not the same. She's the daughter of a headmaster, you must understand. My father's just a farmer . . . But she's very nice, kind . . . '

'What happened?'

'There are lots of lectures here . . . It's just a small town, population five thousand. But people like to keep up with ideas. And last Thursday, Professor Duclos was here, from Nancy. You've heard of him?'

She was amazed that Maigret didn't know of the professor, whom she had assumed to be a national celebrity in France.

12

'He's a top lawyer. A specialist on crime, and what's the right word? Psychology of crime? He was giving this talk on the responsibility of criminals. That's right, is it? You must correct me if I make mistakes. Madame Popinga chairs the committee and the lecturers always stay at her house.

'At ten p.m. there was a small private party. Professor Duclos, Conrad Popinga and his wife. Wienands and his wife and children. And me . . . It was at the Popingas'. About a kilometre from here, it's on the Amsterdiep like this house. The Amsterdiep is the canal you can see. We had a glass of wine and some cakes. Conrad switched on the wireless. Oh yes, I nearly forgot, Any was there, Madame Popinga's sister, she's a lawyer too . . . Conrad wanted people to dance. They rolled back the carpet. The Wienands family left early because of the children. The little one was crying. They live next door to the Popingas. And at midnight, Any was feeling sleepy. I had my bike. Conrad saw me back home, he took his bike too.

'When I got back here, my father was waiting up for me. And it was only next day that we heard what had happened. All of Delfzijl was in an uproar.

'I don't think it was my fault. When Conrad got back home, he went to put his bike in the shed behind the house. And someone shot him with a revolver! He fell down, and in half an hour he was dead. Poor Conrad! With his mouth open.'

She wiped away a tear, which looked

13

incongruous on that smooth cheek as pink as a rosy ripe apple.

'And that's all?'

'Yes. The police came from headquarters at Groningen to help the local gendarmes. They said the shot had been fired from inside the house. Apparently, the professor was seen right afterwards holding a revolver in his hand. And that was the gun that had been fired.'

'Professor Jean Duclos?'

'Yes! So they didn't let him leave.'

'So, in all, in the house at that time, there were just Madame Popinga, her sister Any and Professor Duclos?'

'*Ja!*'

'And that evening, the other people present were the Wienands family, yourself and Conrad . . . '

'And oh yes, there was Cor . . . I forgot.'

'Cor?'

'Short for Cornelius, a pupil at the Naval College. He was taking private lessons.'

'When did he leave?'

'The same time as Conrad and me. But he would have turned left on his bike, to get back to the college boat, which is moored on the Ems Canal. Do you take sugar?'

Steam rose from the teacups. A car had just stopped at the foot of the three steps up to the house. Shortly afterwards, a large burly man, grey-haired, with a serious expression, entered the room: his bulk emphasizing his calm presence.

This was Farmer Liewens, waiting for his

daughter to introduce the visitor.

He shook Maigret's hand vigorously, but without saying anything.

'My father doesn't speak French.'

She served the farmer a cup of tea, which he drank standing up, with small sips. Then she told him about the calf's birth, speaking in Dutch.

She must also have mentioned the part played by the inspector in that event, since her father looked at him in astonishment tinged with irony, before, with a stiff bow, going off to the cowshed.

'So, is the professor in prison?' Maigret asked.

'No, he's at the Van Hasselt Hotel, with a gendarme attached to him.'

'And Conrad?'

'His body has been taken to Groningen . . . Thirty kilometres away. A big town with a university, population a hundred thousand. Where Jean Duclos had been welcomed the day before. It's all so dreadful, isn't it? Nobody can understand it.'

Dreadful, perhaps. But it was hard to feel that way! No doubt because of the clear air, the cosy, welcoming surroundings, the tea steaming on the table and the little town itself, looking like a toy village someone had set down by the seaside for fun.

By leaning out of the window one could see, looming over the brick houses, the smokestack and gangway of a large cargo vessel being unloaded. And the boats floating down the Ems towards the sea.

'Did Conrad usually accompany you home?'

15

'Every time I went to their house. He was a good friend.'

'And Madame Popinga didn't mind?'

Maigret made the remark almost at random, since his gaze had fallen on the young woman's tempting bosom, and perhaps because the sight of it had brought some warmth to his own cheeks.

'Why would she?'

'I don't know. Night time . . . the two of you . . .'

She laughed, showing healthy teeth.

'In Holland, it's always . . . Cor used to see me home too.'

'And *he* wasn't in love with you?'

She didn't say yes or no. She chuckled. A little chuckle of satisfied coquettishness.

Through the window, her father could be seen taking the calf out of the shed, carrying it like a baby and placing it on the grass in the field, in the sunlight.

The creature wobbled on its slender legs, almost fell to its knees, then suddenly tried to gallop for a few metres before stopping still.

'And Conrad never kissed you?'

Another laugh, accompanied by a very slight blush.

'Yes, he did.'

'And Cor?'

This time she was more formal, looking away for a moment.

'Yes, he did too, but why do you ask?'

She looked at him oddly. Perhaps she was expecting Maigret to kiss her as well.

Her father was calling from outside. She opened the window. He spoke to her in Dutch. When she turned back, it was to say:

'Excuse me, please. I have to go to town to find the mayor, about the calf's pedigree. It's very important. You're not going to Delfzijl too?'

He went out with her. She took the handlebars of her nickel-plated bicycle and walked alongside him, swinging her hips, already those of a mature woman.

'It's so beautiful here, isn't it? Poor Conrad! He will never see it again. The swimming opens tomorrow. He used to come every day, other years. He'd stay in the water for an hour.'

Maigret, as he walked, kept his eyes on the ground.

2

The Baes's Cap

Contrary to his usual habit, Maigret noted down a few physical details, mainly topographical, and that was in fact a true case of intuition, since, in the end, the solution proved to be a matter of minutes and metres.

Between the Liewens farm and the Popinga residence, the distance was about twelve hundred metres. Both buildings were on the bank of the canal, and to go from one to the other, the only route was the towpath.

This canal had more or less fallen into disuse, following the construction of a much wider and deeper channel, the Ems Canal, linking Delfzijl to Groningen.

The smaller canal, the Amsterdiep, silted up, meandering and shaded by fine trees, was now used almost exclusively for floating timber, and by the occasional boat of low tonnage.

A few farms scattered about. A boatyard for repairs.

On leaving the Popinga house to go to the farm, the next building one reached, just thirty metres away, was the Wienands villa. Then came a plot under construction. After that, a long empty stretch, and the timber yard with its stacks of wood.

Beyond the yard came another uninhabited

section, preceded by a bend in the canal and the path. From there, the Popinga windows were clearly visible, as was, just to the left, the white-painted lighthouse on the far side of the town.

'Does the lighthouse have a revolving beam?' Maigret asked.

'Yes.'

'So at night, it must light up this part of the road . . . '

'Yes,' she exclaimed again, with a little laugh, as if it brought back some happy memory.

'Not too good for courting couples!' he concluded.

She left him before they reached the Popinga house, claiming that she could take a short cut, but probably so as not to be seen in his company.

Maigret did not stop. The house was modern, brick-built, with a small garden in front, a vegetable plot behind, a path along the right-hand side, and a patch of waste ground on the left.

He preferred to head for the town, only five hundred metres further along. His steps took him to the lock separating the canal from the harbour. The basin was crammed with boats of between a hundred and three hundred tons, moored side by side, masts in the air, forming a floating world.

On the left was the Van Hasselt Hotel, into which he walked.

★ ★ ★

A dark lounge with varnished woodwork, and a complex smell of beer, genever and furniture polish. A large billiard table. Another table with newspapers stretched on brass rods.

A man sitting in the corner stood up as soon as Maigret arrived and came to meet him.

'Are you the man the French police have sent me?'

He was tall and gaunt, with a long face, sharp features, horn-rimmed glasses and a crew cut.

'You must be Professor Duclos,' Maigret replied.

He hadn't expected him to look so young. Duclos was about thirty-five to thirty-eight. But there was something slightly unusual about him that struck Maigret.

'You're from Nancy?'

'I have the chair of sociology in the university there.'

'But you weren't born in France?'

It was as if a little tussle had started.

'I was born in French Switzerland. But I've been naturalized a French citizen. I completed all my studies in Paris and Montpellier.'

'And you're a Protestant?'

'How can you tell?'

By nothing and everything! Duclos belonged to a category of men that the inspector knew well. Men of science. Study for study's sake. Ideas for ideas. A certain austerity of manner and lifestyle, combined with a taste for international contacts. A passion for lectures, conferences and exchanges of letters with foreign correspondents.

He seemed rather on edge, if this could be said of a man whose expression never changed. On his table stood a bottle of mineral water, together with two fat books and a sheaf of papers.

'I don't see the policeman who's supposed to be keeping you under observation.'

'I gave my word of honour I wouldn't leave here. Although, I have to tell you, I'm expected by literary and scientific gatherings in Emden, Hamburg and Bremen. I was due to give my lecture in those three towns, before . . .'

A large blonde woman, the hotel proprietress, appeared and Jean Duclos explained to her in Dutch who the visitor was.

'I just took a chance in asking for a French policeman to be sent here. In fact, I am hoping to be able to shed light on this mystery myself.'

'Can you tell me what you know?'

And Maigret slumped into a chair before ordering:

'A Bols . . . in a big glass.'

'Here are some diagrams, done exactly to scale. I can give you a copy. The first is the ground floor of the Popinga house. With the corridor on the left, the parlour and dining room on the right. The kitchen at the back, and behind it a shed where Popinga kept his boat and the bicycles.'

'Were you all in the parlour?'

'Yes. Madame Popinga and Any went twice into the kitchen to make tea, because the housemaid had gone to bed. And here's the first floor: at the back, over the kitchen, is a bathroom; at the front of the house there are two

21

rooms: on the left, the Popingas' bedroom; on the right a study, where Any slept on a divan. And at the back was the bedroom they had given me.'

'Which rooms could the shot have been fired from?'

'My bedroom, the bathroom and the dining room downstairs.'

'So tell me about the evening.'

'My lecture was a triumph. I gave it in the hall you can see there.'

A long room, decorated with paper chains, and evidently used for dances, banquets and dramatic productions. A stage with scenery representing the grounds of a chateau.

'Then we went to the Amsterdiep.'

'Along the canal bank? Can you tell me what order you went in?'

'I went ahead with Madame Popinga, who is a highly educated woman. Conrad Popinga was flirting with that silly little girl from the farm, who can only giggle and hadn't understood a word of my talk. Then there were the Wienands, and Any, and some pupil of Popinga's, an anaemic-looking boy.'

'You arrived at the house . . . '

'They will have told you that my lecture was about the responsibility of murderers. Madame Popinga's sister, Any, who has finished her law degree and will start teaching in the autumn, asked me for some details. We were led to discuss the role of the lawyer in criminal cases. Then we talked about forensics, and I remember I suggested she read some books by Professor

22

Grosz of Vienna. I maintained that to commit a crime with impunity is virtually impossible. I talked about fingerprints, the analysis of all kinds of material traces and calculations . . . But Conrad Popinga kept pressing me to listen to Radio-Paris!'

Maigret showed only the shadow of a smile.

'And he succeeded. They were playing some jazz. Popinga went to fetch a bottle of cognac, and was amazed to find a Frenchman who didn't drink it. He took some himself, and so did the girl from the farm . . . They were very merry . . . They started dancing. 'Just like in Paris!' Popinga was shouting.'

'You didn't like him!' Maigret remarked.

'An uncouth fellow, of no interest! Wienands, although he is mostly concerned with mathematics, was listening to us. A baby started to cry. The Wienands left. The farmer's daughter was in high spirits. Conrad offered to see her home, and they both went off on their bicycles. Madame Popinga showed me to my room. I sorted out some papers from my briefcase. I was just going to take notes for a book I'm writing when I heard a gunshot, from so close by that it could almost have been fired in my room. I rushed outside. The bathroom door was ajar. I pushed it. The window was wide open. And someone was groaning in the garden, near the bicycle shed.'

'Was the light on in the bathroom?'

'No. I leaned out of the window. And my hand touched the butt of a revolver, which I automatically picked up . . . I thought I saw

23

someone lying on the ground near the shed. I made to go downstairs. And I bumped into Madame Popinga, who was coming out of her room, in shock. We both ran downstairs. We had got as far as the kitchen when we were joined by Any, who was so alarmed that she had come down in nothing but her petticoat. You'll see what I mean when you meet her.'

'And Popinga?'

'Half-dead. He looked up at us with great agonized eyes, clutching at his chest with one hand. At the moment I tried to lift him up, he stiffened. He was dead, a bullet through the heart.'

'And that's all you know?'

'We telephoned the gendarmerie, and the doctor. We called Wienands out, and he came to help us ... I sensed a certain awkwardness around me. I'd forgotten that I had been seen holding the revolver. The gendarmes reminded me of this and asked me to explain. Then they requested me politely to remain available for further questioning.'

'And that was six days ago.'

'Yes. I've been working on the problem, trying to resolve it, because it *is* a problem. See these papers?'

Maigret tapped out his pipe, without looking at the papers in question.

'And you haven't left the hotel?'

'I could do, but I prefer to avoid any incidents. Popinga was very popular with his pupils and you meet them all the time around town.'

'And no physical clue has been found.'

'Ah yes, sorry. Any, who is carrying out her own investigation and hoping to identify the killer too, although she doesn't go about it methodically, sometimes brings me some more information. You ought to know that the bath in the Popinga bathroom is covered with a wooden lid, which converts it into an ironing board. The day after the murder, they took the lid off and found a shabby seaman's cap, which had never been seen in the house before. On the ground floor, a police search found the end of a cigar on the dining room carpet, very dark tobacco, Manila I think, such as none of them smoked, Popinga, Wienands or the young pupil. And I never smoke. And yet the dining room had been swept after dinner.'

'From which you deduce . . . '

'Nothing,' said Jean Duclos. 'I'll draw my conclusions in my own good time. I apologize for bringing you all the way here. And they could have picked a policeman who knew the language. You can be useful to me only in the event that they take any measures regarding me, in which case you would have to make an official protest.'

Maigret stroked his nose, while smiling a truly delicious smile.

'Are you married, Monsieur Duclos?'

'No.'

'And before this you were not acquainted with the Popingas, or the little sister Any, or any of the other people present?'

'No, none of them. They knew me, by reputation . . . '

'Naturally! Of course!'

And Maigret picked up the two carefully plotted diagrams, stuffed them in his pocket, touched his hat and went out.

★   ★   ★

The police station was modern, well-lit and comfortable. Maigret was expected. The station master had reported his arrival and they were astonished not to have seen him yet.

He went in as if to his own office, took off his light spring overcoat and placed his hat on a chair.

The inspector who had been sent from Groningen spoke French slowly and rather pedantically. A tall, blond, clean-cut young man, of remarkably affable manner, he underlined every sentence with a little nod, which seemed to indicate: 'You get my meaning? We are agreed on this?'

Although in truth Maigret hardly gave him time to start speaking.

'Since you've been on this case for six days,' he said, 'you must have checked the times.'

'What times?'

'It would be interesting for instance to know exactly how many minutes the victim took to escort Mademoiselle Beetje home, and then return. Wait! I'd also like to know what time Mademoiselle Beetje actually set foot back in the farm, where her father was waiting up for her, and he ought to be able to tell you that. And lastly, the time that young Cor arrived back at the college boat, where there is no doubt a night watchman.'

The Dutch inspector looked annoyed, stood up suddenly as if struck by inspiration, went towards the back of the room, and returned carrying a very shabby seaman's cap. Then, enunciating his words with exaggerated slowness, he said:

'We have found the owner of this item which was discovered in the bath . . . He is . . . He is a man we call 'the Baes'. In French you'd say '*le patron*', the boss.'

Was Maigret even listening?

'We have not arrested him, because we wish to keep him under observation, and he is popular in the district. You know the mouth of the Ems? When you reach the North Sea, about ten sea miles from here, you come to some sandy islands, which can be more or less completely submerged in the high equinoctial tides. One of these islands is called Workum. This man has settled there with his family and some farmhands, and taken it into his head to raise livestock. That's 'the Baes' for you. He's been granted a state subsidy, because he has established squatter's rights. And he has even been appointed mayor of Workum, of which he is the only Dutch citizen. He has a motor launch, and comes and goes between his island and Delfzijl.'

Maigret still did not budge. The Dutchman winked.

'An odd fellow! Sixty years old, and as solid as a rock. He has three sons, all pirates like himself.

27

Because . . . Listen! This is not the sort of thing to shout out loud. You know that Delfzijl is a port for handling timber from Finland and Riga . . . The steamboats that bring the logs here have part of the cargo on deck, held down with chains. But in emergencies, the captains have orders to cut the chains and jettison the deck cargo into the sea, to save the boat. You still don't see what I am driving at?'

And certainly Maigret gave no sign of being at all interested in this story.

'The Baes is a cunning man. He knows all the sea captains who come in here. He has his little arrangements with them. So when they are in sight of the islands, there's always a reason to be found for cutting at least one chain. Then several tons of timber go into the sea and the tide throws them up on Workum sands. Wreckers' rights. Now do you understand? And the Baes shares the proceeds with the captains. And it was *his* cap that they found in the bath. Just one problem. He only smokes a pipe. But he may not have been alone.'

'And that's it?'

'No. Ah no! Monsieur Popinga, who has contacts everywhere, or rather who *had*, was appointed Finnish vice-consul in Delfzijl a couple of weeks ago.'

The skinny young man was triumphant now, puffing with satisfaction.

'And where was the Baes's boat on the night of the crime?'

This time it was almost a shout.

'In Delfzijl. Moored at the quayside. Near the

28

lock! In other words, fifty metres from the Popinga house.'

Maigret tamped more tobacco into his pipe, and paced up and down in the office, looking with a jaundiced eye at the reports, of which he could understand not a damned word.

'And you haven't anything else to go on,' he said suddenly, thrusting both hands into his pockets.

He was hardly surprised to see the other policeman blush.

'You know already?'

He checked himself.

'Of course, you have spent all afternoon in Delfzijl . . . French tactics.'

He seemed hesitant.

'I don't know yet what this statement means. It was on the fourth day. Madame Popinga turned up. She told me that she had consulted the minister, to see whether she ought to say anything. You know the layout of the house? Not yet? I can show you a diagram?'

'Thanks! But I've got one,' said Maigret, taking it from his pocket.

The other man, looking startled, went on:

'You see the Popingas' bedroom? From the window, you can glimpse only a little section of the road leading to the farm. Just the stretch that is lit up by the lighthouse every fifteen seconds.'

'And Madame Popinga was jealous, so she was spying on her husband?'

'She was looking out. She saw the two bikes on the way to the farm. Then her husband cycling back. Then about a hundred metres behind him, Beetje Liewens's bicycle.'

'In other words, after Conrad Popinga saw her home, Beetje returned on her own towards the Popinga house. So what does she say about this?'

'Who?'

'The girl.'

'Nothing so far. I didn't want to question her right away. It's very serious, and you may have chosen the right word. Jealousy. You understand? Monsieur Liewens is a member of the Council.'

'What time did Cor get back to the Naval College?'

'That we do know, five minutes past midnight.'

'And the shot was fired . . . ?'

'Five minutes before midnight . . . But there's the cap and the cigar . . . '

'And he has a bike?'

'Yes. Everybody cycles everywhere here. It's practical. I do it myself . . . But that night, he didn't have his bike with him.'

'The revolver has been examined?'

'Ja! It's Conrad Popinga's own gun. His service revolver. It was always loaded with six bullets, and inside a drawer of his bedside table.'

'And the shot was fired from how many metres away?'

'About six. The distance from the bathroom window. And also the distance from Monsieur Duclos's bedroom. And perhaps the shot wasn't fired from up above. We don't know, because Popinga, who was putting his bike away, could have been bending down. But there's the cap. And the cigar. Don't forget.'

'Cigar, phooey,' muttered Maigret to himself.
And out loud:
'Is Mademoiselle Any aware of her sister's
statement?'

'Yes.'

'And what does she say about it?'

'She hasn't said anything. She's highly
educated. She doesn't talk much. She's not like
other girls.'

'Is she ugly?'

Every one of Maigret's interruptions had the
knack of disconcerting the Dutch policeman.

'Well . . . not pretty.'

'Very well, she's ugly. And you were saying
that . . . '

'She wants to find the murderer. She's
working on it. She has asked to see the reports.'

Chance took a hand. A young woman came in,
with a leather briefcase under her arm: she was
dressed austerely, almost to the point of
eccentricity.

She marched straight up to the Groningen
police officer. She began speaking volubly in her
own language, either not seeing the stranger, or
taking no notice of him.

The Dutchman reddened, shifted from one
foot to the other, shuffling his papers to give
himself an air of authority and indicating
Maigret with his eyes. But she did not deign to
pay any attention to the Frenchman.

In despair, the Dutch inspector spoke in
French, as if with regret.

'She says the law forbids you to question
anyone on Dutch territory.'

31

'This is Mademoiselle Any?'

Irregular features. If not for the large mouth and uneven teeth, she wouldn't have been worse-looking than average. Flat-chested. Large feet. But above all, the forbidding self-confidence of the suffragette.

'Yes. According to the statutes, she's right. But I've told her that in practice . . . '

'Mademoiselle Any understands French, I believe?'

'I think so.'

The young woman didn't react, but waited, chin held high, for the end of this consultation between the two men, which did not appear to concern her.

'Mademoiselle,' said Maigret, with exaggerated gallantry, 'please accept my respects. Detective Chief Inspector Maigret, from Police Headquarters in Paris. All I wanted to know is what you thought about Mademoiselle Beetje and her relationship with Cornelius.'

She tried to smile. A shy, forced smile. She looked from Maigret to her compatriot and stammered in poor French:

'I not . . . I not understand very well.'

And the effort was enough to make her blush scarlet to the tips of her ears, while everything in her expression pleaded for release.

3

The Quayside Rats Club

There were about a dozen of them, all men, wearing heavy blue woollen jackets, seaman's caps and varnished clogs, some lounging against the town gates, others leaning their elbows on bollards, others again just standing around, their wide trousers making their legs look monumental.

They were smoking, chewing tobacco, spitting a lot, and now and then something made them all burst out laughing, slapping their thighs.

Four metres away from them floated the boats. Beyond lay the smug little town, surrounded by its dykes. Further along, a crane was unloading a collier.

At first the men did not notice Maigret strolling along the wharf. So he had plenty of time to observe them.

He had learned that in Delfzijl this group was known ironically as 'the Quayside Rats Club'. Without even being told, he could have guessed that most of these sailors spent the greater part of their days on the same spot, rain or shine, chatting lazily and sending jets of saliva to the ground.

One of them was the owner of three clippers, handsome vessels of four hundred tons equipped with sails and engines, one of which was just moving up the Ems and would soon be in port.

Other men seemed less distinguished; a ship's caulker who probably didn't do much caulking and the keeper of a disused lock, still wearing his government service cap.

But in the middle of the group, one figure eclipsed all the rest, not only because he was the most massively built and the reddest of face, but because one sensed in him a man of stronger character.

Clogs, a jacket. And on his head a brand-new cap, which had not yet had time to mould itself to the shape of his skull, and consequently looked faintly ridiculous.

This was Oosting, commonly known as the Baes, smoking a short clay pipe as he listened to his neighbours talking.

A vague smile played on his face. From time to time, he removed the pipe from his mouth to allow the smoke to flow gently from his lips.

He reminded Maigret of a small-scale rhinoceros. A heavily built brute, but with mild eyes and something at the same time tough and gentle about his whole person.

His eyes were fixed on a boat about fifteen metres long, moored to the quayside. A swift boat with clean lines, probably a former yacht, though now dirty and cluttered.

This belonged to him, and from here it was possible to see the Ems estuary, twenty kilometres wide, and the distant glimmer of the North Sea: out there somewhere lay a golden brown sandbank known as the island of Workum, Oosting's domain.

Night was falling: the crimson rays of the setting sun painted the brick-built town even redder and glinted in fiery flashes on the scarlet lead paint of a cargo vessel undergoing repairs, reflected in the water of the harbour.

The Baes's gaze, as it wandered calmly across the scene, contrived to take in Maigret as part of the landscape. His blue-green eyes were very small. They remained focused on the French inspector for a short while, after which the man tapped out his pipe against his wooden clog, spat, felt in his pockets for the pig's bladder he used to hold his tobacco, and settled himself more comfortably up against the wall.

From that point on, Maigret felt that gaze resting continuously on him, conveying neither bravado nor distrust: a cool and yet concerned gaze, one that was weighing up, appreciating and calculating.

★ ★ ★

Maigret had been the first to leave the police station, having arranged a later meeting with the Dutch inspector, whose name was Pijpekamp.

Any had remained inside, and presently went past, clutching her briefcase under her arm, leaning forward slightly, like a woman with no interest in anything happening in the street.

It wasn't Any that Maigret was watching, but the Baes, who followed her for a while with his eyes, then, with a more puckered brow, turned towards Maigret.

So, without really knowing why, Maigret

moved towards the group, which fell silent. Ten faces turned in his direction, expressing a degree of surprise.

He addressed Oosting:

'Excuse me. Do you understand French?'

The Baes did not budge, appearing to be thinking. A lanky seaman standing alongside him explained in English and Dutch:

'*Frenchman! Frans politie.*'

The next minute was perhaps one of the strangest in Maigret's career.

The man he had spoken to, turning briefly towards his boat, seemed to hesitate.

It was clear that he wanted to ask the inspector to come aboard with him. One could see a small oak-panelled cabin, with its swinging lamp, a compass.

The other men waited. He opened his mouth.

Then suddenly he shrugged his shoulders, as if deciding: 'No, that's ridiculous!'

But that wasn't what he said. In a hoarse voice issuing from his throat, he uttered: 'No understand. *Hollands . . . English . . .* '

They could still see Any's dark silhouette, with her crepe mourning veil, crossing the bridge over the canal before taking the towpath along the Amsterdiep.

The Baes intercepted Maigret's glance at his new cap, but did not flinch. Rather, the shadow of a smile crossed his lips.

At that moment, the inspector would have given good money to be able to have a chat with this man in his own language, even for five minutes. His goodwill was such that he stammered out a few sentences in English, but his accent was so strong that nobody understood.

'No understand. Nobody understand!' repeated the man who had spoken.

So they resumed their conversation, while Maigret walked away with the vague feeling that he had been very close to the heart of the enigma and that now, for want of mutual comprehension, he was getting further away from it.

He turned round a few minutes later. The Quayside Rats were still chatting as the sun set, and its last rays cast a rosier glow over the heavy-jowled face of the Baes, still turned in Maigret's direction.

* * *

Until then, Maigret had in some sense been circling round the drama, saving until last the visit, always a painful one, to the house of mourning.

He rang the doorbell. It was just after six. He hadn't realized that this was the time when Dutch people eat their evening meal, and when a young housemaid opened the door, he could see in the dining room the two women sitting at the table.

They both stood up in a simultaneous movement with the slightly stiff air of well-brought-up schoolgirls.

They were dressed in black. The table was laid with teacups, wafer-thin slices of bread and cold meats. Despite the gathering dusk, the lamp was not lit but a gas-fired stove, its flames visible through its mica panes, was struggling against the dark.

It was Any who immediately thought to switch on the electric light, while the maid closed the curtains.

'Please forgive me,' said Maigret. 'I'm so sorry to disturb you at supper time.' Madame Popinga vaguely gestured towards an armchair and looked around her distractedly, while her sister retreated as far as possible into the room.

A similar atmosphere to the farm. Some modern furniture, but very conservatively modern. Muted colours combining in an elegant but gloomy harmony.

'You've come to . . . '

Madame Popinga's lower lip trembled, and she had to put her handkerchief to her mouth to stifle a sob that had suddenly broken out. Any didn't move.

'Forgive me. I'll come back . . . '

Madame Popinga shook her head. She was struggling to regain her composure. She must have been a good few years older than her sister. A tall woman, much more feminine. Regular features, a hint of broken veins in the cheeks, the odd grey hair.

And a modest dignity in every gesture. Maigret recalled that she was the daughter of a headmaster, spoke several languages and was well educated. But that didn't affect her timidity, the timidity of a respectable woman in a small town, liable to take fright at the slightest thing.

He also remembered that she belonged to the

most austere of Protestant sects, and that she presided over all the Delfzijl charities and hosted the women's literary circles.

She regained her self-control. She looked at her sister as if asking for help.

'I'm sorry! But it's just so unbelievable, isn't it? Conrad! A man everyone loved.'

Her gaze fell on the wireless loudspeaker, standing in a corner, and she almost burst into tears.

'That was his only distraction,' she stammered. 'And his little boat on the Amsterdiep, on summer evenings. He worked so hard. Who could have done this?'

And as Maigret said nothing, she added, turning a little pink, in the tone she might have used if someone had argued with her:

'I'm not accusing anyone. I don't know. I just can't believe it, do you understand? The police thought of Professor Duclos, because he came out holding the revolver. But I don't know what happened. It's too horrible! Someone killed Conrad. But why? Why him? It wasn't even a burglary. So . . . '

'And you told the police what you saw from the window?'

She blushed deeper. Standing upright, one hand leaning on the dinner-table, she said:

'I didn't know if I should . . . I don't think Beetje did anything. It was just that by chance I saw. They told me the smallest little detail might help their enquiries. I asked the minister for advice. He told me to speak up. Beetje's a perfectly nice girl. Really, I don't see who

. . . Somebody who should be in a lunatic asylum!'

She had no need to search for the right words. Her French was perfect, pronounced with a very slight accent.

'Any told me you've come from Paris. Because of Conrad! Are we to believe that?'

She had calmed down. Her sister, still standing in a corner of the room hadn't stirred, and Maigret could only partly see her, by way of a mirror.

'You'll need to look over the house, I assume?'

She was resigned to it. But she sighed:

'Could you go with . . . Any?'

A black dress moved in front of the inspector. He followed it up a staircase fitted with brand-new carpeting. The Popinga home, no more than ten years old, was built like a doll's house, with lightweight materials, hollow bricks and pine boards. But the paint which had been applied to all the woodwork gave it a fresh and bright look.

The bathroom door was the first to be opened. There was a wooden lid over the bath, transforming it into an ironing board. Maigret leaned out of the window, and saw the bicycle shed, the well-kept kitchen garden, and across the fields the town of Delfzijl, few of whose houses had two storeys, and none three.

Any was waiting at the door.

'I hear you're carrying out your own investigation,' Maigret said.

She shuddered, but didn't answer, and hurried to open the door of Professor Duclos's room.

40

A brass bedstead. A pitch-pine wardrobe. Lino on the floor.

'And this is whose bedroom?'

She had to make an effort to speak French.

'Of me . . . When I am here.'

'And you've often stayed here?'

'Yes . . . I . . . '

She was really very shy. The words stuck in her throat. Her eyes looked around for help.

'So since the professor was a guest here, you slept in your brother-in-law's study?'

She nodded yes and opened the door. A table laden with books, including new publications on gyroscopic compasses and on radio communication with ships. Some sextants. On the walls, photos of Conrad Popinga in the Far East and Africa in his uniform as first lieutenant or captain.

There was a display of Malayan weapons. Japanese enamels. On trestles lay some precision tools and a ship's compass in pieces, which Popinga must have been repairing.

A divan covered with a blue bedspread.

'And your sister's room?'

'Here, next door.'

The study communicated both with the professor's room and the Popingas' bedroom, which was furnished more stylishly. An alabaster lamp over the bed. A rather fine Persian carpet. Wooden colonial furniture.

'And you were in the study,' said Maigret thoughtfully.

A nod, yes.

'So you couldn't come out without going

either through the professor's room or your sister's?'

Another nod.

'And the professor was in his room. And your sister in hers.'

She opened her eyes wide, her jaw dropped as if she'd had a terrible shock.

'And, you think . . . ?'

Maigret muttered as he paced through the three rooms:

'I don't think anything. I'm searching. I'm eliminating possibilities! And up to now, you are the only one who can logically be eliminated, unless we assume some complicity between you and either Duclos or Madame Popinga.'

'You . . . you . . . '

But he was carrying on talking to himself.

'Duclos might have fired the shot either from his room or the bathroom, that's clear. Madame Popinga could have gone into the bathroom. But the professor, who went in there immediately after hearing the shot, didn't see her. On the contrary, he saw her coming out of her room only a few seconds later.'

Perhaps she was now emerging a little from her shell. The student was taking over from the timid girl, as if inspired by this technical hypothesis.

'Maybe, someone shot from downstairs?' she said, her gaze now more focused and her thin body alert. 'The doctor says . . . '

'True, but that doesn't alter the fact that the revolver that killed your brother-in-law was certainly the one Duclos was holding. Unless the murderer threw the gun upstairs through the window.'

'Why not?'

'Obviously. Why not?'

And he went down the stairs, which seemed too narrow for him, the steps creaking under his bulk.

He found Madame Popinga standing in the dining room, apparently on the spot where he had left her. Any followed him in.

'Did Cornelius come here often?'

'Almost every day. He only had lessons three times a week, Tuesdays, Thursdays and Saturdays. But he came on the other days. His parents are in the East Indies. A month ago, he was told that his mother had died. She was dead and buried by the time he got the letter. So . . . '

'What about Beetje Liewens?'

There was a slightly awkward silence. Madame Popinga looked at Any. Any looked down.

'She used to come . . . '

'Often?'

'Yes.'

'Did you invite her?'

His questions were getting brusquer, more pointed. Maigret had the feeling he was making progress, if not in discovering the truth, at least in his penetration of the life in this house.

'No . . . yes.'

'She's a different kind of person from you and Mademoiselle Any, shall we say?'

'She's, well, she's very young, isn't she? Her father is a friend of Conrad's. She used to bring us apples, raspberries, cream . . . '

'And she wasn't in love with Cornelius?'

'No!'

That sounded definite.

'You didn't like her much?'

'Why wouldn't I? She came here, she laughed. She chattered all day long. Like a bird, you understand?'

'Do you know Oosting?'

'Yes.'

'Did he have any dealings with your husband?'

'Last year Oosting put a new engine into his boat. So he consulted Conrad. My husband drew up some plans for him. They went hunting for *zeehonden* — what do you call them in French? — seals, out on the sandbanks.'

And then suddenly:

'Oh, you think . . . The cap perhaps? It's impossible! Oosting!'

And she wailed, in distress once again:

'No, not Oosting. No! Nobody . . . Nobody could have killed Conrad. You didn't know him. He was . . . he . . . '

She turned her head aside, because she was weeping. Maigret preferred to leave. No one shook his hand and he simply bowed, muttering his apologies.

Outside, he was surprised by the damp coolness rising from the canal. And on the other bank, not far from the boatyard, he saw the Baes, talking to a student wearing the uniform of the Naval College.

They were both standing in the gathering dusk. Oosting seemed to be speaking insistently. The young man was looking down and only the

44

pale oval of his face could be made out.

Maigret realized that this must be Cornelius. He was sure of it when he glimpsed a black armband on the blue woollen sleeve.

4

Logs on the Amsterdiep

He wasn't strictly speaking tailing them. At no time did Maigret have the feeling he was spying on anyone. He had been coming out of the Popinga house. He had walked a few steps. He had seen two men on the other side of the canal and had quite simply stopped to observe them. He wasn't hiding. He was there in full view on the bank, pipe in mouth and hands in pockets.

But perhaps it was precisely because he wasn't hiding, and because nevertheless the other men had not seen him as they carried on their intense conversation, that there was something poignant about that moment.

The bank on which the two men were standing was otherwise deserted. A shed loomed up in the centre of a dry dock where two boats were propped on stays, and a few dinghies lay rotting, hauled up out of the water.

On the canal itself, the floating tree trunks allowed only a metre or two of the liquid surface to be seen, giving the scene a slightly exotic feel.

It was evening now. In the semi-darkness, however, the air was still limpid, allowing the colours to retain all their clarity.

The tranquillity was surprisingly intense, so that the croaking of a frog in a distant marsh was startling.

The Baes was doing the talking. He did not raise his voice. But he appeared to be enunciating each syllable clearly, wanting to be understood, or obeyed. Head lowered, the young man in his cadet uniform was listening. He was wearing white gloves, showing as the only bright spots in the failing light.

Suddenly there came an ear-splitting sound. A donkey had started to bray in a field somewhere behind Maigret. It was enough to break the charmed silence. Oosting, looking across in the direction of the animal, which was now beseeching the heavens, noticed Maigret, and let his gaze wander over him, but without showing any reaction.

He said a few more words to his companion, stuck the stem of his clay pipe in his mouth and set off towards the town.

It meant nothing, proved nothing. Maigret walked on as well, and the two men progressed in step together, one on either bank of the Amsterdiep.

But the path Oosting was taking soon diverged from the canalside. And the Baes presently disappeared behind some more sheds. For almost a minute, the heavy tread of his wooden clogs could still be heard.

It was night time now, scarcely a shred of light in the sky. The lamps had just been lit in town and along the canal, where the street lighting stopped at the Wienands' house. The other bank, uninhabited, remained in darkness.

Maigret turned round, without knowing why. He groaned as the donkey launched into another bout of desperate heehawing.

And he glimpsed further along, beyond the houses, two little white patches dancing on the far side of the canal. Cornelius's gloves.

To a casual observer, especially one who forgot that the surface of the water was covered with logs, the sight would have been ghostly. Hands waving in the emptiness. The rest of the body melting into the night. And on the water the reflection of the furthest street lamp.

Oosting's footsteps could no longer be heard. Maigret walked back towards the outlying houses, passing once more in front of the Popingas' and then the Wienands' residence.

He was still making no effort to hide, but he realized that he too would have been swallowed up by the darkness. He followed the gloves with his eyes. Now he understood. To avoid going by way of Delfzijl, where there was a bridge over the canal, Cornelius was crossing the water using the floating logs as a raft. In the middle, there was a gap of about two metres. The white hands moved more quickly, went up in a rapid arc and the water splashed.

A few seconds later, he was walking along the bank, and being followed, scarcely a hundred metres behind, by Maigret.

It was not deliberate on either side, and in any case, Cornelius could not have been aware of the inspector's presence. All the same, from the first, they were walking in step, so that their crunching footfalls on the cinder path sounded in unison.

Maigret realized this, because his foot hit a stone at one point, and the synchronicity failed for a micro-second.

He didn't know where he was heading. And yet his pace quickened as the young man speeded up. More than that: he felt he was gradually being dragged along in a sort of trance.

At first the steps ahead of him were long and regular. Then they shortened and became hurried.

Just as Cornelius was passing the timber yard, a veritable chorus of frogs broke out and the steps stopped abruptly.

Was Cornelius afraid of something? The footsteps continued, but even less regularly, sometimes hesitating, then on the contrary there would be two or three rapid paces, so that it seemed he might break into a run.

And now the silence was truly broken, as the frog chorus intensified. It filled the whole night air.

The steps accelerated. The same process started again. Maigret, by dint of walking in step with the other man, could literally sense his state of mind.

Cornelius was frightened! He was walking fast because he was afraid. He was anxious to get somewhere. But whenever he passed close to an unfamiliar-looking shadow, a stack of timber, a dead tree, a bush, his foot remained in the air a tenth of a second longer.

They reached a bend in the canal. A hundred metres ahead, going towards the farm, was the short stretch illuminated intermittently by the beam from the lighthouse. The young man seemed to be disconcerted by the bright swathe of light. He looked behind him. Then he rushed across it, again turning his head.

He had passed it, and was still casting backward glances, when Maigret calmly entered the illuminated zone, with all his bulk, presence and weight.

The cadet could not fail to see him. He stopped. Long enough to catch his breath. Then he set off again.

The light was behind them now. Ahead was a lit window, in the farm. Was the sound of the frogs following them? Although they were moving forward, it stayed close by, surrounding them, as if there were scores of the creatures escorting them.

A hundred metres from the house, a sudden final stop. A shadow detached itself from a tree trunk. A voice whispered.

Maigret had no wish to turn round and go back. That would be ridiculous. Nor did he want to hide. In any case it was too late, since he had walked through the lighthouse beam.

They knew he was there. He went forward slowly, unsettled now that there were no footsteps to echo his own.

The gloom was intense because of the thick foliage either side of the path. But a white glove showed up ahead, in movement.

An embrace. Cornelius's hand around the waist of a girl: Beetje.

Another fifty metres to go. Maigret paused for a moment, took some matches from his pocket and struck one to light his pipe, thus indicating his exact position.

Then he stepped forward. The lovers stirred. When he was no more than ten metres away, Beetje's silhouette detached itself and came to stand in the middle of the path, her face turned towards him, as if waiting for him. Cornelius stayed behind, flattening himself against a tree trunk.

Eight metres.

The window at the farm was still lit behind them. A plain reddish rectangle.

Suddenly there came a strangled cry, an indescribable cry of fear, indicating a loss of nerve, an utterance such as often precedes an outbreak of tearful sobs.

It was Cornelius weeping, his head in his hands, pressing himself against the tree as if for protection.

Beetje was standing in front of Maigret. She was wearing a coat, but the inspector noted that underneath she was in her nightdress, her legs were bare and her feet in bedroom slippers.

'Pay no attention!'

Well, this one was calm at any rate. Indeed she shot a glance at Cornelius, full of reproach and impatience.

The boy turned his back on them, trying to calm down. He couldn't manage it and was ashamed of his emotion.

'He's on edge . . . He thinks . . . '

'What does he think?'

'That he's going to be accused . . . '

Cornelius was still keeping his distance. He wiped his eyes. Was he about to make a break for it?

'I haven't accused anyone yet!' announced Maigret, for the sake of saying something.

'Of course not!'

And turning towards her companion, she spoke to him in Dutch. Maigret thought he understood, or guessed, that she was saying:

'You see? The inspector isn't accusing you. Calm down. This is childish!'

Then she suddenly stopped speaking. She stayed still, listening. Maigret hadn't heard anything. A few seconds later, he thought he too could hear the snapping of a twig coming from the farm's direction. It was enough to rouse Cornelius, who looked round, his features drawn and his senses alerted.

Nobody spoke.

'Did you hear?' Beetje whispered. Cornelius tried to move towards the sound, with the bravado of a young cock. He was breathing heavily.

Too late. The enemy was nearer than they had realized.

Ten metres away, a figure loomed up, immediately recognizable: Farmer Liewens, in his carpet slippers.

'Beetje!' he called.

She did not dare answer at once. But as he repeated her name, she sighed, tremulously:

'Ja.'

Liewens was still coming forward. He walked past Cornelius, affecting not to notice him. Perhaps he had not yet seen Maigret?

But it was in front of the latter that he stopped four-square, eyes blazing and nostrils quivering with anger. He managed to contain himself, however. And stood quite still. When he spoke, his words were addressed to his daughter, in a harsh, peremptory voice.

Two or three sentences. She hung her head. Then he repeated the same word several times, in a commanding tone. Beetje spoke in French:

'He wants me to say to you . . . '

Her father was watching her as if to guess whether she was translating his words exactly.

' . . . that in Holland the police do not make arrangements to meet unmarried girls after dark out in the countryside.'

Maigret blushed as he had rarely had occasion to before. The rush of warm blood made his ears buzz.

What an idiotic accusation! And made in such bad faith!

Because there was Cornelius, skulking in the shadows, his eyes anxious and his shoulders hunched!

And Beetje's father must surely have known that it was to meet him that she had gone out. So? . . . What could he say in reply? Especially since he would have to go through an interpreter!

In any event, nobody waited for his answer. The father snapped his fingers as if to call a dog, and pointed out the path to his daughter, who hesitated, turned towards Maigret, did not dare look at her young admirer, and finally trudged away ahead of her father.

Cornelius hadn't moved. He raised a hand as if to stop the farmer's progress, but let it fall.

Father and daughter disappeared into the distance. Shortly afterwards the farmhouse door slammed shut.

Had the frogs stopped croaking during this scene? It was hard to be sure, but their chorus now reached a deafening pitch.

'Do you speak French?'

' . . . Little bit.'

The cadet was looking at Maigret with dislike, opening his mouth to speak only reluctantly, and was standing sideways as if to offer less purchase to an attacker.

'Why are you so frightened?'

Tears sprang to his eyes, but there were no sobs. Cornelius blew his nose at length. His hands were shaking. Was he going to have another panic attack?

'Do you really think you're going to be accused of killing your tutor?'

And Maigret added in a gruff voice:

'Come on, let's go.'

He pushed Cornelius in the direction of the town. He spoke slowly, sensing that his listener could only grasp about half his words.

'Is it for yourself that you're afraid?'

He was just a kid! A thin face with still unformed features, pale skin. Slender shoulders under the tight-fitting uniform. The cadet's cap was the finishing touch, making him look like a little boy dressed up as a sailor.

And distrust in his whole attitude, in the expression on his face. If Maigret had shouted at him, he would probably have raised his arms to fend off blows.

The black armband contributed a sombre and pitiful note to his appearance. It was only a month ago, wasn't it, that this boy had learned that his mother had died in the East Indies, perhaps one night when he had been enjoying himself in Delfzijl, possibly even at the annual college ball?

He would be going home in two years, with the rank of third officer, and his father would show him a grave already overgrown, and maybe another woman installed in the family home.

And his life would begin on some great steamship: watches on deck, ports of call, Java-Rotterdam, Rotterdam-Java, two days here, five or six hours there.

'Where were you when your teacher was shot?'

Now a terrible heart-wrenching sob. The boy seized Maigret's lapels in his white-gloved hands, which were trembling convulsively.

'No, not true! Not true,' he repeated a dozen or more times. '*Nee!* You not understand. No, no. Not true!'

They had reached the patch of light beamed out by the lighthouse once more. The brightness dazzled them, outlining their shapes, making every detail stand out.

'Where were you?'

'Over there.'

Over there was the Popinga house, and the canal, which he must have been in the habit of crossing by jumping from log to log.

This was an important detail. Popinga had died at five to midnight. Cornelius had reported back to his ship at five past midnight. The usual route, through the town, would take at least thirty minutes.

But it would take only six or seven minutes crossing the canal this way, avoiding the long detour!

Maigret kept walking with his deliberate, heavy tread, beside the young man, who was trembling like a leaf, and when the donkey started braying again, Cornelius jumped, quivering from head to toe as if he were about to run away.

'You're in love with Beetje?'

A stubborn silence.

'And you saw her come back, after your tutor had seen her home?'

'That's not true. Not true.'

Maigret was on the point of calming him down with a good shaking.

And yet he looked at him with an indulgent, perhaps affectionate air.

'You see Beetje every day?'

Another silence.

'What time are you supposed to be back on the college boat?'

'Ten . . . If not permission. When I went my tutor, me can . . .'

'Be back later? But not tonight?'

They were standing on the bank, near the place where Cornelius had crossed the canal. Maigret headed for the tree trunks, in the most natural way in the world, put his foot on the first and almost fell into the water, because he wasn't used to it and the log rolled under his foot.

'Come on. It'll soon be ten o'clock.'

The boy looked astonished. He must have been expecting never to see his college boat again, and to be arrested and thrown into jail.

And now this terrible French inspector was escorting him back, and preparing, like him, to jump over the two-metre gap in the middle of the canal. They splashed each other. On the other bank, Maigret stopped to wipe his trouser leg.

'Where is it?'

He hadn't explored this bank yet. There was a large area of wasteland between the Amsterdiep and the new canal, which was wide, deep and navigable by sea-going vessels.

Looking behind him, the inspector could see a single window lit on the first floor of the Popinga house. A figure, Any's, was moving behind the curtains. It must be Popinga's study. But he couldn't guess what the young lawyer was doing.

Cornelius had calmed down a little.

'I swear . . . ' he began.

'No!'

That took him aback.

He stared at the inspector with such a wild-eyed expression that Maigret tapped him on the shoulder, saying:

'Never swear to anything. Especially in your situation. Would you have wanted to marry Beetje?'

'*Ja, oh ja!*'

'And would her father have agreed to that?'

Silence. Head down, Cornelius kept on walking, threading his way among the old boats hauled up on the shore.

The broad surface of the Ems canal came into sight. At the bend a large black-and-white vessel loomed up, with every porthole illuminated. A high prow. Mast and rigging.

It was a former Dutch navy vessel, a hundred years old, now no longer seaworthy but moored here as accommodation for the students at the Naval College.

Around it moved some dark silhouettes and the glow of cigarette ends. The sound of a piano came from the games room.

Suddenly the peal of a hand bell was heard, and all the silhouettes on the bank merged into a crowd around the gangway, while further down the path from the town, four stragglers were returning at a run.

It was like the sight at a school gate, except that all these young men aged between sixteen and twenty-two were in the uniform of naval officers, with white gloves and stiff peaked caps trimmed with gold braid.

A grizzled quartermaster, leaning on the guardrail, watched them filing in while he smoked his pipe.

A youthful scene, lively and full of fun. Jokes that Maigret couldn't understand were exchanged. Cigarettes were flung down as the gangway was reached. And on board there were mock fights, chases.

The last arrivals, out of breath, were reaching the foot of the gangway. Cornelius, red-eyed, his features drawn and his expression anguished, turned to Maigret.

'Go on, get along with you,' grunted the inspector.

The boy understood his gesture better than his words, put his hand to his peaked cap, made a clumsy military salute and opened his mouth to say something.

'That'll do! Get going.'

Because the quartermaster was on the point of going inside, while a student was taking up his post as sentry. Through the portholes, the young men could be seen shaking out hammocks, throwing their clothes around with abandon.

Maigret stayed where he was until he had seen Cornelius go timidly into the dormitory, looking awkward, with hunched shoulders — and receive a pillow full in the face before he went over to a hammock at the back of the cabin.

Another scene was about to begin, a more picturesque one. The inspector had gone no more than a dozen paces towards the town when he saw Oosting who, like himself, had come to watch the cadets going back.

The two men were both middle-aged, heavily built and calm.

They surely looked ridiculous, both of them, observing the youngsters climbing into their hammocks and having pillow-fights.

They were for all the world like mother-hens, weren't they, keeping watch over a wayward chick?

They glanced at each other. The Baes did not move, but touched the peak of his cap.

They knew that any conversation was impossible, since neither spoke the other's language.

But, '*Goedenavond*,' muttered the man from Workum.

'*Bonne nuit*,' said Maigret, as if echoing him.

They were going in the same direction, following a path which after about two hundred metres turned into a road, leading into town.

They were now walking along side by side. To separate, one of them would have had to slow his pace deliberately, and neither wanted to do so.

Oosting in his clogs, Maigret in his city clothes. Both men were smoking pipes, only Maigret's was a briar, the Baes's made of china clay.

The third building they came to was a café, and Oosting went in, after stamping his clogs and then leaving them on the doormat, as was the Dutch custom.

Maigret thought for no more than a second before entering in turn.

A dozen or so seamen and bargees sat around the same table, smoking pipes and cigars, and drinking beer or genever.

Oosting shook a few hands, pulled up a chair on which he sat down heavily, and listened to the general conversation.

Maigret settled himself off to one side, well aware that in fact attention was focused on him. The proprietor, who was sitting with the group, waited a few moments before coming to ask him what he would have to drink.

The genever came from a porcelain and brass fountain. This was the predominant smell, peculiar to all Dutch cafés, making the atmosphere very different from a café in France.

Oosting's small eyes were full of laughter every time he looked at the inspector.

Maigret stretched his legs, brought them back under his chair, stretched them again, and stuffed his pipe, all to give himself an impression of composure. The café owner got up to come and offer him a light in person.

'*Mooi weer!*'

Maigret, having no idea what this meant, frowned, and had it repeated.

'*Mooi weer, ja . . . Oost wind.*'

Everyone else waited, nudging each other. Someone pointed at the window, at the starry sky.

'*Mooi weer* . . . Fair weather.'

And he tried to explain that the wind was in the east, which was a very good sign.

Oosting was selecting a cigar from a box. He fingered five or six placed in front of him. He conspicuously chose a Manila one, as black as coal, and spat the end on the floor before lighting up.

Then he showed his new cap to his companions.

'*Vier gulden.*'

Four florins! Forty francs! His eyes were still laughing.

But someone came in, opening a newspaper and talking about the latest freight prices on the Amsterdam Stock Exchange.

And in the animated conversation that followed, which sounded like a quarrel because of the deep voices and harsh syllables, they forgot about Maigret, who took some change

61

from his pocket, then went off to bed in the Van Hasselt Hotel.

5

Jean Duclos's Theories

From the hotel café, as he ate his breakfast next morning, Maigret witnessed the search, about which he had not been informed in advance. Admittedly, he hadn't attempted more than a brief meeting with the Dutch police.

It was about eight o'clock. The mist had not quite cleared, but one sensed that the sun was about to break through, ushering in a fine day. A Finnish cargo ship was leaving port, pulled by a tug. In front of the little café on the corner of the quayside, a large conclave of men had gathered, in their clogs and seaman's caps, talking in small groups.

This was the daily commodities exchange of the *schippers*, the owners of the sea-going barges of every size, crowded with wives and children, which filled one basin in the harbour.

Further along stood another handful of men: the Quayside Rats. And two uniformed gendarmes had just arrived. They had stepped on to the deck of Oosting's boat, and he himself had emerged from the forward hatch, since when he was in Delfzijl he always slept on board.

A man in civilian clothes now arrived: Inspector Pijpekamp, officially in charge of the case. He took off his hat and spoke politely. The two gendarmes vanished inside.

The search was beginning. All the *schippers* had seen it. But there wasn't the slightest movement from them, not even any show of curiosity.

Nor did the Quayside Rats budge an inch. Just a few glances, that was all.

It lasted a good half-hour. When they emerged, the gendarmes gave a military salute. Pijpekamp seemed to be apologizing.

Only, this particular morning, the Baes did not seem to want to come ashore. Instead of joining his friends on the quay, he sat down on a thwart, crossed one leg over the other, looked out to sea, where the Finnish vessel was moving heavily along, and remained there motionless, smoking his pipe.

⋆ ⋆ ⋆

When Maigret turned round, Jean Duclos was coming downstairs from his room, carrying a briefcase and an armful of books and folders, which he placed on the table he had reserved.

He merely looked questioningly at Maigret, without any greeting.

'Well?'

'Well, I think I should wish you good morning.'

The other man stared at him in some surprise and shrugged his shoulders, as if to say: not worth getting bothered about.

'Have you discovered anything?'

'Have you?'

'You know that, in theory, I'm not supposed to

leave here. Your Dutch colleague has fortunately understood that my knowledge might be helpful to him, so I have been kept informed of the results of the investigation. That's a practice the French police might like to take as an example . . . '

'Oh for goodness' sake!'

The professor hurried towards Madame Van Hasselt as she entered the room with her hair in rollers, greeted her as he would have done in a polite drawing room and apparently enquired after her health.

Maigret looked at the papers spread out on the table and recognized a new set of plans and diagrams, not only of the Popinga house but of almost the whole town, with dotted lines drawn on them which must indicate the paths taken by certain persons.

The sun, shining through the multicoloured stained-glass windows, filled the glossy-panelled room with green, red and blue shafts of light. A brewer's dray had pulled up at the door, and during the entire conversation that followed, two gigantic men were rolling barrels continuously across the floor under the eye of Madame Van Hasselt in her early-morning attire. Never had the mingled aromas of genever and beer been so overpowering. And never had Maigret been so aware of the smell of Holland.

'You've identified the murderer, then?' he asked with a sly smile, pointing to the papers.

A sharp glance from Duclos. And his reply:

'I'm beginning to think the foreigners are right. A Frenchman is above all someone who

65

cannot resist irony. Well, in this case, monsieur, it is out of place.'

Maigret looked at him, still smiling, and in no way put out of countenance. The other man went on:

'No, I haven't found the murderer. But I have perhaps done more. I've analysed the situation, I've dissected it. I have isolated each element of it . . . and now . . . '

'Now . . . ?'

'Now, someone like you will no doubt profit from my deductions and wrap up the case.'

He had seated himself. He was determined to talk, in spite of the atmosphere which he himself had made unfriendly. Maigret sat down opposite him and ordered a Bols.

'I'm listening.'

'You will notice in the first place that I am not even asking you what you have done, or what you think. I'll start with the first potential suspect: myself. I had, if I may say so, the best strategic position to shoot Popinga, and besides I was seen holding the murder weapon a few moments after the attack.

'I'm not a rich man, and if my name is known throughout the whole world, or almost, it is only by a small number of intellectuals. I am a man of modest means and sometimes living in straitened circumstances. But there was no theft, and in no way could I have hoped to benefit from the death of a lecturer at the Naval College.

'But wait! That doesn't mean that charges against me can be dropped. And people will not fail to recall that in the course of the evening, since we were discussing forensic science, I defended the proposition that an intelligent man who wished to commit a crime in cold blood might, using all his faculties, outwit a poorly educated police force.

'From which they might deduce that I had sought to illustrate my theory by example. Between ourselves, I can categorically state that if that were the case, the possibility of suspecting me would never have arisen.'

'Your good health,' said Maigret, who was watching the bull-necked brewers' men come and go.

'To continue. I postulate that if I did not commit the crime, and yet the crime was nevertheless committed, as everything seems to indicate, by someone in the house, then the whole family is guilty.

'Don't look startled! Examine my plan of the house. And above all, try to understand the psychological considerations, which I am about to develop.'

This time, Maigret could not suppress a smile at the professor's scornful condescension.

'You have no doubt heard that Madame Popinga, née Van Elst, belongs to the strictest sect in the Reformed Church. In Amsterdam, her father is known as the fiercest of conservatives. And her sister Any, already, at twenty-five, has similar ideas in politics.

'You only arrived here yesterday, and there are many aspects of Dutch life with which you are not yet familiar. Did you know that a teacher at the Naval College would receive a severe reprimand from his superiors if he were seen entering a café like this one? One of them lost his job, merely because he persisted in subscribing to a newspaper suspected of advanced views.

'I met Popinga only that one evening. But it was enough, especially after having heard what people said about him. A likely lad, you might call him. A rollicking likely lad! With his round cheeks and his bright eyes full of fun . . .

'You need to understand he had been a sailor. And when he came back ashore, he had, in a sense, put on the uniform of austerity. But the uniform was bursting at the seams.

'Do you see what I mean? It will make you smile. Because you're French. A couple of weeks ago, the club he belongs to held one of its regular meetings. Since Dutchmen don't go out to cafés at night, they get together in a hired room, under the pretext of club membership, to play billiards or skittles.

'Well, two weeks ago, by eleven at night, Popinga was quite drunk. In the same week, his wife had been organizing collections to buy clothes for the native peoples in the East Indies. And there was Popinga, with his red cheeks and shiny eyes, saying: 'Waste of time! They look much better with no clothes on! Instead of buying clothes for them, we should do as they do . . . '

'Well, of course you're smiling. A silly remark that means nothing at all. But the scandal is still raging, and if Popinga's funeral is held in Delfzijl, some people will avoid going to it.

'And that's just one little incident. Plenty

more where that came from! As I said, every one of the seams of Popinga's uniform of respectability was bursting open. Just try to work out what a sin it is here to get drunk! And his pupils had seen him in that state. That was probably why they were so fond of him!

'And now, try to imagine the atmosphere in that house on the banks of the Amsterdiep. Think of Madame Popinga and Any.

'Look out of the window. On both sides you can see to the edge of the town. It's tiny. Everyone knows everyone else. Scandal takes about an hour to reach the entire population. Including Popinga's relations with the man they call the Baes, and who is a kind of brigand, I have to say. They went seal-hunting together. And Popinga used to knock back spirits on Oosting's boat.

'I'm not asking you to come to a conclusion right away. I would just repeat this sentence: *if the crime was committed by someone in the house, the whole house is guilty.*

'Then there is that silly little girl, Beetje. Popinga never missed a chance of seeing her home. Shall I give you an idea of what she's like? Beetje is the only female round here who goes swimming every day, and not wearing a decent bathing-dress with a skirt, like all the other ladies, but in a skin-tight costume. Bright red, what's more!

'I'll let you carry on with your inquiries. I just wanted to give you a few elements that the police tend to overlook.

'As for Cornelius Barens, as I see it, he's part

69

of the family, on the female side.

'So on one hand, if you like, you have Madame Popinga, her sister Any and Cornelius. On the other, Beetje, Oosting and Popinga. If you have understood what I've told you, you might get somewhere.'

'Can I ask you a question?' said Maigret gravely.

'Yes, I'm listening.'

'Are you a Protestant too?'

'I am, yes, but I don't belong to the *Dutch* Reformed Church. It isn't the same . . . '

'So which side of the barricades are you on?'

'I didn't like Popinga . . . '

'So . . . '

'I disapprove of crime, of whatever kind.'

'Didn't he play jazz music and dance while you were talking to the ladies?'

'That's another aspect of his character that I didn't think to tell you about.'

Maigret looked splendidly serious, solemn indeed, as he stood up, saying:

'So in sum, who do you advise me to arrest?'

Professor Duclos gave a start.

'I didn't mention arresting anyone. I have given you some general indications in the realm of pure ideas, if I may say so.'

'Of course. But in my place . . . ?'

'I'm not the police. I am looking for truth for truth's sake and even the fact that I am myself under suspicion is not capable of influencing my judgement.'

'So I shouldn't arrest anyone?'

'I didn't say that, I . . . '

'Thank you,' said Maigret, extending his hand.

And he tapped his glass with a coin to call Madame Van Hasselt over. Duclos looked at him disapprovingly.

'Not the kind of thing one should do here,' he murmured. 'At least not if you want to be taken for a gentleman.'

The trapdoor for rolling the beer barrels into the cellar was being closed. Maigret paid his bill, and gave a last glance at the plans.

'So, either you, or the whole family . . . '

'I didn't say that. Listen . . . '

But Maigret was already at the door. Once his back was turned, he allowed his features to relax, and if he didn't burst out laughing at least he had a delighted smile on his face.

Outside he found himself bathed in sunlight, gentle warmth and calm. The ironmonger was at the door of his workshop. The little Jewish chandler was counting his anchors and marking them with red paint.

The crane was still unloading coal. Several *schippers* were hoisting their sails, not because they were leaving, but to allow the canvas to dry. And among the forest of masts they looked like great curtains, brown and white, flapping gently in the breeze.

Oosting was smoking his clay pipe on the afterdeck of his boat. A few Quayside Rats were chatting quietly.

But turning towards the town, one could see the smug residences of the local bourgeoisie, freshly painted, with their sparkling panes, immaculate net curtains and pot plants in every window. Beyond those windows, impenetrable shadows.

Perhaps the scene had taken on a new meaning since his conversation with Jean Duclos.

On one hand, the port, the men in clogs, the boats and sails, the tang of tar and salt water.

On the other, those houses with their polished furniture and dark wall-hangings, where people could gossip behind closed doors for a fortnight about a lecturer at the Naval College who had had a glass too many one evening.

The same sky, of heavenly limpidity. But what a frontier between these two worlds!

Then Maigret imagined Popinga, whom he had never seen, even in death, but who had had a ruddy round face, reflecting his crude appetites.

He imagined him standing at that frontier, gazing at Oosting's boat, or at some five-master whose crew had put in to every port in South America, or perhaps at the Dutch steamers that had plied in China alongside junks full of slim women who looked like beautiful porcelain dolls.

And all he had was an English dinghy, highly varnished and fitted with brass trimmings, to sail the flat waters of the Amsterdiep, where you had to navigate through floating tree trunks from Scandinavia or some tropical rainforest!

It seemed to Maigret that the Baes was looking at him meaningfully, as if he would have liked to come over and talk to him. But that was impossible! They would have been unable to exchange two words.

Oosting knew that, and stayed where he was, simply puffing a little faster on his pipe, his eyelids half-closed in the sunlight.

At this time of day, Cornelius Barens would be sitting on a college bench, listening to a lecture on trigonometry or astronomy. No doubt he was still pale in the face.

Maigret was about to go and sit on a bronze bollard when he saw Pijpekamp coming towards him, hand held out.

'Did you find anything this morning aboard the boat?'

'Not yet . . . It's just a formality.'

'You suspect Oosting?'

'Well, there was the cap . . . '

'And the cigar!'

'No. The Baes only smokes Brazilian cigars, and that was a Manila.'

'So?'

Pijpekamp drew him further along the quay, so as not to be under the nose of the overlord of Workum Island.

'The compass on board used to belong to a ship from Helsingfors. The lifebelts came from an English collier . . . And there's plenty more like that . . . '

'Stolen?'

'No. It's always the way. Whenever a cargo vessel comes into the port, there's invariably someone, an engineer, a third officer, an ordinary seaman, sometimes even the captain, who wants to sell something. You see? They tell the company that the lifebelts were swept overboard in a storm, or that the compass didn't work. Emergency flares, whatever you can think of. Sometimes even a dinghy!'

'So that doesn't prove anything.'

'No. See the Jewish chandler over there, he makes his living from this second-hand trade.'

'So your investigation . . . '

Pijpekamp turned away, looking awkward.

'I told you that Beetje Liewens hadn't gone straight home. She retraced her footsteps. That's how you say it, yes? In French?'

'Yes, yes, go on!'

'Maybe she didn't fire the gun . . . '

'Ah.'

The Dutchman was definitely ill at ease. He felt the need to drop his voice, and to take Maigret towards a completely deserted part of the quayside before going on.

'There's that timber yard . . . You see what I mean. The *timmerman* . . . In French you say the sawyer, so, yes, the sawyer claims he saw Beetje and Monsieur Popinga. Yes. The two of them.'

'Hiding behind a stack of timber, you mean?'

'Yes, and I think . . . '

'You think . . . ?'

'There may have been two other people nearby. That's the thing. The boy from the college, Cornelius Barens. He's been wanting to marry that girl. We found a photo of her in his satchel.'

'Really?'

'And also Monsieur Liewens, Beetje's father. Very important man. He raises cattle for export. He even sends some to Australia. He's a

74

widower, and she's his only child.'

'So *he* might have killed Popinga?'

Pijpekamp was so embarrassed that Maigret almost felt sorry for him. It was clearly very painful for him to accuse an important man, someone who raised cattle for export to Australia, no less.

'If he saw, you know . . . '

Maigret was relentless.

'If he saw what?'

'Near the timber stacks. Beetje and Popinga . . . '

'Ah yes.'

'This is completely confidential . . . '

'Good Lord, yes. But what about Barens?'

'He might have seen them too. And perhaps he was jealous. But he was back in college five minutes after the shooting. That's what I don't understand.'

'So to sum up,' said Maigret, in the same solemn tones he had used when speaking to Duclos, 'you suspect both Beetje's father and her admirer, Cornelius.'

There was an awkward silence.

'And you also suspect Oosting, whose cap was found in the bath.'

Pijpekamp made a gesture of discouragement.

'And of course, there's also the man who left a Manila cheroot in the dining room. How many cigar shops are there in Delfzijl?'

'Fifteen.'

'That doesn't help. And finally, you suspect Professor Duclos.'

'Because he was holding the gun. I can't allow

him to leave. You do see that.'

'Absolutely!'

They walked on about fifty metres in silence.

'So what do you think?' said the Groningen policeman, at last.

'That is the question. And that's the difference between us. You think something. In fact, you think a great many things. But I'm not aware of thinking anything yet.'

Then suddenly a question:

'Did Beetje Liewens know the Baes?'

'I don't know. I don't think so.'

'Did Cornelius know him?'

Pijpekamp rubbed his forehead.

'Maybe, maybe not. Probably not. I can find out.'

'That's it. Try to find out if they were acquainted at all before the murder.'

'You think . . . ?'

'I don't think anything at all. One more question. Can they get wireless reception on Workum?'

'No idea.'

'Another thing to find out, then.'

It was hard to say quite how it had happened, but now there was a kind of hierarchy between Maigret and his companion, who was looking up to him almost as if he were his superior officer.

'So, concentrate on those two things. I'm going to pay a visit . . . '

Pijpekamp was too polite to ask any questions about the visit, but his eyes were full of curiosity.

' . . . to Mademoiselle Beetje,' Maigret went on. 'What's the quickest way?'

'Along the Amsterdiep.'

They could see the Delfzijl pilot boat, a handsome steam vessel of some 500 tons, describing a curve on the Ems before entering port. And the Baes, walking with a slow but heavy tread, full of pent-up emotion, on the deck of his boat, a hundred metres from where the Quayside Rats were soaking up the sunshine.

6

The Letters

It was purely by chance that Maigret did not follow the Amsterdiep, but took the cross-country path.

The farm, in the morning sunshine of eleven o'clock, reminded him of his first steps on Dutch soil, the girl in her shiny boots in the modern cowshed, the prim and proper parlour and the teapot in its quilted cosy.

The same calm reigned now. Very far away, almost at the limit of the infinite horizon, a large brown sail floated above the field looking like some ghost ship sailing in an ocean of grassland.

As it had the first time, the dog barked. A good five minutes passed before the door opened, and then only a few centimetres wide, enough to let him guess at the red-cheeked face and gingham apron of the maidservant.

And even so, she was on the point of shutting the door before Maigret could even speak.

'Mademoiselle Liewens!' he called.

The garden separated them. The old woman stayed in the doorway and the inspector was on the other side of the gate. Between them, the dog was watching the intruder and baring its teeth.

The servant shook her head. 'She isn't here . . . *Niet hier.*'

Maigret had by now picked up a few words in Dutch.

'And monsieur . . . *Mijnheer?*'

A final negative sign and the door closed. But as the inspector did not go away immediately, it budged, just a few millimetres this time, and Maigret guessed the old woman was spying on him.

If he was lingering, it was because he had seen a curtain stir at the window he knew to be that of the daughter of the house. Behind the curtain, the blur of a face. Hard to see, but what Maigret did make out was a slight hand movement, which might have been a simple greeting, but more probably meant: 'I'm here. Don't insist. Watch out.'

The old woman behind the door meant one thing. This pale hand another. As did the dog jumping up at the gate and barking. All around, the cows in the fields looked artificial in their stillness.

Maigret risked a little experiment. He took a couple of steps forward, as if to go through the gate after all. He could not resist a smile, since not only did the door shut hurriedly, but even the dog, so fierce before, withdrew, tail between its legs.

This time the inspector did leave, taking the Amsterdiep towpath. All that this reception had told him was that Beetje had been confined to the house, and that orders had been given by the farmer not to let the Frenchman in.

Maigret puffed thoughtfully at his pipe. He looked for a moment at the stacks of timber where Beetje and Popinga had stopped, probably many times, holding their bicycles with one hand, while embracing each other with a free arm.

And what still dominated the scene was the calm. A serene, almost too perfect calm. A calm that might make a Frenchman believe that all of life here was as artificial as a picture postcard.

For instance, he turned round suddenly and saw only a few metres away a high-stemmed boat, which he had not heard approaching. He recognized the sail, which was wider than the canal. It was the same sail he had seen only a short time ago far away on the horizon, and yet it was here already, without it seeming possible that it could have covered the distance so quickly.

At the helm was a woman, a baby at her breast, nudging the tiller with her hip. And a man sat astride the bowsprit, legs hanging over the water, while he repaired the bobstay.

The boat glided past first the Wienands' house, then that of the Popingas, and the sail was higher than either roof. For a moment, it hid the entire façade, with its huge moving shadow.

Once again, Maigret stopped. He hesitated. The Popingas' maidservant was on her knees, scrubbing the front step, head down, hips in the air, and the door stood open.

She gave a start as she sensed him behind her. The hand holding the floor cloth was shaking.

'Madame Popinga?' he said, indicating the

interior of the house.

She tried to go ahead of him, but she got up awkwardly, because of the cloth, which was dripping with dirty water. He was the first to enter the corridor. Hearing a man's voice in the parlour, he knocked at the door.

There was a sudden silence. A total, uncompromising silence. And more than silence: expectation, as if life had been momentarily suspended.

Then footsteps. A hand touched the doorknob from inside. The door began to move. Maigret saw first of all Any, who had just opened it for him, and who gave him an unfriendly stare. Then he made out the silhouette of a man standing at the table, wearing a thick tweed suit and tawny gaiters.

Farmer Liewens.

And finally, leaning her elbow on the mantelpiece and shielding her face with her hand, Madame Popinga.

It was clear that the intruder's arrival had interrupted an important conversation, a dramatic scene, probably an argument.

On the table covered with a lace cloth, some letters were randomly scattered, as if they had been thrown down violently.

The farmer's face was the most animated, but it was also the countenance that froze most immediately.

'I'm afraid I'm disturbing you . . . ' Maigret began.

Nobody spoke. Not a word from anyone. Only Madame Popinga, after a tearful glance round,

81

left the room and went almost at a run towards the kitchen.

'Please believe that I am very sorry to have interrupted your conversation.'

At last Liewens spoke, in Dutch. He addressed a few evidently cutting remarks to the young woman, and Maigret could not help asking:

'What does he say?'

'That he will be back. That the French police . . . '

She looked embarrassed as she cast about for a way to continue.

' . . . have incredibly bad manners, perhaps,' Maigret finished the sentence. 'We have already had occasion to meet, Monsieur Liewens and I.'

The other man tried to guess what they were saying, paying attention to Maigret's intonation and expression. And the inspector, for his part, let his eyes fall on to the letters and on the signature at the bottom of one of them: *Conrad*.

The embarrassment was now at its height. The farmer moved to pick up his cap from a chair, but could not resign himself to leaving.

'He has just brought you letters that your brother-in-law wrote to his daughter.'

'How did you know?'

For heaven's sake! The scene was so easy to reconstruct, in that atmosphere thick with emotion: Liewens arriving, holding his breath in his efforts to contain his anger. Liewens being shown into the parlour, and into the presence of the two terrified women, then suddenly speaking to them and throwing the letters on the table.

Madame Popinga, distraught, hiding her face in her hands, perhaps refusing to believe the evidence, or so distressed that she was unable to speak. And Any trying to stand up to the man, arguing . . .

And it was at this point that he had knocked on the door. Everyone had frozen and Any had let him in.

★ ★ ★

In his reconstruction of events, Maigret was mistaken in one respect at least, the character of one of the people concerned. For Madame Popinga, whom he imagined to be in the kitchen, devastated by this revelation, completely overcome and without any strength, entered the room a few moments later with a calm bearing such as is reached only at a high pitch of emotion.

And slowly, she too put some letters on the table. She did not throw them down. She placed them deliberately. She looked at the farmer and then at the inspector.

She opened her mouth several times before managing to speak and then said:

'You will have to judge for yourselves . . . Someone should read these out . . . '

At that moment, Liewens blushed a deep scarlet as blood rushed to his cheeks. He was too Dutch to fall on the letters at once, but they drew him as if by an irresistible spell.

A woman's handwriting. Blue paper . . . Letters from Beetje, obviously. One thing was immediately striking: the disproportion between the two piles of letters. There were perhaps ten notes from Popinga, always written on a single sheet of paper, and usually consisting of four or five lines.

There were about thirty letters from Beetje, long and closely written!

Conrad was dead. And there remained these two unequal piles of letters, as well as the stack of timber that had protected the couple's rendezvous, on the banks of the Amsterdiep.

'Best if everyone calms down,' said Maigret. 'And perhaps it would be preferable to read out these letters without getting too angry.'

The farmer stared at him, with remarkable sharpness, and must have understood since he took a step towards the table, in spite of himself.

Maigret leaned on to the table with both hands, and picked up a note from Popinga at random.

'Would you have the goodness to translate this, please, Mademoiselle Any?'

But the young woman did not seem to hear him. She looked down at the writing, without speaking. Her sister, serious and dignified, took the letter from her hands.

'It was written at college,' she said. 'There's no date, just six o'clock. This is what it says:

Dear little Beetje,
   Better if you don't come tonight as the college principal is coming round for a cup of tea. See you tomorrow.
   Love and kisses.

84

She looked around with an air of calm defiance. Then she picked up another note. She read it out slowly:

Dear pretty little Beetje,
You must calm down. And remember that life is long. I've got a lot of work to do with the third-year exams. I can't come tonight.
Why do you keep saying I don't love you? I can't leave the college. What on earth would we do?
Take it easy, I beg you. We've got plenty of time.
With affectionate kisses.

And as Maigret seemed to say that that was enough, Madame Popinga took up another letter:
'There's this one, probably the last.'

My dear Beetje,
It's impossible. I beg you to be sensible. You know perfectly well that I don't have any money and that it would take a long time to find employment abroad.
You must be more careful and not get so wrought up. And above all, trust me.
Don't be afraid. If what you are worried about happens, I'll do my duty.
I'm anxious because I've got a lot of work on just now, and when I think of you, I can't work properly. The principal passed a critical remark yesterday and I was very upset.

I'll try to get out tomorrow evening, and tell them I'm going to visit a Norwegian ship in port.

I embrace you fondly, little Beetje.

Madame Popinga looked at each of them in turn, wearily, her eyes hooded. Her hand moved to the other pile, the one she had brought in, and the farmer gave a start. She pulled out a letter.

Dear Conrad, that I love so much,

Good news: Papa has put another thousand florins in my bank account for my birthday present. That's enough to get to America, because I looked up the boat fares in the newspaper. And we could travel third class!

But why don't you hurry up? I can't live here any more. Holland is stifling me to death. The people in Delfzijl seem to be staring at me with disapproval all the time.

But I'm so proud and happy to belong to a man like you! We must absolutely get away before the holidays because Papa wants me to spend a month in Switzerland and I don't want to. Otherwise our big project would have to wait till winter.

I've been buying English books. I can say lots of sentences already. Hurry up, do! We'll have such a lovely time, the two of us. Won't we? We can't stay here. Especially now. I think Madame Popinga is giving me the cold shoulder. And I'm still afraid of

Cornelius, who is courting me, and I don't seem able to discourage him. He's a nice boy and polite, but really stupid.

And of course he's not a man, Conrad, not a real man like you: you've been everywhere, you know everything.

Remember, a year ago, I used to try and meet you on the road and you didn't even look at me!

And now, maybe I'm going to have your child! Or anyway, it's possible.

But why are you being so cool? Don't you love me as much as before?

That wasn't the end of the letter, but Madame Popinga's voice had died away in her throat and she stopped speaking. She leafed through the pile of correspondence with her fingers. She was looking for something.

She read out one more sentence from the middle of a letter:

. . . and I'm starting to think you love your wife more than me, I'm beginning to feel jealous of her and to hate her. If that isn't the reason, why would you be saying now you don't want to go away?

The farmer could not understand the French words, but he was paying such close attention that anyone would have sworn he could guess. Madame Popinga swallowed hard, picked up one last sheet, and read in an even more strained voice:

I've heard rumours that Cornelius is more in love with Madame Popinga than with me, and that they are getting on very well. If only that were true! Then we'd be left in peace and you wouldn't have to feel bad about it.

The sheet dropped from her hands and floated down on to the carpet in front of Any, who stared at it fixedly.

There was another silence. Madame Popinga was not weeping. But everything about her was tragic: her contained pain, her dignity, maintained only through incredible effort, the admirable sentiment which had inspired her.

She had come to defend Conrad! She was waiting for an attack. She would fight if she had to.

'When did you discover these letters?' Maigret asked, awkwardly.

'The day after . . . '

She choked. She opened her mouth for a gulp of air. Her eyelids were swollen.

' . . . after Conrad . . . '

'I see.'

He understood. He looked at her with sympathy. She was not pretty. And yet she had regular features. Her face had none of the flaws that made Any's so unprepossessing.

Madame Popinga was a tall woman, well-built, but not fat. A glossy helmet of fine hair framed her delicately pink Dutch face.

But would he perhaps have preferred it if she had been ugly? Those regular features and her controlled, sensible expression somehow conveyed a total lack of enthusiasm for life.

Even her smile had to be a sensible, measured smile, her joy a sensible joy, always under control.

Already at six years old, she must have been a serious child. And by sixteen, much as she was today.

One of those women who seem born to be sisters, or aunts, or nurses, or widows patronizing good causes.

Conrad was no longer there, and yet Maigret had never felt him to be so alive as at this moment, with his hearty open face, his greed or rather appetite for life, his shyness, his fear of offending people and his wireless set, with which he fiddled for hours in order to pick up jazz from Paris, gypsy music from Budapest, an operetta from Vienna, or perhaps even faraway boat-to-boat calls on short wave.

Any approached her sister, as one would someone who is ill and about to collapse. But Madame Popinga went towards Maigret, or at least took a couple of steps.

'I never dreamed . . . ' she whispered. 'Never. I lived . . . I . . . And when he died, I . . . '

He guessed, from her breathing, that she had a heart condition, and a moment later she confirmed his hypothesis by standing still for a long moment, pressing her hand to her chest.

Someone else moved in the room: the farmer, with wild eyes and a fevered expression, had gone over to the table and snatched up the letters from his daughter, with the nervous gesture of a thief fearing to be caught.

She let him go ahead. Maigret did the same.

But Liewens did not yet dare leave. He could be heard speaking, without addressing anyone in particular. Maigret caught the word *Fransman*, and it was as if he could understand Dutch in the same way that Liewens, that day, had understood French.

He could more or less work out the sentence: 'And you think it was necessary to tell the Frenchman all this?'

Liewens dropped his cap, picked it up, bowed to Any, who was standing in his way, but to her alone, muttered a few more unintelligible syllables and went out. The maid must have finished cleaning the step since they heard the door open and shut and his footsteps going away.

In spite of the younger woman's presence, Maigret asked some further questions, with a gentleness one might not have suspected in him.

'Have you already shown these letters to your sister?'

'No. But when that man . . . '

'Where were they?'

'In a drawer in the bedside table . . . I never used to open it. It was where the revolver was kept too.'

Any said something in Dutch, and Madame Popinga translated automatically.

'My sister is telling me I ought to go and lie down. Because I haven't slept for three nights. He'd never have gone away from here . . . He must have been imprudent, just one indiscretion, don't you think? He liked to laugh and play. But

90

now that I think of it, some little things come back . . . Beetje used to bring over fruits and home-made cake . . . I thought she was coming to see me. And she would ask us to play tennis . . . Always at a time when she knew quite well I was busy. But I didn't see any harm in it. I was glad Conrad had a chance to relax. Because he worked very hard, and Delfzijl was a bit dull for him. Last year, she nearly came to Paris with us . . . and it was even my idea!'

She said all this simply, but with a weariness in which there was hardly any rancour.

'He can't have wanted to leave here . . . You heard . . . But he was afraid of causing pain to anyone. That was how he was. He used to be reprimanded for giving exam marks that were too generous. That's why my father didn't care for him.'

She put an ornament back in its place, and this precise housewifely act was at odds with the atmosphere in the room.

'I'd just like all this to be over. Because we're not even allowed to bury him. You know that? I don't know . . . I want them to give him back to me. God will see that the guilty one is punished.'

She became more animated. She went on, her voice firmer now:

'Yes! That's what I believe. Things like this, they're a matter between God and the murderer. What can we know?'

She gave a start, as if an idea had just struck her. Pointing to the door, she gasped:

'Perhaps he's going to kill her. He's capable of it. That would be terrible!'

91

Any was looking at her with some impatience. She must have been thinking all these words were of no help, and it was with a calm voice that she asked:

'So now, what do you think, *monsieur le commissaire*?'

'Nothing!'

She didn't insist. But her face showed her dissatisfaction.

'I don't think anything, because above all there is the matter of Oosting's cap!' he said. 'You heard Jean Duclos's theories. You've read the books by Grosz he told you about. One principle! Never allow yourself to be distracted from the truth by psychological considerations. Follow to the end the reasoning resulting from material evidence.'

It was impossible to know whether he was serious or whether he was teasing her.

'And here we have a cap, and the stub of a cigar! Somebody must have brought them or thrown them into the house.'

Madame Popinga sighed to herself:

'I can't believe that Oosting . . . '

Then suddenly, lifting her head:

'That makes me think of something I'd forgotten.'

Then she fell silent, as if fearing she had said too much, terrified by the consequences of her words.

'Tell me.'

'No, no, it's nothing.'

'I would still like . . . '

'When Conrad went seal-hunting on the

Workum sandbanks . . . '

'Yes? What about it . . . ?'

'Beetje went with them. Because she goes hunting too . . . Here in Holland, girls have a lot of freedom.'

'Did they spend the night away?'

'Sometimes one night. Sometimes two.'

She took her head in her hands with a gesture of the most extreme frustration and groaned.

'No! I don't want to think about it! It's too horrible! Too horrible.'

This time, sobs were rising in her throat, ready to break out, and Any took her sister by the shoulders and gently propelled her into the next room.

7

Lunch at the Van Hasselt

When Maigret arrived back at the hotel, he realized that something unusual was happening. The previous day he had dined at the table next to Jean Duclos's.

Now, three places were laid on the round table in the centre of the dining room. A dazzling white cloth, with knife-sharp creases, had been spread. And at each place stood three glasses, which in Holland is only done for a truly ceremonial meal.

As soon as he came in, Maigret was greeted by Inspector Pijpekamp, who advanced towards him, hand outstretched, with the wide smile of a man who has arranged a pleasant surprise.

He was in his best clothes: a wing-collar eight centimetres high! A formal jacket. He was freshly shaved, and must have come straight from the barber's, for around him there still hovered a scent of Parma violets.

Less formally dressed, Jean Duclos stood behind him, looking slightly jaundiced.

'You must forgive me, my dear colleague. I should have warned you this morning . . . I would have liked to invite you back home, but I live in Groningen and I'm a bachelor. So I have taken the liberty of inviting you to lunch here. Just a simple lunch, no fuss.'

And looking, as he pronounced the last words, at the cutlery and crystal glasses, he was obviously waiting for Maigret to contradict him.

He did no such thing.

'I thought that since the professor is your compatriot, you would be happy to . . . '

'Very good! Very good!' said Maigret. 'Would you excuse me while I go to wash my hands.'

He did so, looking grumpy, at the little washbasin in an adjacent room. The kitchen was next door, and he could hear much bustle, the clink of dishes and saucepans.

When he went back to the dining room, Pijpekamp himself was pouring port into the glasses and murmuring with a modest but delighted smile:

'Just like in France, eh? *Prosit!* Your very good health, my dear colleague.'

His goodwill was touching. He was making an effort to find the most sophisticated expressions and show that he was a man of the world to his fingertips.

'I ought to have invited you yesterday. But I was so . . . how would you say? So shaken about by this affair. Have you discovered anything?'

'No, nothing.'

The Dutchman's eyes lit up, and Maigret thought to himself:

'Aha, my little man, you've got some prize exhibit to show me, and you'll bring it out over dessert. If you have the patience to wait that long.'

He was not mistaken. The first course was tomato soup, which was served with a

Saint-Émilion sweet enough to make you feel bilious, and obviously fortified for export.

'Your health!'

What a good show Pijpekamp was putting on! Doing his very best or even better. And Maigret didn't even seem to notice it. He showed no appreciation!

'In Holland, you know, we never drink with the meal, only afterwards. In the evening, on special occasions a little glass of wine with a cigar. And we don't have bread with the meal either.'

And he looked at the bread basket, which he had ordered specially. He had even arranged for port as an aperitif, instead of the national drink of genever.

What more could he have done? He was pink with excitement. He looked at the golden wine bottle with emotion. Jean Duclos was eating as if his mind were elsewhere.

And Pijpekamp had been so anxious to inject some gaiety into this lunch, to create an atmosphere of abandon, a real explosion of Frenchness!

The waiters brought in the national Dutch dish: the *hutspot*. The meat was swimming in litres of gravy, and Pijpekamp assumed a mysterious air to announce:

'Now, you must tell me if you like it.'

Unfortunately, Maigret was not in a good mood. He could indeed sense some kind of mystery in the air, but as yet was unable to fathom it.

It seemed to him that there was a kind of

freemasonry between Duclos and the Dutch policeman. For instance, every time the latter refilled Maigret's glass, he stole a glance at the professor.

A bottle of Burgundy was warming by the stove.

'I thought you'd be drinking more wine.'

'That depends . . . '

Duclos was certainly ill at ease. He avoided joining in the conversation, and was drinking nothing but mineral water, claiming he was on a diet.

Pijpekamp could wait no longer. He'd chatted about the beauties of the harbour, the volume of traffic on the Ems, the University of Groningen, where the greatest scholars in the world came to give lectures.

'And now you know, we've come up with something new.'

'Really?'

'Your health! The health of the French police! Yes, now, the mystery is more or less cleared up.'

Maigret looked at him with his most neutral gaze, showing not the slightest trace of emotion, or even curiosity.

'This morning, at about ten o'clock, I was told that someone was waiting to see me in my office. Guess who?'

'Barens. Yes, go on.'

Pijpekamp was even more crestfallen than over the lack of effect the luxurious meal had had on his guest.

'How did you know? Someone told you, didn't they?'

'Not at all. What did he want?'

'You know him. Very timid, very — what's the French word? Reserved. He didn't dare look me in the eye. You'd have thought he was about to burst into tears. He confessed that on the night of the crime, when he left the Popingas' house, he didn't go straight back to the boat.'

At this point, the Dutch inspector gave a whole series of winks and nudges.

'You get it? He is in love with Beetje. And he was jealous because Beetje had been dancing with Popinga. And he was cross with her, because she'd drunk a cognac. He saw them both leave. He went after them at a distance. Then he followed his tutor back home.'

Maigret remained hard-hearted. And yet he could see that the other man would have given anything to receive some indication on his part of surprise, admiration or indeed discomfiture.

'Your good health, monsieur. Barens didn't tell us at first, because he was frightened. But now, here's the truth! He saw a man running away immediately after the gunshot, towards the timber yard where he must have been hiding.'

'And he described him in detail, I suppose?'

'Yes.'

The Dutchman was dripping with perspiration. He no longer had any hope of astonishing his colleague. His story was falling flat.

'A sailor. Undoubtedly a foreign sailor. Very tall, thin, clean shaven.'

'And naturally, a boat left early next morning.'

'Three have left since then. So it's obvious. The whole thing's as clear as day. It's not in

98

Delfzijl that we should be looking. It was an outsider, no doubt some sailor who used to know Popinga in the past, when he was at sea. A sailor with a grudge, someone he'd punished when he was an officer or captain.'

Jean Duclos was obstinately presenting only his profile to Maigret's observation. Pijpekamp signalled to Madame Van Hasselt, who was sitting at the till in her Sunday best, to bring them another bottle. They still had the dessert to eat, a *pièce de résistance*, a cake decorated with three kinds of cream on which the name Delfzijl was written in chocolate icing.

Pijpekamp lowered his eyes modestly.

'Would you like to cut the first slice?'

'And you let Cornelius go?'

His neighbour started, and looked at Maigret as if wondering whether he had gone mad.

'But . . . '

'If it's all the same to you, we can question him together presently.'

'That will be quite easy. I can phone the college.'

'And while you're at it, you can telephone Oosting, and we'll question him after that.'

'Because of his cap? But now that's explained, isn't it? A passing sailor saw his cap on the deck. Picked it up and . . . '

'Naturally.'

Pijpekamp was close to tears. Maigret's grave yet hardly perceptible irony had unsettled him so much that he bumped into the door-frame of the café's telephone booth as he went to make his call.

Maigret remained alone for a moment with Jean Duclos, who was looking determinedly at his plate.

'You didn't ask him to slip me a few discreet florins perhaps, while you were about it?'

These words were spoken quietly, without bitterness, and Duclos raised his head, opening his mouth to protest.

'Hush. We haven't time to argue. You advised him to offer me a good lunch with plenty of wine. You said, in France that's the way to get round a public employee. Hush, not a word. And after that I'd be putty in his hands.'

'I swear . . .'

Maigret lit his pipe and turned towards Pijpekamp, who was coming back from the telephone, and who, as he looked at the table, stammered:

'You'll, er, accept a little brandy? There's some fine old stuff . . .'

'Please allow me to be the one offering the drinks now. Could you ask Madame to bring over a bottle of her best cognac and some brandy glasses?'

But Madame Van Hasselt brought them some shot glasses. Maigret got up and went over to the counter himself to fetch brandy glasses, which he filled to the brim.

'To the health of the Dutch police!' he said.

Pijpekamp did not dare protest. The alcohol brought tears to his eyes, it was so strong. But Maigret, with a ruthless smile, kept raising his glass and repeating:

'Good health to your police force! . . . What

time will Barens be in your office?'

'In half an hour. A cigar?'

'Thank you, but I prefer my pipe.'

And Maigret refilled the glasses with such authority that neither Pijpekamp nor Duclos dared refuse to drink.

'What a beautiful day!' he said several times. 'Maybe I'm mistaken, but I have the feeling that tonight poor Popinga's murderer will be under arrest.'

'Unless he's sailing in the Baltic,' Pijpekamp replied.

'Bah! You really think he's that far away?'

Duclos looked up, the blood draining from his face.

'Is that an insinuation, inspector?' he asked sharply.

'What kind of insinuation?'

'You seem to be suggesting that if he is not far away, he might be very close at hand.'

'What a lively imagination you have, professor.'

They were within inches of an incident. Due in part, no doubt, to the glasses of cognac. Pijpekamp was scarlet in the face. His eyes were glistening.

As for Duclos, the effect of the alcohol was to make him deathly pale.

'Just one more glass, gentlemen, and we can go and interview this poor boy.'

The bottle was on the table. Every time Maigret poured out a glass, Madame Van Hasselt licked her pencil and noted each measure in her book.

As they stepped outside, hot sunshine and tranquillity engulfed them. Oosting's boat lay calmly at its berth. Pijpekamp clearly felt the need to hold himself straighter than usual.

They had only three hundred metres to walk. The streets were deserted. The shops stretched before them, empty of customers, but as clean and well stocked as if for an international exhibition about to open its gates.

'It will be well-nigh impossible to catch this sailor,' Pijpekamp declared. 'But it's a good thing we know it was him, because now we needn't suspect anyone else. I will write a report so that your compatriot, Monsieur Duclos, can be quite at liberty.'

He entered the local police station with far from steady steps, and bumped into a piece of furniture before sitting down rather too heavily.

He wasn't exactly drunk. But the alcohol had taken away some of the mildness and politeness that characterize most Dutchmen.

With a rather expansive gesture, he tilted back his chair and pressed an electric bell. He spoke in Dutch to a uniformed policeman, who went out, returning a moment later with Cornelius.

Although Pijpekamp welcomed him with the utmost cordiality, the young man seemed to lose confidence as he entered the room, because his eyes had immediately lighted on Maigret.

'The chief inspector from Paris just wants to ask you about a few details,' Pijpekamp said in French.

Maigret was in no hurry. He sauntered across the office, puffing at his pipe.

'Well now, young Barens! What did the Baes say to you last night?'

The young man twisted his thin face in every direction, like a panicking bird.

'I . . . I think . . . '

'Come on, I'll help you. You still have your papa, don't you, out in the Indies? He would be very upset, wouldn't he, if anything were to happen to you? If you were to get into trouble? I'm guessing, but possibly perjury, in an affair like this, could land you several months in prison.'

Cornelius was choking, not daring to make a movement or to look at anyone.

'Come on, admit it, Oosting was waiting for you yesterday on the bank of the Amsterdiep, and he instructed you to tell the police what you in fact told them. Let's have the truth now: you never did see any tall, thin man hanging around the Popinga house.'

'I . . . '

But no. He didn't have the strength to resist. He burst into tears. He was in a state of collapse.

And Maigret looked first at Jean Duclos then at Pijpekamp with that heavy but impenetrable expression that made some people think him an idiot. Because that gaze was so neutral that it appeared completely vacant.

'So you think . . . ?' began the Dutch inspector.

'See for yourself.'

The young man, whose officer's uniform, by its formality, made him look even slighter than he was, blew his nose, and clenched his teeth to try and stifle his sobs, but finally stammered:

'I haven't done anything . . . '

They watched him for some moments, as he tried to regain control.

'That's all,' pronounced Maigret firmly at last. 'I didn't say you had done anything. Oosting asked you to claim you had seen a stranger lurking by the house. He probably told you that it was the only way to save a certain someone . . . Who?'

'I swear on the head of my mother he didn't tell me who. I don't know! I want to die!'

'Tut, tut! At eighteen, everyone wants to die. You don't have any more questions, Monsieur Pijpekamp?'

The Dutch officer shrugged his shoulders, a gesture signifying that he had no idea what was going on.

'All right, young man, you can be off now.'

'You know, it wasn't Beetje . . . '

'Possibly. Time for you to run off and join your college friends.'

And he pushed him outside, muttering:

'Next! Has Oosting arrived? Unfortunately that one doesn't understand French.'

The electric bell rang again. Presently, the duty officer brought in the Baes, who was holding his new cap as well as his pipe, which he had allowed to go out.

He looked in only one direction, at Maigret. And, strange to say, his expression was reproachful. He stood in front of the Dutch inspector's desk and greeted him.

'Would you mind asking him where he was

when Popinga was shot?'

Pijpekamp translated. Oosting embarked on a long speech that Maigret couldn't understand, which didn't prevent him interrupting.

'No! Stop him. Just get him to answer the question in a couple of words.'

Pijpekamp translated. Another reproachful stare. And an answer, translated at once:

'On board his boat.'

'Tell him that is not true.'

And Maigret paced up and down again, hands behind his back.

'What does he say to that?'

'He swears it's true.'

'Right, well in that case, get him to tell you who stole his cap.'

Pijpekamp was all docility. It is true that Maigret was now conveying the impression that he was in charge.

'Well?'

'He was in his cabin. Doing the accounts. He saw through the porthole some legs up on deck. He recognized a seaman's trousers.'

'And he followed the man?'

Oosting hesitated, half-shut his eyes, snapped his fingers and spoke volubly.

'What's he saying?'

'That he prefers to tell the truth. That he is quite sure that his innocence will be recognized. By the time he got up on deck, the seaman was far away. He followed at a distance. And he was led along the Amsterdiep to a point near the Popinga house. Then the sailor hid. Oosting was intrigued, so he hid as well.'

'Did he hear the shot, an hour or two later?'

'Yes, but he couldn't catch the man who was running away.'

'He saw the man enter the house?'

'The garden, at any rate. He supposes he must have climbed to the first floor, using the drainpipe.'

Maigret smiled. The vague, contented smile of a man who is digesting his meal with total satisfaction.

'Would he recognize this man again?'

Translation, shrug of shoulders.

'He doesn't know.'

'He saw Barens spying on Beetje and his tutor?'

'Yes.'

'And since he was afraid he would be accused himself, and since he also wanted to give the police a line to follow, he got Cornelius to testify on his behalf.'

'That's what he says. But I don't have to believe him, do I? He's clearly guilty . . . '

Jean Duclos was showing signs of impatience. Oosting was calm, a man who was now ready for anything. He spoke again and the policeman translated his words.

'He's saying now that we can do what we like with him, but that Popinga was both his friend and his benefactor.'

'And what are you going to do?'

'Hold him in custody. He's admitted he was there.'

Still under the influence of the cognac, Pijpekamp's voice was louder than usual, his gestures less controlled, and his decisions reflected this. He wanted to appear authoritative. He had a foreign colleague opposite him and he was trying to save his own reputation as well as that of Holland.

He assumed a serious expression and pressed the bell again. And when the duty officer hurried in, he gave orders punctuated by little taps of his paper-knife on the desk.

'Arrest this man! Take him away. I'll see to him later.'

All this in Dutch, but it was easy to understand what was being said.

Upon which, he stood up: 'I will try to clear this matter up for good. I shall of course report on the role you have played. And naturally your compatriot is free to leave.'

He did not suspect that Maigret, as he watched his Dutch colleague gesticulating wildly, his eyes bright with drink, was thinking to himself: 'My dear fellow, in a few hours' time, when you've calmed down, you will bitterly regret what you have done.'

Pijpekamp opened the door, but Maigret did not seem ready to leave.

'May I prevail on you for a final favour?' he said, with unaccustomed politeness.

'I am all ears, my dear colleague.'

'It's not yet four o'clock. Tonight we could hold a reconstruction of the drama, with all those who have been connected with it, closely or otherwise. Could you make a list of their names? Madame Popinga, Any, Monsieur Duclos, Barens, the Wienands, Beetje, Oosting and lastly Monsieur Liewens, Beetje's father.'

'You want to . . . '

'Re-enact the events, from the time the lecture ended at the Van Hasselt Hotel.'

There was a silence. Pijpekamp was thinking.

'I'll telephone Groningen,' he said at last, 'and ask my superiors for advice.'

He added, not quite sure how his joke would go down, and watching the faces of the others:

'But you know, someone will be missing. Conrad Popinga won't be able to . . . '

' . . . I will take his place,' Maigret finished the sentence.

And he went out followed by Jean Duclos, having issued his parting shot:

'And thank you for that excellent lunch!'

8

Two Young Women

Instead of going straight through town from the police station to the Van Hasselt, Maigret went round by the quayside, followed by Jean Duclos, whose bearing, expression, and the tilt of his head all indicated ill temper.

'You do realize you're making yourself utterly obnoxious?' he muttered at last, his eyes fixed on the crane unloading a ship in the harbour, as its arm swung across just above their heads.

'Because . . . ?'

Duclos shrugged, and walked on a few paces without replying.

'You wouldn't even understand. Or perhaps you're deliberately refusing to understand. You're like all the French . . . '

'But I thought we were the same nationality.'

'Yes, but I've travelled a lot. My culture is worldwide. I know how to fit in with the country where I find myself. But you, ever since you've been here, you've just been barging ahead without bothering about the consequences.'

'Without bothering to find out, for instance, whether people really want the murderer to be found?'

Duclos reacted angrily.

'Why should they? This wasn't a gangland killing. So the murderer isn't a professional criminal. We're not talking about someone who has to be put away in order to protect society.'

'So in that case . . . ?'

Maigret had a self-satisfied way of puffing at his pipe, with his hands behind his back.

'Just take a look,' Duclos said in an undertone, pointing to the scene all around them, the picture-book town, with everything in its place, like ornaments on the mantelpiece of a tidy housewife, the harbour too small for serious trouble, the placid inhabitants standing there in their yellow clogs.

Then he went on:

'Everyone here earns his living. Everyone's more or less content. And above all, everyone keeps his instincts under control, because that's the rule here, and a necessity if people want to live in society. Pijpekamp will confirm that burglaries are extremely rare. It's true that someone who steals a loaf of bread can expect a jail sentence of at least a few weeks. But where do you see any disorder? There are no prowlers. No beggars. This is a place of clean living and organization.'

'And I'm the bull in the china shop!'

'Hear me out! See the houses on the left, by the Amsterdiep? They're the residences of the city elders, wealthy men, powerful locally. Everyone knows them. There's the mayor, the church ministers, the teachers and civil servants, everyone who sees to it that nothing disturbs the peace of the town, that everyone knows his place and isn't a nuisance to his neighbours. These people, as I think I've already told you, don't

110

even approve of one of their number going to a café, because it would be setting a bad example. Then a crime is committed. And *you* suspect some family quarrel.'

Maigret listened to all this as he watched the boats, their decks riding higher than the quayside now, like a series of brightly coloured walls, since it was high tide.

'I don't know what Pijpekamp thinks,' Duclos went on. 'Certainly he's well-respected. What I do know is that it would be preferable, and in everyone's interest, to announce this evening that Popinga's murderer was some foreign seaman, and that the search is still under way. For everyone's sake. Better for Madame Popinga. For her family. For her father, too, who's an eminent intellectual. For Beetje and *her* father. But above all for the sake of example! For all the people living in the little houses in this town, who watch what happens in the big houses on the Amsterdiep and are ready to do the same. But you, you want truth for truth's sake, for the glory of solving a difficult case.'

'Is that what Pijpekamp said to you this morning? And he took the opportunity, didn't he, to ask you how he could discourage my persistent habit of raising awkward questions? And you told him that in France, men like me can be bought off with a good lunch, or even a tip.'

'No such precise words passed our lips.'

'Do you know what I think, Monsieur Jean Duclos?'

111

Maigret had stopped, the better to admire the panorama. A tiny little boat, kitted out as a shop, was chugging along from ship to ship, barge to yacht trailing petrol fumes and selling bread, spices, tobacco, pipes and genever.

'I'm listening.'

'I think you were lucky to come out of the bathroom holding the revolver.'

'What do you mean?'

'Nothing. Just tell me, again, that you saw nobody in the bathroom.'

'That's right, I didn't see anybody.'

'And you didn't hear anything either?'

Duclos turned his head away.

'Nothing very clearly. Perhaps just a feeling that something moved under the lid of the bath.'

'Oh, excuse me — I see there's someone waiting for me.'

And Maigret strode off briskly towards the entrance of the Van Hasselt, where Beetje Liewens could be seen pacing up and down on the pavement, looking out for him.

★   ★   ★

She tried to smile at him, as she had before, but this time her smile was joyless. She seemed nervous. She went on glancing down the street, as if afraid of seeing someone appear.

'I've been waiting almost half an hour for you.'

'Will you come inside?'

'Not to the café, please.'

In the corridor, he hesitated for a second. He couldn't take her to his room either. He pushed open the door of the ballroom, a huge empty space where voices echoed as if in a church.

In broad daylight, the stage looked dusty and lacklustre. The piano was open. A bass drum stood in a corner and piles of chairs were stacked up to the ceiling.

Behind them hung paper chains, which must have been used for a dance.

Beetje looked as fresh-faced as before. She was wearing a blue jacket and skirt, and her bosom was more enticing than ever under a white silk blouse.

'So you were able to get out of the house?'

She did not reply at once. She obviously had plenty to say, but didn't know where to begin.

'I escaped!' she said at last. 'I couldn't stay there any more, I was scared. The maid came to tell me my father was furious, he was capable of killing me. Already he'd shut me in my room without a word. Because he never says anything when he's angry. The other night, we went home without saying a thing. He locked me in. This afternoon, the maid spoke to me through the keyhole. It seems he came back at midday, white in the face. He ate his lunch, then went stalking off around the farm. After that he visited my mother's grave. That's what he does every time he's going to make an important decision. So I broke a pane of glass in the door, and the maid passed me a screw-driver so that I could take off the lock. I don't want to go back. You don't know my father . . . '

'One question,' Maigret interrupted.

He was looking at the little handbag in glossy

kid leather she was holding.

'How much money did you bring with you?'

'I don't know ... Perhaps five hundred florins.'

'From your own bedroom?'

She reddened and stammered:

'It was in the desk. I wanted to go to the station. But there was a policeman on duty there, so I thought of you.'

They were standing there as if in a waiting room, where an intimate atmosphere is impossible, and it occurred to neither of them to take two of the stacked chairs and sit down.

Beetje might be on edge, but she wasn't panicking. That was perhaps why Maigret was looking at her with some hostility, which found its way into his voice when he asked her:

'How many men have you already asked to run away with you?'

She was entirely taken aback. Turning away, she stammered:

'Wh — What did you say?'

'Well, you asked Popinga. Was he the first?'

'I don't understand.'

'I'm asking you if he was your first lover.'

A longish silence. Then:

'I didn't think you'd be so nasty to me. I came here ... '

'Was he the first? All right, so it had been going on for a little over a year. But before that?'

'I ... I had a bit of a flirtation with my gym teacher at high school in Groningen.'

'A flirtation?'

'It was him, he ... '

'Right. You had a lover before Popinga, then. Any others?'

'Never,' she cried indignantly.

'And you've been Barens's mistress too, haven't you?'

'No, that's not true, I swear . . . '

'But you used to meet him . . . '

'Because he was in love with me. But he hardly dared even kiss me.'

'And the last time you had a rendezvous with him, the one that was interrupted when both I and your father turned up, you suggested running away together?'

'How did you know?'

He almost burst out laughing. Her naivety was incredible. She had regained some of her self-possession. In fact, she spoke of these delicate matters with remarkable frankness!

'But he didn't want to?'

'He was scared. He said he didn't have any money.'

'So you proposed to get some from your house. In short, you've been itching to run away for ages. Your main aim in life is to leave Delfzijl with a man, any man.'

'Not just any man,' she corrected him crossly. 'You're being horrible. You're not trying to understand.'

'Oh yes I am! A five-year-old could understand! You love life! You like men! You like all the pleasures the world has to offer.'

She lowered her eyes and fiddled with her handbag.

'You're bored stiff on your father's model

115

farm. You want something else in life. You start at high school, when you're seventeen, with the gym teacher. But you can't persuade him to leave. In Delfzijl you look around at the available men, and you find one who looks more adventurous than the others. Popinga's travelled the world. He likes life too. And he too is chafing at the prejudices of the local people. You throw yourself at him.'

'Why do you say . . . ?'

'Maybe I'm exaggerating a little. Let's say, here you are, a pretty girl, devilishly attractive, and he starts to flirt a bit with you. But only timidly, because he's afraid of complications, he's afraid of his wife, of Any, of his principal and his pupils.'

'Especially Any!'

'We'll get to her later. So he snatches kisses in corners. I'm prepared to bet he wasn't even bold enough to ask for more. But you think you've hit the jackpot. You engineer meetings every day. You go round to his house with fruit. You're accepted into the household. You get him to see you home on his bike, and you stop behind the timber stacks. You write letters to him about your longing to run away . . . '

'You've read them?'

'Yes.'

'And you don't think it was him that started it?'

She was launched now.

'At first, he told me he was unhappy, Madame Popinga didn't understand him, all she thought about was what people would say, that he was leading a stupid life, and so on.'

'Naturally!'

'So you see . . . '

'Sixty per cent of married men say that kind of thing to the first attractive young woman they meet. Unfortunately for him, he'd come across a girl who took him at his word.'

'Oh you're so horrible, so horrible!'

She was on the point of crying. She restrained herself, and stamped her foot as she said 'horrible'.

'In short, he kept putting off this famous escape, and you started to think it was never going to happen.'

'That's not true!'

'Yes it is. As is proved by your taking out a kind of insurance policy against that happening, by letting young Barens pay his respects. Cautiously. Because he's a shy young man, well brought up, respectful, you have to be careful not to scare him off.'

'That's a mean thing to say!'

'It's merely what happens in real life.'

'You really hate me, don't you?'

'Me? Not at all.'

'You do hate me! But I'm so unhappy. I loved Conrad.'

'And Cornelius? And the gym teacher?'

This time she did shed tears. She stamped her foot again.

'I forbid you . . . '

'To say you didn't love any of them? Why not? You only loved them to the extent that they represented another life for you, the great escape you were always longing for.'

She wasn't listening any more. She wailed:

'I shouldn't have come, I thought . . . '

'That I would take you under my wing. But that's what I am doing. Only I don't consider you a victim in all this, or a heroine. Just a greedy little girl, a bit silly, a bit selfish, that's all. There are plenty of little girls like that around.'

She looked up with tearful eyes, in which some hope already glistened.

'But everyone hates me,' she moaned.

'Who do you mean by everyone?'

'Madame Popinga, for a start, because I'm not like her. She'd like me to be making clothes all day for South Sea islanders, or knitting socks for the poor. I know she's told the girls who work for those charities not to be like me. And she even said out loud that if I didn't find a husband soon, I'd come to a bad end. People told me.'

It was as if a breath of the slightly rancid air of the little town had reached them once more: the gossip, the girls from good families, sitting knitting under the watchful eye of a lady who dispensed good works, advice and sly remarks.

'But it's mostly Any.'

'Who hates you?'

'Yes. When I went round there, she'd usually leave the room and go upstairs. I'm sure she guessed the truth a long time ago. Madame Popinga, in spite of everything, means well. She just wanted me to change my ways, to wear different clothes. And she especially wanted to get me to read something different from novels! But she didn't suspect anything. She was the one who told Conrad to see me home.'

An amused smile floated across Maigret's face.

'But with Any, it's not the same. You've seen her, haven't you? She looks a fright! Her teeth are all crooked. She's never had a man interested in her. And she knows it. She knows she'll be an old maid all her life. That's why she did all that studying: she wanted to have a profession. She's even a member of those feminist leagues.'

Beetje was getting worked up. One sensed an ancient grievance coming to the surface.

'So she was always creeping around the house, keeping an eye on Conrad. Because she doesn't have any choice about being virtuous, she'd like everyone to be in the same boat. You understand? She guessed, I'm sure. She must have tried to get her brother-in-law to give me up. And even Cornelius! She could see that all the men look at me, and that includes Wienands, who's never dared say a word to me, but he goes red when I dance with him. And *his* wife hates me too, because of that. Maybe Any didn't say anything to her sister. But maybe she did. Maybe she's the one that found my letters.'

'And then went on to kill?' said Maigret sharply.

She stammered:

'N-no, I swear I don't know, I didn't say that. Just that Any's poisonous! Is it my fault if she's ugly?'

'And you're sure she's never had a lover?'

Ah, the little smile, or indeed giggle, in Beetje's answer, that instinctively victorious giggle of a desirable woman scorning one who is plain!

It was like little misses in boarding school, squabbling over a trifle.

'Not in Delfzijl, at any rate.'

'And as well as hating you, she didn't like her brother-in-law either, did she?'

'I don't know. That's not the same thing, he was family. And perhaps all the family belonged to her a little. So she had to keep an eye on him, see he didn't get into trouble . . . '

'But not shoot him?'

'What can you be thinking? You keep saying that.'

'I don't think anything. Just answer my questions. Was Oosting aware of your relationship with Popinga?'

'Did they tell you that too?'

'You went on his boat together to the Workum sandbanks. Did he leave you two . . . on your own?'

'Yes, he was up on deck, steering the boat.'

'And he let you have the cabin.'

'Naturally, it was cold outside.'

'You haven't seen him since . . . since Conrad's death?'

'No! I swear I haven't.'

'And he's never made any advances to you?'

She laughed out loud.

'Him?'

And yet she was again on the brink of weeping, clearly distressed. Madame Van Hasselt, having heard their raised voices, put her head round the door, then muttered her apologies and went back to her post behind the till. There was a silence.

'Do you really believe your father's capable of killing you?'

'Yes! He would . . . '

'So he might also have been capable of killing your lover.'

She opened her eyes wide with terror, and protested fiercely:

'No, no! That's not true! Papa wouldn't . . . '

'But when you got home on the night of the crime, he wasn't there.'

'How do you know that?'

'He came in a little later than you, didn't he?'

'Straight afterwards. But . . . '

'In your last letters, you showed signs of impatience. You felt Conrad was getting away from you, that the whole escapade was starting to frighten him, and that, in any case, he wouldn't leave his home to run off abroad with you.'

'What do you mean?'

'Nothing. Just recapping. Your father will soon be here looking for you.'

She looked around in anguish, and seemed to be searching for the exit.

'Don't be afraid. I will be needing you tonight.'

'Tonight?'

'Yes, we're going to stage a reconstruction of what everyone did the night of the crime.'

'He'll kill me!'

'Who?'

'My father.'

'I'll be there, never fear.'

'But . . .'

Jean Duclos came into the room, shutting the door behind him quickly and turning the key in the lock. He stepped forward, looking important.

'Watch out! The farmer's here. He . . .'

'Take her up to your room.'

'To my . . .'

'Or mine, if you prefer.'

They could hear footsteps in the corridor. Near the stage was another door communicating with the service stairs. Duclos and Beetje went out that way. Maigret unlocked the main door, and found himself face to face with Farmer Liewens, who was looking past his shoulder.

'Beetje?'

The language barrier was between them again. They could not understand each other. Maigret merely interposed his large body to obstruct passage and gain time, while trying not to enrage the man in front of him.

Jean Duclos was quickly back downstairs, trying to look casual.

'Tell him he can have his daughter back tonight, and that he will also be needed for the reconstruction of the crime.'

'Do we have to . . .'

'Just translate, for God's sake, when I tell you.'

Duclos did so, in a placatory voice. The farmer stared at the two men.

'Tell him as well that tonight the murderer will be under lock and key.'

This too was translated. Then Maigret just had time to spring forward, knocking over Liewens, who had pulled out a revolver and was trying to press it to his own temple.

The struggle was brief. Maigret was so massive that his adversary was quickly immobilized and disarmed, while a stack of chairs they had collided with collapsed noisily, grazing the inspector's forehead.

'Lock the door!' Maigret shouted to Duclos. 'Don't let anyone in.'

And he stood up, recovering his breath.

9

The Reconstruction

The Wienands family arrived first, at seven thirty precisely. There were, at that moment, only three men waiting in the Van Hasselt ballroom, some distance apart, and not speaking to each other: Jean Duclos, on edge, pacing up and down the room, Farmer Liewens, looking withdrawn and sitting still on a chair, and Maigret, leaning against the piano, pipe between his teeth.

No one had thought to switch on all the lamps. A single large bulb, hanging very high up, cast a greyish light. The chairs were still stacked at the back of the room, except for one row, which Maigret had had lined up at the front.

On the little stage, otherwise empty, stood a table covered in green baize, and a single chair.

Monsieur and Madame Wienands were in their Sunday best. They had obeyed to the letter the instructions they had been given, since they had brought their two children with them. It was easy to guess that they had eaten their evening meal in haste, leaving their dining room uncleared, in order to arrive on time.

Wienands took his hat off as he walked in, looked around for someone to greet and, after thinking better of approaching the professor, shepherded his family into a corner where they waited in silence. His stiff collar was too large

124

and his tie was awry.

Cornelius Barens arrived almost immediately afterwards, so pale and nervous that he looked as if he might run off at the slightest alarm. He also glanced around to see if he could attach himself to some group, but dared not approach anyone, and stood with his back against the stack of chairs.

Pijpekamp came in next, escorting Oosting, whose eyes lighted sternly on Maigret. Then came the last arrivals: Madame Popinga and Any, who walked in quickly, stopped for a second then both headed for the row of chairs.

'Bring Beetje down,' Maigret instructed the Dutch inspector, 'and have one of your men keep an eye on Liewens and Oosting. They weren't in here on the night of the murder. We'll only be needing them later. They can stand at the back for now.'

After Beetje arrived, looking flustered at first, then deliberately stiffening her back with an impulse of pride as she saw Any and Madame Popinga, there was a pause, while everyone seemed to hold their breath.

Not because the atmosphere was tense. Because it wasn't. It was merely sordid.

In that huge empty hall, with the single light bulb hanging from the ceiling, they looked like a random group of human beings.

It was hard to imagine that, a few days earlier, many people, the notable citizens of Delfzijl, had paid for the right to sit on those stacked chairs, had made their entrance hoping to impress others, exchanging smiles and handshakes, had sat down in their best clothes facing the stage and had applauded the arrival of Professor Jean Duclos.

It was as if the same sight were being viewed through the wrong end of a telescope.

Because of having to wait, and the uncertainty they all felt about what was going to happen, their faces expressed neither anxiety nor pain, but something else entirely. Empty, blank eyes, devoid of thought. Drawn features, giving nothing away.

The poor light made everyone look grey. Even Beetje did not seem alluring.

The spectacle was without prestige or dignity. It was pitiful or laughable.

Outside, a crowd had gathered, because the rumour had circulated in late afternoon that something was about to happen. But nobody had imagined it would be so lacking in excitement.

Maigret approached Madame Popinga first.

'Would you kindly sit in the same place as the other evening?' he asked her. At home, a few hours earlier, she had been a pathetic figure. But no longer. She had aged. Her poorly tailored suit made one shoulder look noticeably higher than the other, and she had large feet. And a scar on her neck, under her ear.

Any was in a worse case, her face had never seemed more lopsided than now. Her outfit was ridiculous, a scarecrow with a frumpish hat.

Madame Popinga sat down in the middle of the row of chairs, in the place of honour. The other evening, under the lamps, with all of Delfzijl sitting behind her, she must have been

126

pink with pleasure and pride.

'Who was sitting next to you?'

'The principal of the Naval College.'

'And on the other side?'

'Monsieur Wienands.'

He was asked to come and sit down. He had kept his coat on, and sat down awkwardly, looking away.

'Madame Wienands?'

'At the end of the row, because of the children.'

'Beetje?'

She went to take her place unaided, leaving an empty chair between herself and Any: the one that had been occupied by Conrad Popinga.

Pijpekamp was standing to the side, unsettled, confused, ill at ease and anxious. Jean Duclos was awaiting his turn.

'Go up on the stage!' Maigret told him.

He was perhaps the person who had lost most prestige. He was just a thin man, inelegantly dressed. It was hard to think that a few nights earlier a hundred people had taken the trouble to attend his lecture.

The silence was as distressing as the light, at once revealing and inadequate, being shed from the high ceiling. At the back of the room, the Baes coughed four or five times, expressing the general feeling of disquiet.

Maigret himself did not look entirely at ease. He was surveying the scene he had set. His heavy gaze moved from one person to another, halting at small details, Beetje's posture, Any's over-long skirt, the poorly kept fingernails of

127

Duclos, who was now all alone at the lecturer's table, trying to maintain his dignity.

'You spoke for how long?'

'Three quarters of an hour.'

'And you were reading your lecture from notes?'

'Certainly not! I've given it twenty times before. I never use notes these days.'

'So you were watching the audience.'

And Maigret went to sit for a moment between Beetje and Any. The chairs were quite close together and his knee touched Beetje's.

'What time did the event end?'

'A little before nine. Because first of all a girl played the piano.'

The piano was still open, with a Chopin Polonaise propped on the stand. Madame Popinga began to chew her handkerchief. Oosting shifted at the back. His feet were shuffling all the time on the sawdust-covered floor.

It was a few minutes after eight o'clock. Maigret stood up and paced around.

'Now, Monsieur Duclos, could you summarize for me the subject of your lecture?'

But Duclos was unable to speak. Or rather he seemed to want to recite his usual speech. After clearing his throat a few times, he murmured:

'I would not wish to insult the intelligence of the people of Delfzijl . . . '

'No, stop. You were talking about crime. What approach were you taking?'

'I was talking about criminal responsibility.'

'And your argument was . . . ?'

'That society is responsible for the sins committed within it, which we call crime. We have organized our lives for the good of all. We have created social classes, and every individual belongs in one of them . . . '

He was staring at the green baize table top as he spoke. His voice was indistinct.

'All right, that will do,' snapped Maigret. 'I know how it goes: 'There are some exceptions, they're sick or they're misfits. They meet barriers they can't overcome. They're rejected on all sides, so they turn to a life of crime.' That sort of thing, yes? Not original. With the conclusion: 'We don't need more prisons, we need more rehabilitation centres, hospitals, clinics . . . ' '

Duclos, looking sullen, did not reply.

'Right, so you were talking about this for three quarters of an hour, with a few striking examples. You quoted Lombroso, Freud and company.'

He looked at his watch, then spoke mainly to the row of chairs.

'I'm going to ask you to wait another few minutes.'

Just at that moment, one of the Wienands children started to cry, and her mother, in a state of nerves, gave the little girl a shake to quieten her. Wienands, seeing that this was having no effect, took the child on his knees and first patted her hand, then pinched her arm to make her stop.

The empty chair between Beetje and Any was the only reminder that what had happened was a tragedy. And even then it was hard to take it in.

Was Beetje, with her fresh complexion but quite ordinary features, really worth breaking up a marriage for?

There was just one thing about her that was really seductive, and it was the spell cast by Maigret's staging of the scene that had brought out that pure truth, reducing events to their crudest common denominator: her two splendid breasts, made even more enticing by the shiny silk surface. Eighteen-year-old breasts, quivering a little under her blouse, just enough to make them look even more luscious.

Along the row sat Madame Popinga, who even at the age of eighteen hadn't had breasts like that, Madame Popinga, swathed in too many clothes, layer upon layer of sober, tasteful garments, which took away from her any fleshly allure.

Then there was Any, skinny, ugly, flat-chested, but enigmatic.

Conrad Popinga had met Beetje: Popinga, a man who loved life, a man who had such an appetite for good things. And he hadn't been looking at Beetje's face, with her baby-blue eyes. Nor, above all, had he guessed at the desire to escape lurking beneath that china-doll face.

What he'd seen was that quivering bosom, that attractive young body bursting with health!

As for Madame Wienands, she was no longer a woman in that sense: she was all mother and housewife. Just now she was wiping the nose of her child, who had worn herself out with crying.

'Do I have to stay up here?' asked Duclos from the stage.

'If you please.'

And Maigret approached Pijpekamp, and spoke to him in an undertone. Shortly afterwards, the Dutch policeman went out, taking Oosting with him.

Men were playing billiards in the café. The clash of the billiard balls could be heard.

And in the hall, people's chests were constricted. It felt like a spiritualist session, as if they were waiting for some terrifying thing to happen. Any was the only one who dared stand up, abruptly, and after hesitating for a while she said:

'I don't see what you want us to do. It's . . . '

'It's time now. Excuse me, where is Barens?'

He'd forgotten about him. He located him, standing at the back of the hall, leaning against the wall.

'Why didn't you come and take your seat?'

'You said: the same as the other night . . . '

The boy's gaze shifted around, and his voice came out breathless.

'The other night I was in the cheap seats, with the other students.'

Maigret took no further notice of him. He went to open the door that led to an entry porch giving directly on to the street, making it possible to avoid going through the café. He could see only three or four silhouettes in the darkness outside.

'I presume that when the lecture finished, some people clustered around the foot of the stage: the college principal, the minister, a few elders of the town congratulating the lecturer.'

No one replied, but these few words were enough to conjure up the scene: the bulk of the audience moving towards the exit, the scraping of chairs, conversations and around the stage a little group: handshakes and words of praise for the professor.

As the room emptied, the last handful of people would finally move towards the door. Barens would come to join the Popingas.

'You can come down now, Monsieur Duclos.'

They all stood up. But everyone seemed unsure about the role he or she should play. They were watching Maigret. Any and Beetje were pretending not to see each other. Wienands, looking awkward and embarrassed, was carrying his younger child, a baby.

'Follow me.'

And just before they reached the door:

'We're going to walk to the house in the same order as on the evening of the lecture. Madame Popinga and Monsieur Duclos . . . '

They looked at each other, hesitated, then started to walk along the dark street.

'Mademoiselle Beetje! You were walking with Monsieur Popinga. So go along now, I'll catch up with you.'

She scarcely dared set off alone towards the town, and above all was afraid of her father, at present being guarded in a corner of the hall by a policeman.

'Now Monsieur and Madame Wienands . . . '

These two could behave the most naturally, since they had the children to look after.

'Now Mademoiselle Any and Barens.'

The last named almost burst into tears, but bit his lip and walked out past Maigret.

Then the inspector turned to the policeman guarding Liewens.

'On the evening of the murder, at this time, he was at home. Can you take him there, and get him to do exactly what he did that night?'

It looked like a straggling funeral procession. The first to leave kept stopping and wondering whether they should keep going. There were hesitations and halts.

Madame Van Hasselt was watching the scene from her doorway, while exchanging remarks with the billiard players.

The town was three-quarters asleep, the shops all closed. Madame Popinga and Duclos headed straight for the quayside, the professor seemingly trying to reassure his companion.

Pools of light alternated with darkness, since the street lamps were far apart.

The black waters of the canal were visible, and boats bobbed gently, each with a lamp attached to its mast. Beetje, sensing Any following behind her, was trying to walk casually, but being on her own made that difficult to achieve.

A few paces separated each group. A hundred metres or so ahead, Oosting's boat could easily be seen, since it was the only one with a hull painted white. No light showed from the portholes. The quayside was deserted.

'Please stop where you are now!' Maigret called out, loudly enough to be heard by everyone.

They all froze. It was a dark night. The

luminous beam of the lighthouse passed very high overhead, without illuminating anything.

Maigret spoke to Any:

'This is where you were in the procession?'

'Yes.'

'And what about you, Barens?'

'Yes, I think so.'

'You're sure? You were definitely walking along with Any?'

'Yes. Wait ... Not here but a few metres further on, Any pointed to one of the children's coats, dragging in the mud.'

'And you ran ahead a little way to tell Wienands?'

'Madame Wienands, yes.'

'And that just took a few seconds?'

'Yes. The Wienands family went on, and I waited for Any to catch up.'

'And you didn't notice anything unusual?'

'No.'

'Go on another ten metres, everyone,' Maigret ordered. By that time, Madame Popinga's sister was level with Oosting's boat.

'Now Barens, go and catch up the Wienands family.'

And to Any:

'Pick up that cap from the deck!'

She had only to take three steps and lean across. The cap was clearly visible, black on white: the metallic badge on it was catching the light.

'Why do you want me to . . . ?'

'Just pick it up. '

The others could be glimpsed ahead of them

134

turning round to see what was happening.

'But I didn't . . . '

'That doesn't matter. We haven't got enough people. Everyone will have to act several parts. It's just an experiment.'

She picked up the cap.

'Now hide it under your coat. And go and join Barens.'

Then he went on to the deck of the boat and called:

'Pijpekamp!'

'*Ja!*'

And the Dutch inspector showed himself at the forward hatch. It was where Oosting slept. There wasn't room for a man to stand upright inside it, so it made sense, if you were smoking the last pipe of an evening, say, to lean out and put your elbows on the deck.

Oosting was in precisely this attitude. From the bank, from the level where the cap had been placed, he could not be seen, but he would have been able to see the person who had stolen the cap quite clearly.

'Good. Now get him to act exactly the same as he did the other night.'

And Maigret strode on, overtaking some of the groups.

'Keep walking! I will take Popinga's place.'

He found himself alongside Beetje, with Madame Popinga and Duclos ahead of him, the Wienands family behind him, and Any and Barens bringing up the rear. There was a sound of steps further behind. Oosting, accompanied by Pijpekamp, had started to walk along the bank.

From that point, there was no more street lighting. After the harbour, one went past the lock, now deserted, separating the sea from the canal. Then came the towpath, with trees on the right, and half a kilometre ahead, the Popinga house.

Beetje stammered:

'I . . . I don't see what . . . '

'Hush. It's a quiet night. The others can hear us, just like we can hear the people in front of us and behind us. So Popinga was talking to you out loud about this and that, the lecture probably.'

'Yes.'

'But under your breath you were remonstrating with him.'

'How do you know?'

'Never mind. Wait. During the lecture, you were sitting next to him. You tried to press his hand. Did he push you away?'

'Y-yes,' she stammered, impressed, and looking at him wide-eyed.

'And you tried again.'

'Yes. He wasn't so cautious before, he even kissed me behind a door in his house. And once in the dining room, when Madame Popinga was in the parlour, and saying something to us. It was only recently he started to get scared.'

'So, you were arguing with him. You told him again that you wanted to go away somewhere with him, while you carried on the more innocent conversation in normal voices.'

They could hear the footsteps of the people ahead of them and behind, voices murmuring, and Duclos saying:

'. . . assure you that this does not correspond to any *proper* method of conducting a police investigation.'

And behind them Madame Wienands was telling her child in Dutch to behave herself. Ahead of them, the house loomed up through the darkness. There were no lights on. Madame Popinga stopped at the door.

'You stopped like this the other night too, didn't you, because your husband had the key?'

'Yes.'

The groups all caught up.

'Open the door,' said Maigret. 'Was the maid in bed then?'

'Yes, as she is tonight.'

After opening the door, she pressed an electric switch. The hall, with the bamboo coat-stand on the left, was now illuminated.

'And Popinga was in a good mood at this point?'

'Yes, very, but he was not his usual self. He was speaking too loudly.'

People took off their hats and coats.

'One moment. Did everyone take off their coats here?'

'Everyone except Any and me,' said Madame Popinga. 'We went up to our rooms to tidy ourselves up.'

'And you didn't go into any other room? Who put the light on in the parlour?'

'Conrad.'

'So please go upstairs.'

And he went up with them.

'Any didn't stay in your room, although she

137

had to go through it to get to hers. Is that right?'

'Yes, I think so.'

'Would you be so good as to repeat exactly what you did? Mademoiselle Any, please go and put the cap with your hat and coat in your room. What did you do next, both of you?'

Madame Popinga's lower lip quivered.

'I . . . I just powdered my nose,' she said in a childlike voice. 'And combed my hair. But I can't . . . It's so awful. I seem to . . . I could hear Conrad's voice. He was talking about the wireless, and saying he wanted to listen to Radio-Paris.'

Madame Popinga threw her coat on the bed. She was weeping without tears, from nervous tension. Any, in the study which was her temporary bedroom, was standing still and waiting.

'And you came down together?'

'Yes. No. I can't remember. I think Any came down a little after me. I was thinking about getting the tea made.'

'So in that case, would you go downstairs now, please.'

He remained alone with Any, didn't say a word but took the cap from her, looked around and hid it under the divan.

'Come on.'

'How can you think . . . ?'

'No. Just come along. You didn't powder your nose?'

'No, never!'

There were shadows under her eyes. Maigret made her go down ahead of him. The stairs

138

creaked. Below, there was absolute silence. So much so that when they entered the parlour, the atmosphere was surreal. The room looked like a waxworks museum. Nobody had dared sit down. Madame Wienands was the only one moving, as she tidied her older child's hair.

'Take your places as you did the other night. Where's the wireless?'

He found it himself, and switched it on. There was crackling at first, then some voices and strains of music, and finally he tuned it to a station playing a comedy sketch between two Frenchmen:

So this feller says to the captain . . .

The voice grew louder as the set was tuned. A few more crackles.

. . . And the captain, he's a good sort. But the other feller, nudge nudge, know what I mean? . . .

And this voice, that of a Parisian music-hall performer, echoed around the impeccable parlour, where everyone was standing absolutely still.

'Right, sit down, everyone,' Maigret thundered. 'Let's have some tea. Talk among yourselves.'

He went to look out of the window, but the shutters were closed. He opened the door and called:

'Pijpekamp!'

'Yes,' came a voice from the gloom.

'Is he there?'

'Yes, behind the second tree!'

Maigret came back inside. The door slammed.

The sketch was over and an announcer's voice said:

And now record number 2-8-6-7-5 from Odeon!

Some scratchy sounds. Then jazz music. Madame Popinga was huddled against the wall. Underneath the surface broadcast another voice could be heard, singing nasally in some foreign language, and sometimes there was a further spell of crackling before the music came through once more.

Maigret looked over at Beetje. She had collapsed into an armchair and was weeping bitterly. Through her sobs, she was whispering:

'Oh, poor Conrad, poor Conrad!'

And Barens, all the blood having drained from his face, was biting his lip.

'Tea!' Maigret ordered, looking at Any.

'We didn't bring it yet. They rolled back the carpet. Conrad was dancing.'

Beetje gave an even louder sob. Maigret looked at the carpet, the solid oak table with its lace cloth, the window and Madame Wienands, who didn't know what to do with her children.

10

Someone Waiting for the Right Moment

Maigret dominated them by his size, or rather his bulk. The room was small. Standing with his back to the door, he seemed too big for it. He looked serious. Perhaps he was never more human than when he said slowly, in a neutral voice:

'The music goes on playing. Barens helps Popinga to roll back the carpet. In a corner, Jean Duclos is talking to Madame Popinga and Any and listening to his own voice. Wienands and his wife are thinking it's time to leave because of the children, and are talking about doing so in low voices. Popinga has drunk a glass of brandy. That's enough to make him merry. He laughs. He hums the tune. He goes over to Beetje and asks her to dance.'

Madame Popinga was looking fixedly at the ceiling. Any's piercing eyes were directed at the inspector, who finished what he was saying:

'The murderer knows who is going to be the victim. Someone is watching Conrad dancing and knows that, in two hours, this man who's laughing a bit too loudly, who wants to be jolly in spite of everything, who is hungry for life and emotions, will be nothing more than a corpse.'

The shock made itself felt, literally. Madame

141

Popinga's mouth opened to utter a cry that never came. Beetje was still sobbing.

The atmosphere had changed at a stroke. They might almost have been looking around expecting to see Conrad. Conrad dancing! Conrad, who was being watched by the eyes of the assassin!

Only Jean Duclos spoke, to say:

'That's a bit strong!'

And since no one was listening to him, he went on to himself, hoping Maigret might overhear him:

'Now I see your method, and it isn't original! Terrorize the suspect, suggest certain possibilities, place him in the context of the crime, to force a confession out of him. Sometimes when this is tried, the criminal repeats the same gestures in spite of himself.'

But it came across just as muffled muttering. Such words were hardly appropriate at a moment like this.

Music was still coming through the loudspeaker, and that was enough to lift the atmosphere a little.

Wienands, after his wife had whispered something in his ear, stood up timidly.

'Yes, yes! You can go,' Maigret told him, before he could say anything.

Poor Madame Wienands! A well-brought-up and most respectable citizen, who would have preferred to bid everyone goodbye politely, to get her children to do the same, but who didn't know how to manage it, and ended by shaking hands with Madame Popinga, without finding any of the right words!

There was a clock on the mantelpiece. The time it showed was five past ten.

'Not time for tea yet?' asked Maigret.

'Yes, it is!' Any replied, as she got up and went to the kitchen.

'Excuse me, madame. But didn't you go to make the tea with your sister?'

'A little later.'

'And you joined her in the kitchen?'

Madame Popinga passed her hand across her forehead. She was making an effort not to slump into stupor. She stared despairingly at the loudspeaker.

'I don't know. Wait a minute. I think Any came out of the dining room, because the sugar's kept in the sideboard there.'

'Was the light on?'

'No. Maybe. No, I think not.'

'And you didn't speak to each other?'

'Oh yes! I said: Conrad mustn't have any more to drink or he'll start misbehaving.'

Maigret went into the corridor, just as the Wienands were closing the front door. The kitchen was well lit and meticulously clean. Water was being heated on a gas cooker. Any was taking the top off a teapot.

'Don't bother actually making the tea.'

They were alone. Any looked him in the eye.

'Why did you make me take that cap?' she asked.

'Never mind. Come back in.'

In the parlour, nobody spoke or moved.

'Are you going to let this music go on playing

143

for ever?' Jean Duclos managed nevertheless to protest.

'Perhaps. There's one more person I wish to see: the maid.'

Madame Popinga looked at Any, who answered: 'But she's in bed. She always goes to bed at nine.'

'No matter. Get her to come downstairs for a few minutes. She needn't bother getting dressed.'

And in the same flat voice he had used at first, he repeated obstinately:

'You were dancing with Conrad, Beetje. Over in the corner, other people were having a serious conversation. And someone knew there would be a death. Someone knew this was Conrad Popinga's last night on earth.'

* * *

The sound of steps was heard and a door banged on the second floor of the house, where the attic bedroom was. Then a murmur of voices. Any came in first. A shadow remained standing in the corridor.

'Come on,' said Maigret gruffly. 'Someone tell her not to be afraid to come in.'

The maid had indistinct features in a large plain face, and looked dazed. Over her cream flannelette ankle-length nightdress, she had simply thrown an overcoat. Her eyes were half-closed with sleep and her hair tousled. She smelled of her warm bed.

Maigret spoke to Duclos:

144

'Ask her, in Dutch of course, if she was Popinga's mistress.'

Madame Popinga turned her head away in pain. The sentence was translated.

The maid shook her head energetically.

'Repeat the question. Ask her whether her employer ever made any advances to her.'

More protestations.

'Tell her if she does not tell the truth, she risks a prison sentence. Divide the question up. Did he ever kiss her? Did he sometimes come into her bedroom when she was there?'

The girl standing there in her nightdress burst into tears, and cried out in her own language:

'I haven't done anything. I swear I haven't done anything wrong.'

Duclos translated. With pinched lips, Any was staring at the maid.

'Was she in fact his mistress, then?'

But the maid was unable to speak. She was protesting vehemently and crying. Asking to be forgiven. Her words were half drowned by her sobs.

'No, I don't think so,' the professor finally translated. 'From what I can gather, he did pester her. When they were alone in the house, he kept hanging around her in the kitchen. He kissed her. Once he came into her bedroom when she was getting dressed. He gave her chocolate in secret. But it didn't go any further.'

'She can go back to bed now.'

They heard the girl go back upstairs. A few minutes later, there was the sound of footsteps coming and going on the second floor. Maigret spoke to Any:

'Would you be good enough to go and see what she's doing?'

The answer was not long in coming.

'She wants to leave here at once. She's ashamed. She doesn't want to stay a minute longer in this house. She begs my sister's forgiveness. She says she'll go to Groningen or somewhere. But she won't stay in Delfzijl.'

And Any added aggressively: 'Is that what you wanted to achieve?'

The clock was now showing ten forty. A voice from the loudspeaker announced:

Our programme is over. Good night, ladies and gentlemen.

Then the sound of some other station's music came faintly through.

Maigret irritably switched the wireless off, and there was suddenly total silence. Beetje was no longer weeping, but was still hiding her face in her hands.

'And the conversations went on after that?' asked the inspector, with obvious weariness.

No one replied. Faces now looked even more drawn than in the Van Hasselt ballroom.

'Please accept my apologies for this painful evening.'

Maigret was speaking principally to Madame Popinga.

' . . . but don't forget that your husband was still alive. He was here, in rather high spirits because of the brandy. He probably drank some more . . . '

146

'Yes, he did.'

'He was a condemned man, you understand! Condemned by someone watching him. And others here, now, are refusing to say what they know, and are making themselves accomplices of the murderer.'

Barens gulped and started to shake.

'Aren't they, Cornelius?' said Maigret point-blank, looking him in the eyes.

'No! No! That's not true.'

'So why are you shaking?'

'I . . . I . . .'

He was about to have a panic attack, as he had on the way to the farm.

'Listen to me! It's about the time Beetje went off with Popinga. And *you* went out straight afterwards, Barens. You followed them for a while. And you saw something . . .'

'No. It's not true.'

'Wait. After the three of you had left, the only people in the house were Madame Popinga, Any and Professor Duclos. These three all went upstairs.'

Any nodded.

'And each of them went into his or her bedroom, yes? So tell me what you saw, Barens.'

He was casting about him desperately now. Maigret fixed the squirming boy with a look.

'No, no! Nothing.'

'You didn't see Oosting, hiding behind a tree?'

'No.'

'But all the same, you were hanging around the house. So you saw *something*.'

'I don't know, I don't want to . . . No, it's impossible.'

Everyone was looking at him. He dared not look at anyone. Maigret remained pitiless.

'It was on the road that you first noticed something. The two bikes had gone off together. They would have to pass through the place which is lit up by the lighthouse. You were jealous. You were waiting. And you had to wait a long time . . . A time that didn't correspond to the distance they had to cover.'

'Yes.'

'In other words, the couple stopped in the shelter of the timber stacks. That wasn't enough to frighten you. It would merely have made you angry, and perhaps despair of your chances. So you must have seen something else that frightened you. Something frightening enough, in any case, to make you stay put, although it was time for you to be back at college. You were between here and the timber yard. You could only see one of the windows of the house.'

At these words, Barens gave a start and lost control completely.

'You can't . . . You can't know that. I . . . I . . . '

'The window of Madame Popinga's bedroom. And there was someone at the window. Someone who, like you, had seen that the couple took far too long before they appeared in the beam of light from the lighthouse . . . Someone who knew therefore that Conrad and Beetje had stopped in the shadows for a long time . . . '

'It was me!' said Madame Popinga, in a clear voice.

Now it was Beetje's turn to react, and to stare at her, wide-eyed with terror.

★　★　★

Contrary to expectation, Maigret asked no further questions. Indeed, this created an atmosphere of unease. People in the room felt that having reached a culminating point, everything had stopped dead.

And the inspector went to open the front door, calling:

'Pijpekamp! Come here, please. Leave Oosting where he is. I imagine you have been able to see the lights going on and off in the Wienands house. They must be in bed.'

'Yes.'

'And Oosting?'

'Still behind the tree.'

The Groningen inspector looked around him in astonishment. Everything was very quiet. The faces were those of people who had spent night after night without sleeping.

'Would you stay here for a moment? I'm going to accompany Beetje Liewens outside, as Popinga did. Madame Popinga will go up to her room and so will Any and Professor Duclos. I would ask them just to do exactly what they did the other night.'

And turning to Beetje:

'Come along, please.'

It was cool outside. Maigret went round the building to the shed containing Popinga's bike and two women's bicycles.

'Take one of these.'

Then, as they rode calmly along the towpath towards the timber yard:

'Who suggested stopping?'

'Conrad.'

'He was still in a jolly mood?'

'No. As soon as we got outside, I saw that he was getting sad.'

They had reached the stacks of timber.

'Let's stop here. Was he in an amorous mood?'

'Yes and no. He was unhappy. I think it was because of the brandy, It cheered him up at first. He put his arms round me here. He said he was miserable, that I was a sweet little girl. Yes, those were his words, a sweet little girl, but I'd come along too late, and if we didn't take care, this would end in tears.'

'And the bikes?'

'We leaned them up here. I thought he was going to cry. I'd seen him like that before, when he'd had too much to drink. He said he was a man, so it wasn't so important for him, but a girl like me shouldn't throw away her life by having an affair. Then he swore that he was fond of me, but he didn't have the right to ruin my life, that Barens was a nice boy, and that I'd be happy with him at the end of the day.'

'And then?'

She breathed in deeply. Then she burst out:

'I shouted at him that he was a coward and I went to get on my bike.'

'What did he do?'

'He grabbed the handlebars. He tried to stop me. He said: 'Let me explain . . . It's not because of me . . . It's . . . ' '

'And what did he explain?'

'Nothing. Because I said if he didn't let go of me, I'd scream. He let me go. I pedalled off. He came after me, still talking . . . But I was going faster. All I could hear was him saying: 'Beetje, Beetje, wait, listen!' '

'And that's all?'

'When he saw me reach the farm gate, he turned back. I looked behind me. I saw him bending over his bicycle, looking very sad.'

'And you ran back to him?'

'No! I hated him because he wanted me to marry Barens. He wanted a quiet life, didn't he? But then just as I was going in, I realized I didn't have my scarf. Someone might find it. So I went back to look for it. I didn't meet anyone. But by the time I finally got home, my father wasn't there. He came in later. He didn't say good night to me. He was looking pale and his eyes were angry. I thought he had been spying on us, and that perhaps he'd been hiding behind the timber stack. Next day, he must have searched my room. He found Conrad's letters, because I didn't see them after that. Then he shut me in.'

'Right. Come.'

'Where to?'

He didn't even reply, but cycled back to the Popinga house. There was a light in Madame Popinga's window, but she could not be seen.

'You think *she* did it?'

The inspector was muttering to himself:

'He came back this way, he was worried. He got off his bike, probably about here. He went

151

round the house, wheeling the bike. He knew his peace of mind was threatened, but he was incapable of running away with his mistress.'

And then, suddenly:

'Stay here, Beetje.'

Maigret wheeled the bike along the path around the house. He went into the courtyard and towards the shed, where the varnished boat was a long silhouette.

Jean Duclos's window was lit up. The professor could be glimpsed sitting at a small table. Two metres along was the bathroom window, open, but in darkness.

'He probably wasn't in a hurry to go inside.' Maigret was still talking to himself. 'He bent down to push the bike in under cover.'

Maigret fidgeted. He seemed to be waiting for something. And something did happen, but unexpectedly. A little noise up above, at the bathroom window, a metallic click — the sound of a revolver firing a blank.

And then immediately, there was the sound of a struggle, and of two bodies falling to the ground.

Maigret went into the house through the kitchen door, ran upstairs and into the bathroom, where he switched on the light.

Two shapes were wrestling on the floor: Pijpekamp and Barens, who was the first to give up, as his right hand opened and dropped the revolver.

11

The Light in the Window

'You idiot!'

Those were Maigret's first words, as he literally picked up Barens from the floor and held him upright, supporting him for a second, otherwise the young man would no doubt have fallen over again. Doors opened. Maigret thundered:

'Everyone downstairs!'

He was holding the revolver, handling it without precautions, since he had himself replaced its bullets with blank cartridges.

Pijpekamp was brushing down his dusty jacket with the back of his hand. Jean Duclos asked, pointing to Barens:

'Was it him?' The young naval cadet looked pitiful, not so much a hardened criminal, more a schoolboy caught out in some misdemeanour. He dared not meet anyone's eye, and didn't know what to do with his hands or where to look.

Maigret switched on the lights in the parlour. Any was the last to enter. Madame Popinga refused to sit down, and one sensed that under her dress her knees were trembling.

Then, for the first time, they saw the inspector looking awkward. He filled his pipe, lit it, let it go out, sat down in an armchair, but immediately stood up again.

'I have become involved in a case that has nothing to do with me,' he began hurriedly. 'A French citizen was a suspect, and I was sent to shed light on the matter.'

He relit his pipe to give himself time to think. He turned to Pijpekamp.

'Beetje is outside, as are her father and Oosting. We must either tell them to go home, or to come inside. It depends. Do you want everyone to know the truth?'

The Dutch inspector went to the door. A few moments later, Beetje came in, timid and shamefaced, then Oosting with his obstinate expression, and finally Liewens, pale and wild-eyed.

Then they watched as Maigret opened the door into the dining room. They heard him feeling around in a cupboard. When he came back, he was holding a bottle of cognac and a glass.

He drank alone. His expression was grim. Everyone was standing around him and he seemed reluctant to speak.

'Do *you* want to know, Pijpekamp?'

And suddenly:

'Well, there's no help for it! No help for it, even if your method is the right one. We're different countries, different people. We have different climates. When *you* sense a family drama, you leap on the first bit of evidence that lets you explain away the crime. It must have been committed by some foreign seaman. That would be preferable perhaps, from the point of view of public morale. No scandal! No bad example being set by the bourgeoisie to the lower classes. Only *my* problem is I can still see Popinga, in this very room, turning on the wireless and dancing under the very eyes of his murderer.'

And he muttered crossly, without looking at anyone:

'The revolver was found in the bathroom. So the shot came from inside the house. Because it would be ridiculous to assume that the killer, after committing the crime, had the presence of mind to aim at a half-open window and throw the weapon inside. Let alone go and put a cap in the bath and a cigar in the dining room.'

He began pacing up and down, still avoiding looking anyone in the eye. Oosting and Liewens, neither of whom could understand what he was saying, were gazing at him intently, trying to guess what he was driving at.

'The cap, the cigar butt, and then the revolver taken from Popinga's own bedside table — it was all too much. Do you see? Someone wanted to provide too much evidence. To cause too much confusion. Oosting, or someone like him from outside, might have left half those clues, but not everything.

'Therefore, there was premeditation. Therefore, a desire to escape punishment.

'So we simply have to proceed by elimination. We can eliminate the Baes, first of all. What reason could he possibly have to go into the dining room and drop a cigar, then go up to the bedroom to look for the revolver, and finally to leave a cap in the bath?

'Next we can rule out Beetje, who in the course of the evening never once went upstairs, couldn't have left the cap, and couldn't even have taken it from the boat, because she was walking back from the lecture with Popinga.

'Her father could well have killed Popinga, after surprising him with his daughter. But by that stage, it was too late for him to gain access to the bathroom.

'Then there is Barens. He didn't go upstairs either. He didn't steal the cap. He was jealous of his tutor, but an hour beforehand, he had no certainty of what he suspected.'

Maigret stopped talking, and knocked out his pipe on his heel without worrying about the carpet.

'So that's all. It leaves us a choice between Madame Popinga, Any and Jean Duclos. There is no evidence against any of them. But it's not materially impossible for any of them to have done it either. Jean Duclos came out of the bathroom holding the revolver. We could take that as a sign of his innocence. Or it could be a very clever double bluff. But since he walked back from town with Madame Popinga, he couldn't have stolen the cap. And Madame Popinga, by the same token, being with him, couldn't have done it either.

'The cap could only have been taken by one of the last couple, Barens or Any. And just now, on the way here, I had it confirmed that Any remained alone for a moment or two alongside Oosting's boat.

'As for the cigar, let's not bother about it.

Anyone could pick up an old cigar end anywhere.

'So, of all those who were here the night of the crime, Any is the only person who stayed upstairs without any witnesses, and who, we also know, had been into the dining room.

'But she had a cast-iron alibi concerning the crime.'

And Maigret, still avoiding looking at anyone, placed on the table the plan of the house drawn by Jean Duclos.

'Any could only have reached the bathroom by going through either her sister's bedroom or that of the French visitor. A quarter of an hour before the murder, she was in her own room. How could she get into the bathroom? *And how could she be sure to be able to pass through one of the two bedrooms at the right moment?* Don't forget that she has not only studied the law but also forensic science. She's discussed them with Duclos. They talked together about the possibility of a crime which could be committed with mathematical impunity.'

Any, standing very upright and pale in the face, was nevertheless in control of herself.

'Now I will embark on a digression. I'm the only person here who didn't know Popinga. I have had to construct my idea of him from other people's evidence. He was keen to enjoy himself, but equally he was intimidated by his responsibilities and especially by received standards of proper behaviour. One day, in a jolly mood, he made advances to Beetje. And she became his mistress. Principally because *she* wanted it. I

157

questioned the maid just now. And we know that he snatched kisses from her too, casually, in passing. But it didn't go any further, because he got no encouragement.

'In other words, he was a man attracted to all women. He was capable of taking small risks. A kiss in the corner, the odd caress. But above all, he was keen to ensure his own safety.

'He'd been an ocean-going captain. He'd known the delights of shore leave with no consequences. But he was also a servant of the Dutch Crown, and he wanted to hold on to his position, his house and his wife.

'He was a mixture of appetites and repression, imprudence and caution.

'Beetje, only eighteen years old, didn't understand that, and she believed he was ready to run away with her.

'Any lived in close proximity with him. Never mind that she is not particularly beautiful, she's a woman. A mystery therefore . . . and one day . . . '

The silence around him was painful.

'I'm not suggesting that he became her lover. But with Any, too, he was imprudent enough to make advances. She believed him. And she conceived a passion for him, though not as blind a passion as that of Madame Popinga. So here they were, all living together: Madame Popinga, suspecting nothing, Any more withdrawn, more passionate, more jealous and more subtle.

'She guessed he was having an affair with Beetje. She sensed the presence of the enemy.

Maybe she even looked for the letters and found them.

'She could tolerate sharing him with her sister. But she couldn't accept this pretty girl brimming with good health who was talking of running away.

'She decided to kill.'

And Maigret concluded:

'That's all. Love that had turned to hate. Love-hate. A complex, wild emotion, capable of driving someone to any lengths. She decided to kill Conrad. Decided that in cold blood. To kill, without laying herself open to the least suspicion.

'And that very night the professor had spoken about crimes that were never detected, about unpunished murders.

'She is as proud of her intelligence as she is passionate. She committed the perfect crime. A crime that could easily be blamed on a prowler.

'The cap, the cigar and the unshakeable alibi: she couldn't escape from her room to fire the gun without going through either her sister's room or the Frenchman's. During the lecture, she saw the hands feeling for each other. On the way home, Popinga walked with Beetje. They drank, they danced and they went off together on their bikes.

'All she had to do was get Madame Popinga to stand for a while at her window, and insinuate something to make her suspicious of the pair who had just left.

'And while her sister thought she was in her own room, Any was able to creep behind her,

159

already in her underclothes. Everything was planned. She got into the bathroom. She fired the shot. The lid of the bath was up. The cap was already in it. She just had to slip inside.

'On hearing the shot, Duclos rushed in, found the weapon on the window sill, and rushed out again, meeting Madame Popinga on the landing, and they went downstairs together.

'Any was ready and, half-undressed, she followed them. Who would ever suspect she wasn't coming straight from her room, in a state of panic? Here she was, appearing in public in her underwear, when she was known to be extremely prudish.

'No pity! No remorse! The hatred of a lover extinguishes any other feelings. There remains only the desire to conquer.

'Oosting, who had seen the person who took his cap, kept quiet. Both out of respect for the dead man, and from love of order. He didn't want scandal to surround Popinga's death. He even dictated to Barens what he should say to the police, so that they would just assume that this was a banal crime, committed by an unknown sailor.

'Liewens, who saw his daughter finally return home *after* Popinga had been accompanying her, and who next day read the letters, believed *Beetje* was guilty, so he locked her up and tried to find out the truth. When he thought I was going to arrest her earlier on, he tried to kill himself.

'And lastly we come to Barens. Barens suspected everyone. He was wrestling with the

160

unknown and feeling under suspicion himself. Barens who had seen Madame Popinga at her window. Could it be that she had shot her husband, having discovered that he was unfaithful?

'Cornelius had been received here like a son. Orphaned of his own mother, he had found another in Madame Popinga.

'He wanted to devote himself to her. To save her. We forgot about him during the reconstruction. He fetched the revolver and went into the bathroom. *He wanted to shoot the only man who knew, and no doubt to kill himself afterwards.* A poor, heroic child. Generous as only an eighteen-year-old can be!

'And that's all . . . What time is the next train for France?'

Nobody said a word. They were all struck dumb with amazement, anguish, fear or horror. Finally Jean Duclos spoke:

'Well, a lot of good that has done . . . '

But Madame Popinga was leaving the room with mechanical steps and a few minutes later she was found on her bed, suffering a heart attack.

Any had not budged. Pijpekamp tried to get her to speak:

'Have you anything to say to this?'

'I will speak only in the presence of the examining magistrate.'

She was very pale. The deep circles under her eyes had spread to her cheeks.

Oosting alone remained calm, but he was looking at Maigret with eyes full of reproach.

161

And the fact is that at five o'clock in the morning, Detective Chief Inspector Maigret boarded a train, alone, at the little railway station of Delfzijl. No one had accompanied him. No one had thanked him. Not even Duclos, who had claimed he could only manage to catch the next train!

Day was breaking as the train crossed a bridge over a canal. Boats were waiting to pass, their sails flapping. An official was standing by to swing the bridge open after the train had gone across.

It was not until two years later, in Paris, that Maigret met Beetje again: she was the wife of a representative for Dutch electrical lamps, and had put on weight. She blushed when she recognized him.

She told him she now had two children, but gave him to understand that life with her husband was not up to expectations.

'And what about Any?' he asked her.

'Didn't you hear? It was all over the Dutch papers. She killed herself with a fork on the day of her trial, a few minutes before she was due in court.'

And she added:

'You must come and see us: 28 Avenue Victor Hugo. Don't leave it too late, we're off next week for winter sports in Switzerland.'

That day, when Maigret returned to headquarters, he contrived excuses to shout at all his inspectors.

The Grand Banks Café

Translated by DAVID COWARD

1

The Glass Eater

. . . that he's the finest young man around here there ever was, and that all this could well be the death of his mother. He's all she's got. I am absolutely sure that he's innocent: everybody here is. But the sailors I've talked to reckon he'll be found guilty because civilian courts never understand anything to do with the sea.

Do everything you can, old friend, just as if you were doing it for me. I see from the papers that you've become something very important in the Police Judiciaire, and . . .

★   ★   ★

It was a June morning. The windows of the flat on Boulevard Richard-Lenoir were wide open. Madame Maigret was finishing packing large wicker trunks, and Maigret, who was not wearing a collar, was reading aloud.

'Who's it from?'

'Jorissen. We were at school together. He's a primary-school teacher now in Quimper. Listen, are you still set on passing our week's holiday in Alsace?'

She stared at him, not understanding. The question was so unexpected. For the past twenty

165

years they'd always spent their holidays with family, and always in the same village in eastern France.

'What if we went to stay by the sea instead?'

He read out parts of the letter again, in a half whisper:

. . . you are better placed than I am to get accurate information. Very briefly, Pierre Le Clinche, aged twenty, a former pupil of mine, sailed three months ago on the *Océan*, a Fécamp trawler which was going fishing for cod off Newfoundland. The boat docked back in port yesterday. Hours later, the body of the captain was found floating in the harbour, and all the signs point to foul play. Pierre Le Clinche is the man who's been arrested.

'We'll be able to take it just as easy at Fécamp as anywhere else!' said Maigret, holding out no great hopes.

Objections were raised. In Alsace, Madame Maigret was with her family and helped with making jam and plum brandy. The thought of staying in a hotel by the seaside with a lot of other people from Paris filled her with dread.

'What would I do all day?'

In the end, she packed her sewing and her crocheting.

'Just don't expect me to go swimming! I thought I'd better warn you in advance.'

★ ★ ★

166

They had arrived at the Hôtel de la Plage at five. Once there, Madame Maigret had set about rearranging the room to her liking. Then they'd had dinner.

Later, Maigret, now alone, pushed open the frosted-glass door of a harbour-front café, the Grand Banks Café.

It was located opposite the berth where the trawler the *Océan* was tied up, just by a line of railway trucks. Acetylene lamps hung from the rigging, and in their raw light a number of figures were busily unloading cod, which they passed from hand to hand and piled into the trucks after the fish had been weighed.

There were ten of them at work, men and women, dirty, their clothes torn and stiff with salt. By the weighing scales stood a well-turned-out young man, with a boater over one ear and a notebook in his hand, in which he recorded the weighed catch.

A rank, stomach-churning smell, which distance did nothing to lessen, seeped into the bar, where the heat made it even more oppressive.

Maigret sat down in a free corner, on the bench seat. He was surrounded by noise and activity. There were men standing, men sitting, glasses on the marble-topped tables. All were sailors.

'What'll it be?'

'A beer.'

The serving girl went off. The landlord came up to him:

'I've got another room next door, you know.

For tourists. This lot make such a din in here!'
He winked. 'Well, after three months at sea, it's
understandable.'

'Are these the crew of the *Océan*?'

'Most of them. The other boats aren't back
yet. You mustn't pay any attention. Some of them
have been drunk for three days. Are you staying
put? ... I bet you're a painter, right? We get
them in now and again. They do sketches. There,
see? Over the counter? One of them drew me,
head and shoulders.'

But the inspector offered so little encouragement to his chatter that the landlord gave up and
went away.

'A copper two-*sou* bit! Who's got a copper
two-*sou* bit?' shouted a sailor no taller than a
sixteen-year-old youth and as thin.

His head was old, his face was lopsided, and
he was missing a few teeth. Drink made his eyes
bright, and a three-day stubble had spread over
his jaws.

Someone tossed him a coin. He bent it almost
double with his fingers, then put it between his
teeth and snapped it in two.

'Who's wants to have a go next?'

He strutted around. He sensed that everyone
was looking at him and was ready to do anything
to remain the centre of attention.

As a puffy-faced mechanic produced a coin,
he stepped in:

'Half a mo'. This is what you got to do as
well.'

He picked up an empty glass, took a large bite
out of it and chewed the broken pieces with a

168

show of relish worthy of a gourmet.

'Ha ha!' he smirked. 'You're all welcome to give it a try . . . Fill me up again, Léon!'

He looked round the bar boastfully until his eyes came to rest on Maigret. His eyebrows came together in a deep frown.

For a moment he seemed nonplussed. Then he started to move forwards. He had to lean on a table to steady himself because he was so drunk.

'You here for me?' he blustered.

'Take it easy, Louis boy!'

'Still on about that business with the wallet? Listen, boys. You didn't believe me just now when I told you about my run-ins with the Rue de Lappe boys. Well, here's a top-notch cop who's come out of his way to see yours truly . . . Will it be all right if I have another little drink?'

All eyes were now on Maigret.

'Sit yourself down here, Louis boy, and stop playing the fool!'

Louis guffawed:

'You paying? No, that would be the day! . . . Is it all right with you, boys, if the chief inspector buys me a drink? . . . Make it brandy, Léon, a large one!'

'Were you on the *Océan*?'

The change in Louis was instant. His face darkened so much that it seemed as if he had suddenly sobered up. He shifted his position on the bench seat, backing off suspiciously.

'What if I was?'

'Nothing . . . Cheers . . . Been drunk long?'

'We been celebrating for three days. Ever since

169

we landed. I gave my pay to Léon. Nine hundred francs, give or take. Here until it runs out . . . How much have I got left, Léon, you old crook?'

'Well, not enough for you to go on buying rounds until tomorrow! About fifty francs. Isn't it a stupid shame, inspector! Tomorrow he'll be skint and he'll have to sign as a stoker on the first boat that'll have him. It's the same story every time. Mark you, I don't encourage them to drink! The very opposite!'

'Shut your mouth!'

The others had lost their high spirits. They talked in whispers and kept looking round at the table where the inspector was sitting.

'Are all these men from the *Océan*?'

'All save the big fellow in the cap, who's a pilot, and the one with ginger hair. He's a ship's carpenter.'

'Tell me what happened.'

'I got nothing to say.'

'Watch your step, Louis! Don't forget the wallet business, which ended up with you doing your glass-eating number behind bars.'

'All I'd get is three months, and anyway I could do with a rest. But if you want, why not just lock me up right now?'

'Were you working in the engine room?'

'Sure! As usual! I was second fireman.'

'Did you see much of the captain?'

'Maybe twice in all.'

'And the wireless operator?'

'Dunno.'

'Léon! Same again.'

Louis gave a contemptuous laugh.

'I could be drunk as a lord and still I wouldn't tell you anything I didn't want to say. But since you're here, you could offer to buy the boys a round. After the lousy trip like the one we just been on!'

A sailor, not yet twenty, approached shiftily and tugged Louis' sleeve. They both started talking in Breton.

'What did he say?'

'He said it's time I went to bed.'

'A friend of yours?'

Louis shrugged, and just as the young sailor was about to take his glass off him, he downed it in one defiant gulp.

The Breton had thick eyebrows and wavy hair.

'Sit down with us,' said Maigret.

But without replying the sailor moved to another table, where he sat staring unblinkingly at both of them.

The atmosphere was heavy and sour. The sounds of tourists playing dominoes came from the next room, which was lighter and cleaner.

'Catch much cod?' asked Maigret who pursued his line of thought with the single-mindedness of a mechanical drill.

'It was no good. When we landed, it was half rotten!'

'How come?'

'Not enough salt! . . . Or too much! . . . It was off! There'll not be a third of the crew who'll go out on her again next week.'

'Is the *Océan* going out again?'

'By God, yes! Otherwise what's the point of

boats with engines? Sailboats go out the once, from February to October. But these trawlers can fit in two trips to the Grand Banks.'

'Are you going back on her?'

Louis spat on the floor and gave a weary shrug.

'I'd just as well be banged up at Fresnes . . . You must be joking!'

'And the captain?'

'I got nothing to say!'

He had lit the stump of a cigar he'd found lying about. Suddenly he retched, made a rush for the door and could be seen throwing up on the kerb, where the Breton joined him.

'It's a crying shame,' sighed the landlord. 'The day before yesterday, he had nearly a thousand francs in his pocket. Today, it's touch and go if he doesn't end up owing me money! Oysters and lobster! And that's not reckoning all the drinks he stood everybody, as if he didn't know what to do with his money.'

'Did you know the wireless operator on the *Océan*?'

'He had a room here. As a matter of fact, he'd eat his dinners off this very table and then he'd go off to write in the room next door because it was quieter there.'

'Write to who?'

'Not just letters . . . Looked like poetry or novels. A kid with an education, well brought up. Now that I know you're police, I can tell you that it was a mistake when your lot . . . '

'Even though the captain had been killed?'

A shrug for an answer. The landlord sat down

facing Maigret. Louis came back in, made straight for the counter and ordered another drink. His companion, still talking Breton, continued to tell him to stay calm.

'Pay no attention . . . Once they're back on dry land, they're like that: they booze, they shout, they fight, they break windows. On board they work like the devil. Even Louis! The chief mechanic on the *Océan* was telling me only yesterday that he does the work of two men . . . When they were at sea, a steam joint split. Repairing it was dangerous . . . No one wanted to do it . . . But Louis stepped up to the mark . . . If you keep him away from the bottle . . . '

Léon lowered his voice and ran his eyes over his customers suspiciously.

'Maybe this time they've got different reasons for going on the bottle. They won't tell you anything, not you! Because you're not a seafaring man. But I overhear them talking. I used to be a pilot. There are things . . . '

'What things?'

'It's hard to explain . . . You know that there aren't enough men in Fécamp to crew all the trawlers. So they bring them in from Brittany. Those boys have their own way of looking at things, they're a superstitious lot . . . '

He lowered his voice even further, until he was barely audible.

'It seems that this time they had the evil eye. It started in port, even before they sailed. There was this sailor who'd climbed the derrick to wave to his wife . . . He was hanging on to a rope, which broke, and the next moment he's lying on deck with his leg in a hell of a mess! They had to ferry him ashore in a dory. And then there was the ship's boy who didn't want to go to sea, he was bawling and yelling! Then three days later, they telegraphed saying he'd been washed overboard by a wave! A kid of fifteen! A small lad with fair hair, skinny he was, with a girlish name: Jean-Marie. And that wasn't all . . . Julie, bring us a couple of glasses of calvados . . . The right-hand bottle . . . No, not that one . . . The one with the glass stopper . . . '

'So the evil eye went on?'

'I don't know exactly. It's as if they're all too scared to talk about it. Even so, if the wireless operator has been arrested, it's because the police must have got to hear that during the whole time they were at sea he and the captain never said a word to each other . . . They were like oil and vinegar.'

'And?'

'Things happened . . . Things that don't make any sense. Like for instance when the skipper made them move the boat to a position where no one ever heard of cod being caught! And he went berserk when the head fisherman refused to do what he was told! He got his revolver out. It was like they were off their heads! For a whole month they didn't even net a ton of fish! And then all of a sudden, the fishing was good. But even then, the cod had to be sold at half price because it hadn't been kept right. And on it went. Even when they were coming into the harbour, they lost control twice and sank a rowing boat. It was like there was a curse on the boat. Then the

174

skipper sent all hands ashore without leaving anyone on watch and stayed on board that evening all by himself.

'It was around nine o'clock. They were all in here getting drunk. The wireless operator went up to his room. Then he went out. He was seen heading in the direction of the boat.

'It was then that it happened. A fisherman down in the harbour who was getting ready to leave heard a noise like something falling in the water.

'He ran to see, with a customs man he'd met on the way. They lit lanterns . . . There was a body in the water. It had caught in the *Océan*'s anchor chain.

'It was the skipper! He was dead when they fished him out. They tried artificial respiration. They couldn't understand it. He hadn't been in the water ten minutes.

'The doctor explained the reason. Seems as how somebody had strangled him *before* . . . Do you follow me? And they found the wireless operator on board in his cabin, which is just astern of the funnel. You can see it from here.

'The police came here and searched his room. They found some burned papers . . .

'What do you make of it? . . . Ho! Julie, two calvados! . . . Your very good health!'

Louis, getting more and more carried away, had gripped a chair with his teeth and, in the middle of a circle of sailors, was holding it horizontally while staring defiantly at Maigret.

'Was the captain from around here?' asked the inspector.

'That he was. A curious sort. Not much taller, or wider than Louis. But always polite, always friendly. And always nattily turned out. I don't think he went much to cafés. He wasn't married. He had digs in Rue d'Étretat, with a widow whose husband had worked for customs. There was talk that they'd get wed in the end. He'd been fishing off Newfoundland these fifteen years. Always for the same owners: the French Cod Company. Captain Fallut, to give him his full name. They're in a fix now if they want to send the *Océan* out to the Grand Banks. No captain! And half the crew not wanting to sign on for another tour!'

'Why is that?'

'Don't try to understand! The evil eye, like I told you. There's talk of laying the boat up until next year. On top of which the police have told the crew they have to stay available.'

'And the wireless operator is behind bars?'

'Yes. They took him away the same evening, in handcuffs he was . . . I was standing in the doorway. I tell you God's truth, the wife cried . . . and so did I. But he wasn't a special customer. I used to knock a bit off when I sold him supplies. He wasn't much of a drinker himself.'

They were interrupted by a sudden uproar. Louis had thrown himself at the Breton, presumably because the Breton had insisted on trying to stop him drinking. Both were rolling around on the floor. The others got out of their way.

It was Maigret who separated them, picking

176

them up one in each hand.

'That's enough! You want to argue?'

The scuffle was over quickly. The Breton, whose hands were free, pulled a knife from his pocket. The inspector saw it just in time and with a swift back heel sent it spinning two metres away.

The shoe caught the Breton on the chin, which started to bleed. Louis, still in a daze and still drunk, rushed to his friend and started crying and saying he was sorry.

Léon came up to Maigret. He had his watch in his hand.

'Time I closed up! If I don't we'll have the police on the doorstep. Every evening it's the same story! I just can't kick them out!'

'Do they sleep on board the *Océan*?'

'Yes. Unless, that is, and it happened to two of them yesterday, they sleep where they fall, in the gutter. I found them this morning when I opened the shutters.'

The serving girl went round gathering glasses off the tables. The men drifted off in groups of two or three. Only Louis and the Breton didn't budge.

'Need a room?' Léon asked Maigret.

'No thanks. I'm booked into the Hôtel de la Plage.'

'Can I say something?'

'What?'

'It isn't that I want to give you advice. It's none of my business. But if anyone was feeling sorry for the wireless operator, maybe it wouldn't be a bad idea to *chercher la femme*, as

177

they say in books. I've heard a few whispers along those lines . . . '

'Did Pierre Le Clinche have a girlfriend?'

'What, him? No fear! He'd got himself engaged wherever it was he came from. Every day he'd write home, letters six pages long.'

'Who do you mean, then?'

'I dunno. Maybe it's more complicated than people think. Besides . . . '

'Besides what?'

'Nothing. Behave yourself, Louis! Go home to bed!'

But Louis was far too drunk for that. He was tearful, he had his arms around his friend, whose chin was still bleeding, and he kept saying sorry.

Maigret left the bar, hands thrust deep in his pockets and with his collar turned up, for the air was cool.

In the vestibule of the Hôtel de la Plage, he saw a young woman sitting in a wicker chair. A man got up from another chair and smiled. There was a slight awkwardness in his smile.

It was Jorissen, the primary-school teacher from Quimper. Maigret had not seen him for fifteen years, and Jorissen was not sure whether he should treat him with their old easy familiarity.

'Look, I'm sorry . . . I . . . that is we, Mademoiselle Léonnec and I, have only just got here . . . I did the rounds of the hotels . . . They said you . . . they said you'd be back . . . She's Pierre Le Clinche's fiancée . . . She insisted . . . '

She was tall, rather pale, rather shy. But when Maigret shook her hand, he sensed that behind the façade of small-town, unsophisticated coyness there was a strong will.

She didn't speak. She felt out of her depth. As did Jorissen, who was still just a primary-school teacher who was now meeting up again with his old friend, who now held one of the highest ranks in the Police Judiciare.

'They pointed out Madame Maigret in the lounge just now, but I didn't like to . . . '

Maigret took a closer look at the girl, who was neither pretty nor plain, but there was something touching about her natural simplicity.

'You do know that he's innocent, don't you?' she said finally, looking at no one in particular.

The porter was waiting to get back to his bed. He had already unbuttoned his jacket.

'We'll see about that tomorrow . . . Have you got a room somewhere?'

'I've got the room next to you . . . to yours,' stammered the teacher from Quimper, still unsure of himself. 'And Mademoiselle Léonnec is on the floor above . . . I've got to get back tomorrow, there are exams on . . . Do you think . . . ?'

'Tomorrow! We'll see then,' Maigret said again.

And as he was getting ready for bed, his wife, already half asleep, murmured:

'Don't forget to turn the light out.'

2

The Tan-Coloured Shoes

Side by side, not looking at each other, they walked together first along the beach, which was deserted at that time of day, and then along the quays by the harbour.

Gradually, the silences grew fewer until Marie Léonnec was speaking in a more or less natural tone of voice.

'You'll see! You'll like him straight away! He couldn't be anything but likeable! And then you'll understand that . . . '

Maigret kept shooting curious, admiring glances at her. Jorissen had gone back to Quimper, very early that morning, leaving the girl by herself in Fécamp.

'I can't make her come with me,' he had said. 'She's far too independent for that.'

The previous evening, she was as unforthcoming as a young woman raised in the peace and quiet of a small town can be. Now, it wasn't an hour since she and Maigret had walked out of the Hôtel de la Plage together.

The inspector was behaving in his most crusty manner.

But to no effect. She refused to let herself be intimidated. She was not taken in by him, and she smiled confidently.

'His only fault,' she went on, 'is that he is so

very sensitive. But it's hardly surprising. His father was just a poor fisherman, and for years his mother mended nets to raise him. Now he keeps her. He's educated. He's got a bright future before him.'

'Are your parents well off?' Maigret asked bluntly.

'They are the biggest makers of ropes and metal cables in Quimper. That's why Pierre wouldn't even speak to my father about us. For a whole year, we saw each other in secret.'

'You were both over eighteen?'

'Just. I was the one who told my parents. Pierre swore that he wouldn't marry me until he was earning at least two thousand francs a month. So you see . . . '

'Has he written to you since he was arrested?'

'Just one letter. It was very short. And that from someone who used to send me a letter pages and pages long every day! He said it would be best for me and my parents if I told everyone back home that it was all over between us.'

They passed near the *Océan*, which was still being unloaded. It was high tide, and its black hull dominated the wharves. In the foredeck three men stripped to the waist were getting washed. Among them Maigret recognized Louis.

He also noticed a gesture: one of the men nudged the third man with his shoulder and nodded towards Maigret and the girl. Maigret scowled.

'Just shows how considerate he is!' continued the voice at his side. 'He knows how quickly scandal spreads in a small town like Quimper.

He wanted to give me back my freedom.'

The morning was clear. The girl, in her grey two-piece suit, looked like a student or a primary-school teacher.

'For my parents to have let me come here, they must obviously trust him too. But my father would prefer me to marry someone in business.'

At the police station Maigret left her in the waiting room, sitting some considerable time in the waiting room. He jotted down a few notes.

Half an hour later, they both walked into the jail.

★ ★ ★

It was Maigret in his surly mood, hands behind his back, pipe clenched between his teeth, shoulders bent, who now stood in one corner of the cell. He had informed the authorities that he was not taking an official interest in the investigation, that he was following its progress out of curiosity.

Several people had described the wireless operator to him, and the picture he had formed corresponded exactly to the young man he was now seeing in the flesh.

He was tall and slim, in a conventional suit, though a little on the shabby side, with the half-solemn, half-timid look about him of a schoolboy who is always top of his class. There were freckles on his cheeks. His hair was cropped short.

He had started when the door was opened. For a moment, he stayed well away from the girl who walked straight up to him. She had had to throw herself into his arms, literally, and cling on hard while he looked around in bewilderment.

'Marie! . . . Who on earth . . . ? How . . . ?'

He was quite disoriented. But he wasn't the sort to get excited. The lenses of his glasses clouded over, that was all. His lips trembled.

'You shouldn't have come.'

He caught sight of Maigret, whom he didn't know, and then stared at the door, which had been left half-open.

He wasn't wearing a collar, and there were no laces in his shoes. He also had a beard, gingerish and several days old. He was still feeling awkward about these things, despite the sudden shock he'd had. He felt his bare neck and his prominent Adam's apple with an embarrassed movement of his hand.

'Is my mother . . . ?'

'She didn't come. But she doesn't think you're guilty any more than I do.'

The girl was no more able than he was to give vent to her feelings. The moment fell flat. Maybe it was the intimidating effect of the surroundings.

They looked at each other and, not knowing what to say, groped for words. Then Mademoiselle Léonnec turned and pointed to Maigret.

'He's a friend of Jorissen's. He's a detective chief inspector in the Police Judiciaire and he's agreed to help us.'

Le Clinche hesitated about offering his hand, then did not dare to.

'Thanks . . . I . . . '

Another moment that failed entirely. The girl knew it and felt like crying. She had been counting on a touching interview which would win Maigret over to their side.

She gave her fiancé a look of resentment, even of muted impatience.

'You must tell him everything that might help your defence.'

Pierre Le Clinche sighed, ill at ease and unsettled.

'I've just a few questions for you,' the inspector broke in. 'All the crew say that throughout the voyage your dealings with the captain were more than cool. And yet, when you sailed, you were on good terms with him. What happened to bring about the change?'

The wireless operator opened his mouth, said nothing, then stared at the floor, looking very sorry for himself.

'Something to do with your duties? For the first two days, you ate with the first mate and the chief mechanic. After that you preferred to eat with the men.'

'Yes . . . I know . . . '

'Why?'

Losing patience, Marie Léonnec said:

'Out with it, Pierre! We're trying to save you! You must tell the truth.'

'I don't know.'

He looked limp, cowed, almost without hope.

'Did you have any differences of opinion with Captain Fallut?'

'No.'

'And yet you lived with him for nearly three

184

months cooped up on the same ship without ever saying a single word to him. Everybody noticed. Some of them talked behind his back, saying that there were times when Fallut gave the impression of being mad.'

'I don't know.'

It was all Marie Léonnec could do to choke back her frustration.

'When the *Océan* returned to port, you went ashore with the others. When you got to your room, you burned a number of papers . . . '

'Yes. Nothing of any importance.'

'You keep a regular journal in which you write down everything you see. Wasn't what you burned your journal of the voyage?'

Le Clinche remained standing, head down, like a school-boy who hasn't done his homework and keeps his eyes stubbornly on his feet.

'Yes.'

'Why?'

'I don't remember!'

'And you can't remember why you went back on board either? Though not straight away. You were seen crouching behind a truck fifty metres from the boat.'

The girl looked at the inspector, then at her fiancé, then back to the inspector and began to feel out of her depth.

'Yes.'

'The captain walked down the gangplank on to the quay. It was at that moment that he was attacked.'

Pierre Le Clinche still said nothing.

'Talk to me, dammit!'

'Yes, answer him, Pierre! We're trying to save you. I don't understand . . . I . . . '

Her eyes filled with tears.

'Yes.'

'Yes what?'

'I was there!'

'And you saw?'

'Not clearly . . . There were a lot of barrels, trucks . . . Two men fighting, then one running off and a body falling into the water.'

'What was the man who ran away like?'

'I don't know . . . '

'Was he dressed like a sailor?'

'No!'

'So you know how he was dressed?'

'All I noticed was a pair of tan-coloured shoes under a gas lamp as he ran away.'

'What did you do next?'

'I went on board.'

'Why? And why didn't you try to save the captain? Did you know he was already dead?'

A heavy silence. Marie Léonnec clasped both hands together in anguish.

'Speak, Pierre! Speak . . . please!'

'Yes . . . No . . . I swear I don't know!'

Footsteps in the corridor. It was the custody officer coming to say that they were ready for Le Clinche in the examining magistrate's office.

His fiancée stepped forward, intending to kiss him. He hesitated. In the end, he put his arms round her, slowly, deliberately.

So it was not her lips that he kissed but the fine, fair curls at her temples.

'Pierre!'

'You shouldn't have come!' he told her, his brow furrowed, as he wearily followed the custody officer out.

Maigret and Marie Léonnec returned to the exit without speaking. Outside she sighed unhappily:

'I don't understand . . . I . . . '

Then, holding her head high:

'But he's innocent, I know he is! We don't understand because we've never been in a predicament like his. For three days he's been behind bars, and everybody thinks he's guilty! . . . He's a very shy person . . . '

Maigret was moved, for she was doing her level best to make her words sound positive and convincing, though inside she was utterly devastated.

'You will do something to help despite everything, won't you?'

'On condition that you go back home, to Quimper.'

'No! . . . I won't! . . . Look . . . Let me . . . '

'In that case, take yourself off to the beach. Go and sit by my wife and try to find something to do. She's bound to have something you can sew.'

'What are you going to do? Do you think the tan-coloured shoes are a clue? . . . '

People turned and stared at them, for Marie Léonnec was waving her arms about, and it looked as if they were having an argument.

'Let me say it again: I'll do everything in my power . . . Look, this street leads straight to the Hôtel de la Plage. Tell my wife that I might be back late for lunch.'

187

He turned on his heel and walked as far as the quays. His surly manner had disappeared. He was almost smiling. He'd been afraid there might have been a stormy scene in the cell, heated protests, tears, kisses. But it had passed off very differently, in a way that was more straightforward, more harrowing and more significant.

He had liked the boy, more precisely the part of him that was distant, withdrawn.

As he passed a shop, he ran into Louis, who was holding a pair of gumboots in his hand.

'And where are you off to?'

'To sell these. Do you want to buy them? It's the best thing they make in Canada. I defy you to find anything as good in France. Two hundred francs . . .'

Even so Louis seemed a touch jittery and was only waiting for the nod to be on his way.

'Did you ever get the idea that Captain Fallut was crazy?'

'You don't see much down in a coal bunker, you know.'

'But you do talk. So?'

'There were weird stories going round, of course.'

'What stories?'

'All sorts! . . . Something and nothing! . . . It's hard to put your finger on it. Especially when you're back on dry land again.'

He was still holding the boots in his hand, and the owner of the ship's chandler's shop who had seen him coming, was waiting for him in his doorway.

'Do you need me any more?'

188

'When did those stories start exactly?'

'Oh, straight away. A ship is in good shape or it's in poor shape. I tell you: the *Océan* was sick as a dog.'

'Handling errors?'

'And how! What can I say? Things that don't make any sense, though they happen right enough! The fact is we had this feeling we'd never see port again . . . Look, is it true that I won't be bothered again over that business with the wallet?'

'We'll see.'

The port was almost empty. In summer, all the boats are at sea off Newfoundland, except the smaller fishing vessels which go out after fresh fish in coastal waters. There was only the dark shape of the *Océan* to be seen in the harbour, and it was the *Océan* that filled the air with a strong smell of cod.

Near the trucks was a man in leather gaiters. On his head was a cap with a silk tassel.

'The boat's owner?' Maigret asked a passing customs man.

'Yes. He's head of French Cod.'

The inspector introduced himself. The man looked at him suspiciously but without taking his eyes off the unloading operation.

'What do you make of the murder of your captain?'

'What do I think about it? I think that there's 800 tons of cod that's off, that if this nonsense goes on, the boat won't be going out again for a second voyage, that it's not the police who'll sort out the mess or cover the losses!'

'I assume you had every confidence in Captain Fallut?'

'Yes. And?'

'Do you think the wireless operator . . . ?'

'The wireless operator is neither here nor there: it's a whole year down the chute! And that's not counting the nets they came back with! Those nets cost two million francs, you know! Full of holes, as if someone has been having fun fishing up rocks! On top of which, the crew's been going on about the evil eye! . . . Hoy, you there! What do you think you're playing at? . . . God give me strength! Did I or did I not tell you to finish loading that truck first?'

And he started running alongside the boat, swearing at all the hands.

Maigret stayed a few moments more, watching the boat being unloaded. Then he moved off in the direction of the jetty, where there were groups of fishermen in pink canvas jerkins.

He'd been there only a moment when a voice behind him said:

'Hoy! Inspector!'

It was Léon, the landlord of the Grand Banks Café, who was trying to catch him up by pumping his short legs as fast as he could.

'Come and have a drink in the bar.'

He was behaving mysteriously. It seemed promising. As they walked, he explained:

'It's all calmed down now. The boys who haven't gone home to Brittany or the villages round about have just about spent all their money. I've only had a few mackerel men in all morning.'

They walked across the quays and went into the café, which was empty except for the girl from behind the bar, who was wiping tables.

'Half a mo'. What'll you have? Aperitif? . . . It's almost time for one . . . Not that, as I told you yesterday, I encourage the boys to drink too much . . . The opposite! . . . I mean, when they've had a drop or three, they start smashing the place up, and that costs me more than I make out of them . . . Julie! Pop into the kitchen and see if I'm there!'

He gave the inspector a knowing wink.

'Your very good health! . . . I saw you in the distance and since I had something to tell you . . . '

He crossed the room to make sure the girl was not listening behind the door. And then, looking even more mysterious and pleased with himself, he took something out of his pocket, a piece of card about the size of a photo.

'There! What do you make of that!'

It was indeed a photo, a picture of a woman. But the face was completely hidden, scribbled all over in red ink. Someone had tried to obliterate the head, someone very angry. The pen had bitten into the paper. There were so many criss-crossed lines that not a single square millimetre had been left visible.

On the other hand, below the head, the torso had not been touched. A pair of large breasts. A light-coloured silk dress, very tight and very low cut.

'Where did you get this?'

More knowing winks.

191

'Since there's just the two of us, I can tell you ... Le Clinche's sea-chest doesn't fasten properly, so he'd got into the habit of sliding his girlfriend's letters under the cloth on his table.'

'And you used to read them?'

'They were of no interest to me ... No, it was luck ... When the place was searched, nobody thought of looking under the tablecloth. It came to me last night, and that's what I found. Of course, you can't see the face. But it's obviously not the girlfriend, she isn't stacked like that! Anyway, I've seen a photo of her. So there's another woman lurking in the background.'

Maigret stared at the photo. The line of the shoulders was inviting. The woman was probably younger than Marie Léonnec. And there was something extremely sensual about those breasts.

But also something vulgar too. The dress looked shop-bought. Seduction on the cheap.

'Is there any red ink in the house?'

'No! Just green.'

'Did Le Clinche never use red ink?'

'No. He had his own ink, on account of having a fountain pen. Special ink. Blue-black.'

Maigret stood up and made for the door.

'Do you mind excusing ... ?'

Moments later he was on board the *Océan*, searching first the wireless operator's cabin and then the captain's, which was dirty and full of clutter.

There was no red ink anywhere on the trawler. None of the fishermen had ever seen any there.

When he left the boat, Maigret came in for sour looks from the man in gaiters, who was still bawling at his men.

'Do you use red ink in any of your offices?'

'Red ink? What for? We're not running a school . . . '

But suddenly, as if he'd just remembered something:

'Fallut was the only one who ever wrote in red ink, when he was working at home, in Rue d'Étretat. But what's all this about now? . . . You down there, watch out for that truck! All we need now is an accident! . . . So what are you after now with your red ink?'

'Nothing . . . Much obliged.'

Louis reappeared bootless and a few sheets to the wind, with a roughneck's cap on his head and a pair of scuffed shoes on his feet.

3

The Headless Photograph

. . . and that no one could tell me to my face and that I've got savings, which are at least the equivalent of a captain's pay.

★   ★   ★

Maigret left Madame Bernard standing on the doorstep of her small house in Rue d'Étretat. She was about fifty, very well preserved, and she had just spoken for a full half-hour about her first husband, about being a widow, about the captain, whom she had taken as her lodger, about the rumours which had circulated about their relationship and, finally, about an unnamed female who was beyond a shadow of a doubt a 'loose woman'.

The inspector had looked round the whole house, which was well kept but full of objects in rather bad taste. Captain Fallut's room was still as it had been arranged in readiness for his return.

Few personal possessions: some clothes in a trunk, a handful of books, mostly adventure yarns, and pictures of boats.

All redolent of an uneventful, unremarkable life.

' . . . It was understood though not finally

settled, but we both knew that we would eventually get married. I would bring the house, furniture and bed linen. Nothing would have changed, and we would have been comfortably off, especially in three or four years' time, after he got his pension.'

Visible through the windows were the grocer's opposite, the road that ran down the hill and the pavement, where children were playing.

'And then this last winter he met that woman, and everything was turned upside down. At his age! How can a man lose his head over a creature like that? And he kept it all very secret. He must have been going to see her in Le Havre or somewhere, for no one here ever saw them together. I had a feeling that something was going on. He started buying more expensive underwear. And once, even a pair of silk socks! As there wasn't anything definite between us, it was none of my business, and I didn't want to look as if I was trying to defend my interests.'

The interview with Madame Bernard cast light on one whole area of the dead man's life. The small, middle-aged man who returned to port after a long tour on a trawler and spent his winters living like an upstanding citizen, with Madame Bernard, who looked after him and expected to marry him.

He ate with her, in her dining room, under a portrait of her first husband, who sported a blond moustache. Afterwards, he would go to his room and settle down with an exciting book.

And then that peace was shattered. Another woman burst on to the scene. Captain Fallut went to Le Havre frequently, took more care of his appearance, shaved more closely, even bought silk socks and hid it all from his landlady.

Still, he wasn't married, he had made no promises. He was free and yet he had never appeared once in public in Fécamp with his unknown woman.

Was it the grand passion, his belated big adventure? Or just a sordid affair?

Maigret reached the beach, saw his wife sitting in a red-striped deckchair and, just by her, Marie Léonnec, who was sewing.

There were a few bathers on the shingle, which gleamed white in the sun. A drowsy sea. And further on, on the other side of the jetty, the *Océan* at her berth, and the cargo of cod that was still being unloaded, and the resentful sailors exchanging veiled comments.

He kissed Madame Maigret on the forehead. He nodded politely to the girl and replied to her questioning look:

'Nothing special.'

His wife said in a level voice:

'Mademoiselle Léonnec has been telling me her story. Do you think that her young man is capable of doing such a thing?'

They walked slowly towards the hotel. Maigret carried both deckchairs. They were about to sit down to lunch when a uniformed policeman arrived, looking for the inspector.

'I was told to show you this, sir. It came an hour ago.'

And he held out a brown envelope, which had been already opened. There was no address on it.

196

Inside was a sheet of paper. On it, in a tiny, thin, cramped hand, was written:

No one should be accused of bringing about my death, and no attempt should be made to understand my action.

These are my last wishes. I leave all my worldly goods to Madame Bernard, who has always been kind to me, on the condition that she sends my gold chronometer to my nephew, who is known to her, and that she sees to it that I am buried in Fécamp cemetery, near my mother.

Maigret opened his eyes wide.

'It's signed Octave Fallut!' he said in a whisper. 'How did this letter get to the police station?'

'Nobody knows, sir. It was in the letterbox. It seems that it's his handwriting right enough. The chief inspector informed the public prosecutor's department immediately.'

'Despite the fact that he was strangled! And that it is impossible to strangle yourself!' muttered Maigret.

Close by, guests who had ordered the set menu were complaining loudly about some pink radishes in a hors d'oeuvres dish.

'Wait a moment while I copy this letter. I imagine you have to take it back with you?'

'I wasn't given any special instructions but I suppose so.'

'Quite right. It must be put in the file.'

A moment or two later, Maigret, holding the

copy in his hand, looked impatiently round the dining room, where he was about to waste an hour waiting for each course to arrive. All this time, Marie Léonnec had not taken her eyes off him but had not dared interrupt his grim reflections. Only Madame Maigret reacted, with a sigh, at the sight of pale cutlets.

'We'd have been better off going to Alsace.'

Maigret stood up before the dessert arrived and wiped his mouth, eager to get back to the trawler, the harbour, the fishermen. All the way there, he kept muttering:

'Fallut knew he was going to die! But did he know he would be killed? Was he trying in advance to save his killer's neck? Or was it just that he intended to commit suicide? Then again, who dropped the brown envelope in the station's postbox? There was no stamp on it, no address.'

The news had already got out, for when Maigret had nearly reached the trawler, the head of French Cod called out to him with aggressive sarcasm:

'So, it seems Fallut strangled himself! Who came up with that bright idea?'

'If you've got something to say, you can tell me which of the *Océan*'s officers are still on board.'

'None of them. The first mate has gone on the spree to Paris. The chief mechanic is at home, at Yport and won't be back until they've finished unloading.'

Maigret again looked round the captain's quarters. A narrow cabin. A bed with a dirty quilt over it. A clothes press built into the bulkhead. A blue enamel coffee-pot on an oilcloth-covered table. In a corner, a pair of boots with wooden soles.

It was dark and clammy and permeated with the same acrid smell which filled the rest of the ship. Blue-striped knitted pullovers were drying on deck. Maigret nearly lost his footing as he walked across the gangway, which was slippery with the remains of fish.

'Find anything?'

The inspector gave a shrug, took yet another gloomy look at the *Océan*, then asked a customs officer how he could get to Yport.

Yport is a village built under the cliffs six kilometres from Fécamp. A handful of fishermen's cottages. The odd farm round about. A few villas, most let furnished during the summer season, and one hotel.

On the beach, another collection of bathing costumes, small children and mothers busily knitting and embroidering.

'Could you tell me where Monsieur Laberge lives?'

'The chief mechanic on the *Océan* or the farmer?'

'The mechanic.'

He was directed to a small house with a small garden round it. As he came up to the front door, which was painted green, he heard the sound of an argument coming from inside. Two voices: a man's and a woman's. But he could not make out what they were saying. He knocked.

It all went quiet. Footsteps approached. The door opened and a tall, rangy man appeared looking suspicious and cross.

'What is it?'

A woman in housekeeping clothes was quickly tidying her dishevelled hair.

'I'm from the Police Judiciaire and I'd like to ask you a few questions.'

'You'd better come in.'

A little boy was crying, and his father pushed him roughly into the adjoining room, in which Maigret caught sight of the foot of a bed.

'You can leave us to it!' Laberge snapped at his wife.

Her eyes were red with crying too. The argument must have started in the middle of their meal, for their plates were still half full.

'What do you want to know?'

'When did you last go to Fécamp?'

'This morning. I went on my bike. It's no fun having to listen to the wife going on all day. You spend months at sea, working your guts out, and when you get back . . . '

He was still angry. However, his breath smelled strongly of alcohol.

'Women! They're all the same! Jealous don't say the half of it! They imagine a man's got nothing else on his mind except running after skirts. Listen to her! That's her giving the kid a hiding, taking it out on him!'

The child could be heard yelling in the next room, and the mother's voice getting louder.

'Stop that row, you hear! . . . Just stop it!'

Judging by the sounds, the words were accompanied by slaps and thumps, for the crying started up again, with interest.

'Ah! What a life!'

200

'Had Captain Fallut told you he was worried about anything in particular?'

Laberge scowled at Maigret, then moved his chair.

'Who made you think he had?'

'You'd been sailing with him for a long time, hadn't you?'

'Five years.'

'On board you took your meals together.'

'Except this last time! He got the idea that he wanted to eat alone, in his cabin . . . But I'd rather not talk any more about that damned trip!'

'Where were you when the crime was committed?'

'In the café, with the others . . . They must have told you.'

'Do you think the wireless operator had any reason for attacking the captain?'

Suddenly, Laberge lost his temper.

'Where are all these questions leading? What do you want me to say? Look, it wasn't my job to keep everybody in order, was it? I'm fed up to the back teeth, fed up with this business and all the rest of it! So fed up that I'm wondering if I'm going to sign up for the next tour!'

'Obviously the last one wasn't exactly a roaring success.'

Another sharp glance at Maigret.

'What are you getting at?'

'Just that everything went wrong! A ship's boy was killed. There were more accidents than usual. The fishing wasn't good, and when the cod arrived back in Fécamp it was off . . . '

201

'Was that my fault?'

'I'm not saying that. I merely ask if in the events at which you were present there was anything that might explain the captain's death. He was an easy-going sort, led a quiet life . . . '

The mechanic smiled mockingly but said nothing.

'Do you know anything about him that says otherwise?'

'Look, I told you I don't know anything, that I've had enough of the whole business! Is everybody trying to drive me crazy? . . . What more do you want now?'

He had it in most for his wife. She had just come back into the room and was hurrying to the stove, where a saucepan was giving off a smell of burning.

She was about thirty-five. She wasn't pretty and she wasn't ugly.

'I'll only be a minute,' she said meekly. 'It's the dog's dinner . . . '

'Get on with it, woman! . . . Haven't you finished yet?'

And turning to Maigret:

'Shall I give you a piece of good advice? Let it alone! Fallut is well off where he is! The less said about him, the better it'll be! Now listen: I don't know anything. You can ask me questions all day, and I wouldn't have anything else to say . . . Did you get the train here? If you don't catch the one that leaves in ten minutes, you'll not get another until eight this evening.'

He had opened the door. Sunshine flooded into the room.

When he got to the doorway, the inspector asked quietly: 'Who is your wife jealous of?'

The man gritted his teeth and did not speak.

'Do you know who this is?'

Maigret held out the photo with the head obscured by the red scribble. But he kept his thumb over the face. All that was visible was the cleavage in the silk dress.

Laberge glanced up at him quickly and tried to grab the picture.

'Do you recognize her?'

'Why should I recognize her?'

His hand was still open when Maigret put the photograph back in his pocket.

'Will you be coming to Fécamp tomorrow?'

'I don't know . . . Will you be needing me?'

'No. I was just asking. Thanks for the information you gave me.'

'But I didn't tell you anything!'

Maigret had not gone ten paces from the door when it was kicked shut and voices were raised inside the house, where the argument would now start up again, even more acrimoniously.

★ ★ ★

The chief mechanic was right: there were no trains to Fécamp until eight in the evening, and Maigret, having time on his hands, was inevitably drawn to the beach, where he sat down on the terrace of a hotel.

There was the usual holiday atmosphere: red sun umbrellas, white dresses, white trousers and a group of sightseers clustered around a fishing boat that was being winched up on to the pebble beach with a capstan.

To right and left, light-coloured cliffs. Straight ahead, the sea, pale green with white combers, and the regular murmur of wavelets lapping the shoreline.

'A beer!'

The sun was hot. A family were eating ice-creams on the next table. A young man was taking photos with a Kodak, and somewhere there were the shrill voices of little girls.

Maigret allowed his eyes to wander over the view. His thoughts grew hazy, and his brain sluggishly started weaving a daydream around Captain Fallut, who became increasingly insubstantial.

'Thanks a million!'

The words went round and round in his head, not on account of their meaning, but because they had been pronounced curtly, with biting sarcasm, by a woman somewhere behind the inspector.

'But Adèle, I told you . . . '

'Shut up!'

'You're not going to start all that again . . . '

'I'll do exactly as I please!'

It was obviously a good day for arguments. First thing that morning, Maigret had encountered a man who bristled: the head man from French Cod.

At Yport, there had been that domestic scene between the Laberges. And now on the hotel terrace an unknown couple were exchanging heated words.

'Why don't you stop and think!'

'Get lost!'

'Do you think it's clever to talk like that?'

'Damn and blast you! Haven't you got the message yet? . . . Waiter, this lemonade is warm. Get me another!'

The accent was common, and the woman was speaking more loudly than was necessary.

'But you must make up your mind!' the man said.

'Just go by yourself! I told you! And leave me alone.'

'You know, what you're doing is pretty shabby.'

'So are you!'

'Me? You dare . . . Listen, if we weren't here, I don't think I'd be able to keep control of myself!'

She laughed. Much too loudly.

'You tell a girl the nicest things!'

'Be quiet! Please!'

'Why should I?'

'Because!'

'Now that really is a clever answer, I must say!'

'Are you going to shut up?'

'If I feel like it.'

'Adèle, I'm warning you I'll . . . '

'You'll what? Kick up a fuss in front of everybody? And where would that get you? People are already listening.'

'If only you'd stop and think for a moment, you'd understand.'

She sprang to her feet like someone who has had enough. Maigret had his back turned to her but saw her shadow grow bigger on the tiled floor of the terrace.

Then he saw her, from the back, as she walked off in the direction of the sea.

From behind, she was just a silhouette against the sky, which was now turning red. All Maigret could make out was that she was quite well-dressed, but not for the beach, not with silk stockings and high heels.

It was an outfit which made it difficult for her to walk elegantly over the pebble beach. At any moment she could twist an ankle, but she was furiously, stubbornly determined to forge ahead.

'Waiter, what do I owe you?'

'But I haven't brought the lemonade which the lady . . . '

'Forget it! What's the damage?'

'Nine francs fifty . . . Won't you be having dinner here?'

'No idea.'

Maigret turned round to get a sight of the man, who was looking very awkward because he was well aware that everyone nearby had heard everything.

He was tall and flashily elegant. His eyes looked tired, and his utter frustration was written all over his face.

When he stood up, he hesitated about which way to go and in the end, trying to look as if he didn't give a damn about anything, he set off in the direction of the young woman, who was now walking along the winding edge of the sea.

'Another pair that aren't married, for sure!' said a voice at a table where three women were busy doing crochet work.

'Why couldn't they wash their dirty linen somewhere else? It's not setting the children a very good example.'

The two silhouettes joined at the water's edge. Their words were no longer audible. But the way they stood and moved made it easy to guess what was going on.

The man pleaded and threatened. The woman refused to give an inch. At one point he grabbed her by the wrist, and it seemed as if they would come to blows.

Instead, he turned his back on her and walked away quickly towards a street nearby, where he started the engine of a small grey car.

'Waiter! Another beer!'

Then Maigret noticed that the young woman had left her handbag on the table. Imitation crocodile-skin, full to bursting, brand new.

Then a shadow coming towards him on the ground. He looked up and got a front view of the owner of the handbag, who was coming back to the terrace.

The inspector gave a start. His nostrils flared slightly.

He could be wrong, of course. It was more an impression than a certainty. But he could have sworn he was looking at the person in the headless photo.

Cautiously, he took the photo out of his pocket. The woman had sat down again.

'Well, waiter? Where's my lemonade?'

'I thought . . . The gentleman said . . . '

'I ordered lemonade!'

It was the same slightly fleshy line of the neck,

the same full but firm breasts, the same voluptuous buoyancy . . .

And the same style of dressing, the same taste for very glossy silk in loud colours.

Maigret dropped the photo in such a way that the woman at the next table could not fail to see it.

And see it she did. She stared at the inspector as though she were trawling through her memories. But if she was disconcerted, her feelings did not show in her face.

Five minutes, ten minutes went by. Then there was the distant thrum of an engine. It grew louder. It was the grey car heading back to the terrace. It stopped, then set off again, as though the driver could not make up his mind to drive away and not come back.

'Gaston!'

She was on her feet. She waved to the man. This time she grasped her bag firmly and the next moment she was getting into the car.

The three women at the next table followed her with their eyes and a disapproving air. The young man with the Kodak turned round.

The grey car was already vanishing in a roar of acceleration.

'Waiter! Where can I get hold of a car?'

'I don't think you'll find one in Yport . . . There is one which sometimes takes people to Fécamp or Étretat, but now that I think I saw it drive off this morning with some English people in it.'

The inspector's thick fingers drummed rapidly on the tabletop.

'Bring me a road map. And get me the chief inspector of Fécamp police on the phone . . . Have you ever seen those two before?'

'The couple who were arguing? Almost every day this week. Yesterday they had lunch here. I think they're from Le Havre.'

There were now only families left on the beach, which exuded all the warmth of a summer evening. A black ship moved imperceptibly across the line of the horizon, entered the sun and emerged on the other side, as if it had jumped through a paper hoop.

4

The Mark of Rage

'Speaking for myself,' said the chief inspector of Fécamp's police department as he sharpened a blue pencil, 'I'll admit I have few illusions left. It's so rarely that we manage to clear up any of these cases involving sailors. And that's being optimistic! Just you try getting to the bottom of one of those mindless brawls that happen every day of the week down by the harbour. When my men get there, they're all beating seven bells out of each other. Then they spot uniforms and they close ranks and go on the offensive. Question them and they all lie, contradict each other and muddy the waters to the point that in the end we give up.'

There were four of them smoking in the office, which was already filled with tobacco fumes. It was evening. The divisional head of Le Havre's flying squad, who was officially in charge of the investigation, had a young inspector with him.

Maigret was there in a private capacity. He sat at a table in a corner. He hadn't yet spoken.

'It looks straightforward enough to me,' ventured the young inspector, who was hoping to earn the approval of his chief. 'Theft wasn't the motive for the crime. So it was an act of revenge. On which member of the crew did Captain

210

Fallut come down hardest when they were away at sea?'

But the chief inspector from Le Havre gave a shrug, and the junior inspector turned red and fell silent.

'Still . . . '

'No, no! It's something else. And top of the list is this woman you unearthed for us, Maigret. Did you give the boys in uniform all the information they need to find her? Dammit, I can't for the life of me work out what part she played in all this. The boat was at sea for three months. She wasn't there when it docked, because no one has reported seeing her get off it. The wireless operator is engaged to be married. By all accounts, Captain Fallut didn't seem the kind of man who'd do anything silly. And yet he wrote his will just before he got himself murdered.

'It would also be interesting to know who exactly went to the trouble of delivering the will here,' sighed Maigret. 'There's also a reporter — he's the one who wears a beige raincoat — who claims in *L'Éclair de Rouen* that the owners of the *Océan* had sent it to sea to do something other than fish for cod.'

'They always say that, every time,' muttered the Fécamp chief inspector.

The conversation languished. There was a long silence during which the spittle in Maigret's pipe could be heard sizzling. He got stiffly to his feet.

'If anyone asked me what the distinctive feature of this case is,' he said, 'I'd say that it has the mark of rage on it. Everything to do with the

211

trawler is acrimonious, tense, overheated. The crew get drunk and fight in the Grand Banks Café. I bring the wireless operator's fiancée to see him, and he could barely conceal his irritation and gave her a pretty cool reception. He almost as good as told her to mind her own business! At Yport, the chief mechanic calls his wife all sorts and treats me like some dog he can kick. And then I come across two people who seem to have the same mark on them: the girl called Adèle, and her boyfriend. They make scenes on the beach, and no sooner do they settle their differences than they disappear together . . . '

'And what do you make of it all?' asked the chief inspector from Le Havre.

'Me? I don't make anything of it. I merely remark that I feel as if I'm going round in circles surrounded by a lot of mad people . . . Anyway, I'll say good night. I'm just an observer here. Besides, my wife is expecting me back at the hotel. You'll let me know, chief inspector, if you locate the Yport woman and the man in the grey car?'

'Of course! Good night!'

Instead of walking through the town, Maigret went via the harbour, hands in pocket, pipe between his teeth. The empty port was a large black rectangle where the only lights that showed were those of the *Océan*, which was still being unloaded.

' . . . the mark of rage!' he muttered to himself.

No one paid attention when he climbed on

board. He walked along the deck, with no obvious purpose, he saw a light in a foredeck hatchway. He leaned over it. Warm air blew up into his face, a combined smell of doss-house, canteen and fish market.

He went down the iron ladder and found himself face to face with three men who were eating from mess tins balanced on their knees. For light, there was an oil lamp hung on gimbals. In the middle of their quarters was a cast-iron stove caked with grease.

Along the walls were four tiers of bunks, some still full of straw, the others empty. And boots. And sou'westers hanging on pegs.

Of the three, only Louis had stood up. The other two were the Breton and a black sailor with bare feet.

'Enjoying your dinner?' growled Maigret.

He was answered with grunts.

'Where are your mates?'

'Gone home, haven't they,' said Louis. 'You gotta have nowhere to go and be broke to hang about here when you're not at sea.'

Maigret had to get used to the semi-darkness and especially the smell. He tried to imagine the same space when it was filled by forty men who could not move a muscle without bumping into somebody.

Forty men dropping on to their bunks without taking their boots off, snoring, chewing tobacco, smoking . . .

'Did the captain ever come down here?'

'Never.'

And all the while the throb of the screw, the

smell of coal smoke, of soot, of burning hot metal, the pounding of the sea . . .

'Come with me, Louis.'

Out of the corner of his eye, Maigret caught the sailor, full of bravado, making signs to the others behind his back.

But once aloft, on the deck now flooded with shadow, his swagger evaporated.

'What's up?'

'Nothing . . . Listen . . . Suppose the captain died at sea, on the way home. Was there someone who could have got the boat safely back to port?'

'Maybe not. Because the first mate doesn't know how to take a bearing. Still they say that, using the wireless, the wireless operator could always find the ship's position.'

'Did you see much of the wireless operator?'

'Never saw him at all! Don't imagine we walk around like we're doing now. There are general quarters for some, others have separate quarters of their own. You can go for days without budging from your small corner.'

'How about the chief mechanic?'

'Him? Yes. I saw him more or less every day.'

'How did he seem?'

Louis turned evasive.

'How the devil should I know? Look, what are you driving at? I'd like to see how you make out when everything's going wrong, a lad goes overboard, a steam valve blows, the captain's mind is set on anchoring the trawler in a station where there's no fish, a man gets gangrene and the rest of it . . . You'd be effing and blinding nineteen to the dozen! And for the smallest thing

214

you'd take a swing at someone! And to cap it all, when you're told the captain on the bridge is off his rocker . . . '

'Was he?'

'I never asked him. Anyway . . . '

'Anyway what?'

'At the end of the day, what difference will it make? There'll always be someone who'll tell you. Look, it seems there were three of them up top who never went anywhere without their revolvers. Three of them spying on each other, all afraid of each other. The captain hardly ever came out of his cabin, where he'd ordered the charts, compass, sextant and the rest to be brought.'

'And it went on like that for three months?'

'Yes. Anything else you want to ask me?'

'No, that's it. You can go . . . '

Louis walked away almost regretfully. He stopped for a moment by the hatch, watching the inspector, who was puffing gently at his pipe.

Cod was still being extracted from the gaping hold in the glare of the acetylene lamps. But Maigret had had enough of trucks, dockers, the quays, the jetties and the lighthouse.

He was standing on a world of plated steel and, half-closing his eyes, he imagined being out on the open sea, in a field of surging swells through which the bows ploughed an endless furrow, hour after hour, day after day, week after week.

'Don't imagine we walk around like we're doing now . . . '

Men below serving the engines. Men in the

forward crew quarters. And on the after deck, a handful of God's creatures: the captain, his first mate, the chief mechanic and the wireless operator.

A small binnacle light to see the compass by. Charts spread out.

Three months!

When they'd got back, Captain Fallut had written his will, in which he stated his intention to put an end to his life.

An hour after they'd berthed, he'd been strangled and dumped in the harbour.

And Madame Bernard, his landlady, was left grieving because now there would be no marriage of two ideally suited people. The chief mechanic shouted at his wife. The girl called Adèle defied an unknown man, but ran off with him the moment Maigret held a picture of herself scribbled on in red ink under her nose.

And in his prison cell the wireless operator Le Clinche in a foul temper.

The boat hardly moved. Just a gentle motion, like a chest breathing. One of the three men he'd seen in the foredeck was playing the accordion.

As he turned his head, Maigret made out the shapes of two women on the quayside. Suddenly galvanized, he hurried down the gangway.

'What are you doing here?'

He felt his face burn because he had sounded gruff, but especially because he was aware that he too was being infected by the frenzy which filled all those involved in the case.

'We wanted to see the boat,' said Madame Maigret with disarming self-effacement.

'It's my fault,' said Marie Léonnec. 'I was the one who insisted on . . . '

'All right! That's fine! Have you eaten?'

'It's ten o'clock . . . Have you?'

'Yes, thanks.'

The windows of the Grand Banks Café were more or less the only ones still lit. A few shadowy figures could be made out on the jetty: tourists dutifully out for their evening stroll.

'Have you found out anything?' asked Le Clinche's fiancée.

'Not yet. Or rather, not much.'

'I don't dare ask you a favour.'

'You can always ask.'

'I'd like to see Pierre's cabin. Could I?'

He shrugged and took her there. Madame Maigret refused to walk over the gangway.

Literally a metal box. Wireless equipment. A steel table, a seat and a bunk. Hanging on a wall, a picture of Marie Léonnec in Breton costume. Old shoes on the floor and a pair of trousers on the bed.

The girl inhaled the atmosphere with a mixture of curiosity and delight.

'Yes! But it isn't at all how I'd imagined. His shoes have never been cleaned . . . Oh look! He kept drinking from the same glass without ever washing it . . . '

A strange girl! An amalgam of shyness, delicacy and a good upbringing on the one hand and dynamism and fearlessness on the other. She hesitated.

'And the captain's cabin?'

Maigret smiled faintly, for he realized that

deep down she was hoping to make a discovery. He led the way. He even fetched a lantern he found on deck.

'How can they live with this smell?' she sighed.

She looked carefully around her. He saw her become flustered and shy as she said:

'Why has the bed been raised up?'

Maigret stopped drawing on his pipe. She was right. All the crew slept in berths which were more or less part of the architectural structure of the boat. Only the captain had a metal bed.

Under each of its legs a wooden block had been placed.

'You don't think that's strange? It's as if . . . '

'Go on.'

All trace of ill-humour had gone. Maigret saw the girl's pale face lighten as her mind worked and her elation grew.

'It's as if . . . but you'll only laugh at me . . . as if the bed's been propped up so that someone could hide underneath . . . Without those pieces of wood, the bedstead would be much too low, but the way it is now . . . '

And before he could stop her, she lay down flat on the floor regardless of the dirt on the floor and slid under the bed.

'There's enough room!' she said.

'Right. You can come out now.'

'Just a minute, if you don't mind. Pass me that lamp for a minute, inspector.'

She went quiet. He couldn't work out what she was doing. He lost patience.

'Well?'

She reappeared suddenly, her grey suit

covered with dust and eyes shining.

'Pull the bed out . . . You'll see.'

Her voice broke. Her hands shook. Maigret yanked the bed away from the wall and looked at the floor.

'I can't see anything . . . '

When she didn't answer he turned and saw that she was crying.

'What did you see? Why are you crying?'

'There . . . Read it.'

He had to bend down and place the lamp against the wall. Then he could make out words scratched on the wood with a sharp object, a pin or a nail.

Gaston — Octave — Pierre — Hen . . .

The last word was unfinished. And yet it did not look as if it had been done in a hurry. Some of the letters must have taken an hour to inscribe. There were flourishes, little strokes, the sort of doodling that's done in an idle moment.

A comic note was struck by two stag's antlers above the name 'Octave'.

The girl was sitting on the edge of the bed, which had been pulled into the middle of the cabin. She was still crying, in silence.

'Very curious!' muttered Maigret. 'I'd like to know if . . . '

At this point, she stood up and said excitedly:

'Of course! That's it! There was a woman here! She was hiding! . . . All the same, men would come looking for her . . . Wasn't Captain Fallut called Octave?'

The inspector had rarely been so taken off guard.

'Don't go jumping to conclusions!' he said, though there was no conviction in his words.

'But it's all written down! . . . The whole story is there! Four men who . . . '

What could he say to calm her down?

'Look, I've a lot of experience, so take it from me. In police matters, you must always wait before making judgements . . . Only yesterday, you were telling me that Le Clinche is incapable of killing.'

'Yes,' she sobbed. 'Yes, and I still believe it! Isn't it . . . '

She still clung desperately to her hopes.

'His name is Pierre . . . '

'I know. So what? One sailor in ten is called Pierre, and there were fifty men on board . . . There's also a Gaston . . . And a Henry . . . '

'So what do you think?'

'Nothing.'

'Are you going to tell the examining magistrate about this? And to think it was me who . . . '

'Calm down! We haven't found out anything, except that the bed was raised for one reason or another and that someone has written names on a wall.'

'There was a woman there.'

'Why a woman?'

'But . . . '

'Come on. Madame Maigret is waiting for us on the quay.'

'You're right.'

She wiped her tears, meek now, and sniffled.

'I shouldn't have come . . . But I thought

. . . But it's not possible that Pierre . . . Listen! I must see him as soon as I can! I'll talk to him, alone . . . You can arrange it, can't you?'

Before starting down the gangway, she looked back with eyes full of hate at the dark ship, which was no longer the same to her now that she knew that a woman had been hiding on board.

Madame Maigret watched her, intrigued.

'Come! You mustn't cry! You know everything will all turn out all right.'

'No, it won't,' she said with a despairing shake of her head.

She couldn't speak. She could hardly breathe. She tried to look at the boat one more time. Madame Maigret, who did not understand what was going on, looked inquiringly at her husband.

'Take her back to the hotel. Try and calm her down.'

'Did something happen?'

'Nothing specific. I expect I'll be back quite late.'

He watched them walk away. Marie Léonnec turned round a dozen times, and Madame Maigret had to drag her away like a child.

Maigret thought about going back on board. But he was thirsty. There were still lights on in the Grand Banks Café.

Four sailors were playing cards at a table. Near the counter, a young cadet had his arm round the waist of the serving girl, who giggled from time to time.

The landlord was watching the card game and was offering suggestions.

He greeted Maigret with: 'Hello! You back again?'

He did not look overjoyed to see him. The very opposite. He seemed rather put out.

'Look sharp, Julie! Serve the inspector! Whatever's your poison. It's on me.'

'Thanks. But if it's all the same to you, I'll order like any other customer.'

'I didn't want to get on the wrong side of you . . . I . . . '

Was the day going to end with the mark of rage still on it? One of the sailors muttered something in his Norman dialect which Maigret translated roughly as:

'Watch out, I smell more trouble.'

The inspector looked him in the eye. The man reddened then stammered:

'Clubs trumps!'

'You should have played a spade,' declared Louis for something to say.

5

Adèle and Friend

The phone rang. Léon snatched the receiver, then called Maigret. It was for him.

'Hello?' said a bored voice on the other end of the line. 'Detective Chief Inspector Maigret? It's the duty desk officer at Fécamp police station. I've just phoned your hotel. I was told you might be at the Grand Banks Café. I'm sorry to disturb you, sir. I've been glued to the phone for half an hour. I can't get hold of the chief anywhere. As for the head of the Flying Squad, I'm wondering if he's still actually here in Fécamp . . . Thing is, I've got a couple of odd customers who've just turned up saying they want to make statements, all very urgent, apparently. A man and a woman . . . '

'Did they come in a grey car?'

'Yes, sir. Are they the pair you're looking for?'

Ten minutes later, Maigret was at the police station. All the offices were closed except for the inquiries area, a room divided in two by a counter. Behind it the duty officer was writing. He smoked as he wrote. A man was waiting. He was sitting on a bench, elbows on knees, chin in his hands.

And a woman was walking up and down, beating a tattoo on the floorboards with her high heels

The moment the inspector appeared, she walked right up to him, and the man got to his feet with a sigh of relief and growled between gritted teeth:

'And not a minute too soon!'

It was indeed the couple from Yport, both a little crosser than during the domestic shouting-match Maigret had sat through.

'Come next door with me.'

Maigret showed them into the office of the chief inspector, sat down in his chair and filled a pipe while he took a good look at the pair.

'Take a seat.'

'No thanks,' said the woman, who was clearly the more highly strung of the two. 'What I've got to say won't take long.'

He now had a frontal view of her, lit by a strong electric light. He did not need to look too hard to situate her type. Her picture with the head removed had been enough.

A good-looking girl, in the popular sense of the expression. A girl with alluring curves, good teeth, an inviting smile and a permanent come-hither look in her eye.

More accurately, a real bitch, a tease, on the make, always ready to create a scandal or burst into gales of loud, vulgar laughter.

Her blouse was pink silk. To it was pinned a large gold brooch as big as a 100-sou coin.

'First off, I want to say . . . '

'Excuse me,' interrupted Maigret. 'Please sit down as I've already asked. You will answer my questions.'

She scowled. Her mouth turned ugly.

'Look here! You're forgetting I'm here because I'm prepared to . . . '

Her companion scowled, irritated by her behaviour. They were made for each other. He was every inch the kind who is always seen with girls like her. His appearance was not exactly sinister. He was respectably dressed, though in bad taste. He wore large rings on his fingers and a pearl pin in his tie. Even so, the effect was disturbing. Perhaps because he gave off a sense of existing outside the established social norms.

He was the type to be found at all times of day in bars and brasseries, drinking cheap champagne with working girls and living in third-class hotels.

'You first. Name, address, occupation . . . '

He started to get to his feet.

'Sit down.'

'I just want to say . . . '

'Just say nothing. Name?'

'Gaston Buzier. At present, I'm in the business of selling and renting out houses. I'm based mainly in Le Havre, in the Silver Ring Hotel.'

'Are you a registered property agent?'

'No, but . . . '

'Do you work for an agency?'

'Not exactly . . . '

'That's enough. In a word you dabble . . . What did you do before?'

'I was a commercial traveller for a make of bicycle. I also sold sewing machines out in the sticks.'

'Convictions?'

'Don't tell him, Gaston!' the woman broke in.

'You've got a nerve! It was us who came here to . . . '

'Be quiet! Two convictions. One suspended for passing a dud cheque. For the other I got two months for not handing over to the owner an instalment I'd received on a house. Small-time stuff, as you see.'

Even so, he gave the impression that he was used to having to deal with policemen. He stayed relaxed, with something in his eye that suggested he could turn nasty.

'You next,' said Maigret, turning to the woman.

'Adèle Noirhomme. Born in Belleville.'

'On the Vice Squad register?'

'I was put on it five years ago in Strasbourg because some rich cow had it in for me on account of me having snatched her husband off her . . . But ever since . . . '

' . . . you've never been bothered by the police! . . . Fine! . . . Now tell me in what capacity you signed on for a cruise on the *Océan.*'

'First we'd better explain,' the man replied, 'because if we're here, it means we've got nothing to be ashamed of. At Yport, Adèle told me you had a picture of her. She was sure you were going to arrest her. Our first thought was to hop it so we wouldn't get into trouble. Because we both know the score. When we got to Étretat, I saw policemen stopping cars up ahead and I knew they'd go on looking for us. So I decided to come in voluntarily.'

'Now you, lady! I asked what you were doing on board the trawler.'

'Dead simple! I was following my boyfriend.'

'Captain Fallut?'

'Yes, the captain. I'd been with him, so to say, since last November. We met in Le Havre, in a bar. He fell for me. He used to come back to see me two or three times a week. Though from the start I thought he was a bit odd, because he never asked me to do anything. It's true! He was ever so prissy, everything had to be just so! He set me up in a room in a nice little hotel, and I started thinking that if I played my cards right he'd end up marrying me. Sailors don't get rich, but it's steady money, and there's a pension.'

'Did you ever come to Fécamp with him?'

'No. He wouldn't have that. It was him who came to me. He was jealous. He was a decent enough sort who can't have been around much because he was fifty and was as shy with women as a schoolboy. That plus the fact that he'd got me under his skin . . . '

'Just a moment. Were you already the mistress of Gaston Buzier?'

'Sure! But I'd introduced Gaston to Fallut. Said he was my brother.'

'I see. So in short you were both being subsidized by the captain.'

'I was working!' protested Buzier.

'I can see you now, hard at it every Saturday afternoon. And which of you came up with the scheme for sending you to sea on the boat?'

'Fallut. He couldn't bear the thought of leaving me by myself while he was away playing sailors. But he was also scared witless, because the rules about that sort of thing are strict, and he was a stickler for rules. He held out until the very last minute. Then he came and fetched me. The night before he was to set sail, he took me to his cabin. I quite fancied the idea because it made a change. But if I'd known what it was going to be like, I'd have been off like a shot!'

'Buzier didn't try to stop you?'

'He couldn't make up his mind. Do you understand? We couldn't go against what the old fool wanted. He'd promised me he'd retire as soon as he got back after that trip and marry me. But the whole set-up was nothing to write home about! It was no fun being cooped up all day in a cabin that stank of fish! And on top of that, every time anybody came in, I had to hide under the bed! We'd been at sea no time when Fallut started regretting he'd taken me along. I never saw a man have the jitters like him! A dozen times a day he'd check to see if he'd locked the door. If I spoke, he shut me up in case anyone overheard. He was grumpy, on pins . . . Sometimes he'd stare at me for minutes on end as if he was tempted to get rid of me by throwing me overboard.'

Her voice was shrill, and she was waving her arms about.

'Not to mention the fact that he got more and more jealous! He asked me about my past . . . he tried to find out . . . then he'd go three days without talking to me, spying on me like I was his enemy. Then all of a sudden, he'd be madly in love with me again. There were times when I was really scared of him!'

'Which members of the crew saw you when

228

you were on board?'

'It was the fourth night. I felt like a breath of air out on deck. I'd had enough of being locked up. Fallut went outside and checked to make sure there was no one about. It was as much as he could do to let me walk five steps up and down. He must have gone up on the bridge for a moment, and it was then that the wireless operator showed up and spoke to me . . . He was shy but got worked up. Next day he managed to get into my cabin.'

'Did Fallut see him?'

'I don't think so . . . He didn't mention anything.'

'Did you sleep with Le Clinche?'

She did not answer. Gaston Buzier sneered.

'Admit it!' he barked in a voice full of spite.

'I'm free to do as I please! Especially seeing as how you didn't exactly abstain from female company while I was away! Don't deny it! Are you forgetting the girl from the Villa des Fleurs? And what about that photo I found in your pocket?'

Maigret sat as solemn and impassive as the oracle.

'I asked if you slept with the wireless operator.'

'And I'm telling you to go to blazes!'

She smiled provocatively. Her lips were moist. She knew men desired her. She was counting on the promise of her pouting mouth, her sensuous body.

'The chief mechanic saw you too.'

'What's he been telling you?'

'Nothing. I'll recap. The captain kept you

hidden in his cabin. Pierre Le Clinche and the chief mechanic would come to you there, on the quiet. Was Fallut aware of this?'

'No.'

'Although he had his suspicions and prowled round you and never left you alone except when he absolutely had to.'

'How do you know?'

'Did he still talk about marrying you?'

'I don't know.'

In his mind's eye, Maigret saw the trawler, the firemen down in the bunkers, the crew crammed into the foredeck, the wireless room, the captain's cabin aft, with the raised bed.

And the voyage had lasted three months!

All that time three men had prowled round the cabin where this woman was shut away.

'I've done some pretty stupid things, but that . . . ' she exclaimed. 'Hand on heart, if I had to do it again . . . A girl should always be on her guard against shy men who talk about marriage!'

'If you'd listened to me,' said Gaston Buzier.

'You shut your trap! If I'd listened to you, I know what kind of accommodation I'd be in now! I don't want to speak ill of Fallut, because he's dead. But all the same he was cracked. He had peculiar ideas. He'd have thought he'd done something wrong just because he'd broken some rules. And it went from bad to worse. After a week, he never opened his mouth except to go on at me or ask if anybody had been in the cabin. Le Clinche was the one he was most jealous of. He'd say:

' ''You'd like that, wouldn't you! A younger

man! Say it! Admit that if he came in when I wasn't here you wouldn't turn him away!'

'And he'd laugh so nastily that it hurt.'

'How many times did Le Clinche come to see you?' Maigret asked slowly.

'Oh, all right, the hell with it. Once. On the fourth day. I couldn't even tell you how it happened. After that, it wasn't on the cards, because Fallut kept such a close eye on me.'

'And the mechanic?'

'Never! But he tried! He'd come and look at me through the porthole. When he did that, he looked as white as a sheet . . . What sort of life do you think that was? I was like an animal in a cage. When the sea was rough I was sick, and Fallut didn't even try to look after me. He went for weeks without touching me. Then the urge would come back. He'd kiss me as if he wanted to bite me and held me so tight I thought he was trying to suffocate me.'

Gaston Buzier had lit a cigarette and was now smoking it with a sarcastic expression on his face.

'Please note, inspector, all this had nothing to do with me. While it was going on, I was working.'

'Oh give it a rest, will you?' she said, losing patience.

'What happened when you got back? Did Fallut tell you that he was intending to kill himself?'

'What, him? He didn't say anything. When we got back to port, he hadn't said a single word to me for two weeks. To tell the truth, I don't think

231

he spoke to anyone. He'd stay put for hours with his eyes just staring in front of him. Meantime I'd made up my mind to leave him. I was fed up with it all, wasn't I? I'd have sooner starved to death: I'd never give up my freedom . . . I heard somebody walking along the quayside. Then he came in the cabin and said just a few words:

' "Wait here until I come to fetch you." '

'Spoken like a captain. Didn't he ever speak more . . . fondly?'

'At the finish, no!'

'Go on.'

'I don't know anything else. Or rather, the rest I learned from Gaston. He was there, down at the harbour.'

'Talk!' Maigret ordered the man.

'Like she said, I was down by the harbour. I saw the crew go into the bar. I waited for Adèle. It was dark. Then after a while, the captain came on shore by himself. There were trucks parked nearby. He started walking, and as he did a man jumped him. I don't know exactly what happened but there was a noise like a body falling into the water.'

'Would you recognize the man?'

'No. It was dark, and the trucks stopped me seeing much.'

'Which way did he go when he left?'

'I think he walked along the quay.'

'And you didn't see the wireless operator?'

'I don't know . . . I've no idea what he looks like.'

'And you,' said Maigret, turning to the woman, 'how did you get off the boat?'

'Somebody unlocked the door of the cabin where I was shut in. It was Le Clinche. He said: ' 'Go quickly!' '

'Was that all?'

'I tried to ask him what was happening. I heard people running along the quayside and a boat with a lantern being rowed across the harbour.

' 'Get going!' he repeated.

'He pushed me on to the gangway. Everybody was looking the other way. No one paid any attention to me. I had the feeling that something horrible was going on but I preferred to make myself scarce. Gaston was waiting for me a little further along.'

'And what did the two of you do after that?'

'Gaston was as white as a sheet. We went into bars and drank rum. We spent the night at the Railway Inn. The next day all the papers were full of the death of Fallut. So first we took ourselves off to Le Havre, just in case. We didn't want to get mixed up in that business.'

'But that didn't stop her wanting to come back and nose around here,' snapped Gaston. 'I don't know whether it was on account of the wireless operator or . . . '

'Just shut up! That's enough! Of course I was curious about what had happened. So we came back here to Fécamp three times. So that we wouldn't attract attention, we stayed at Yport.'

'And you never saw the chief mechanic again?'

'How do you know about that? One day, in Yport . . . I was scared by the way he looked at me . . . He followed me quite a long way.'

'Why were you arguing earlier this afternoon with Gaston?'

She gave a shrug.

'Because! Look, haven't you got it yet? He thinks I'm in love with Le Clinche, that the wireless operator killed because of me and I don't know what else. He keeps going on and on until I'm sick to death of it. I had my fill of scenes on that damned boat . . . '

'But when I showed you that photo of you, on the hotel terrace . . . '

'Oh very clever! Of course I knew straight off that you were police. I told myself Le Clinche must have talked. I got scared and told Gaston to get us out of there. Only on the way, we thought there was no point because in the end they'd collar us round the next corner. Not to mention the fact that we'd only got two hundred francs between us. What are you going to do with me? . . . You can't send me to jail!'

'Do you think the wireless operator is the killer?'

'How should I know?'

'Do you own a pair of tan-coloured shoes?' Maigret suddenly asked Gaston Buzier.

'I . . . Yes. Why?'

'Oh, nothing. Just asking. Are you absolutely sure you wouldn't be able to recognize the man who killed the captain?'

'All I saw was a man's outline in the dark.'

'Well now, Pierre Le Clinche, who was also there, hidden by the trucks, reckons the murderer was wearing tan shoes.'

Gaston was on his feet like a shot. His eyes

were hard, and his lips curled in a snarl.

'He said that? You're sure he said that?'

His anger almost choked him, reduced him to a stammer. He was no longer the same man. He banged the desk with his fist.

'I'm not having this! Take me to him! . . . Where is he? By God! We'll soon see who's lying! Tan-coloured shoes! And that makes me the killer, right? . . . He's the one who took my girl! He's the one who let her off the boat! And he has the nerve to say . . . '

'Calm down.'

He could scarcely breathe. He gasped:

'Did you hear that, Adèle? . . . That's just like all your lover-boys!'

Tears of rage filled both eyes. His teeth chattered.

'This is too much! . . . It wasn't me who . . . ha ha ha . . . this takes the biscuit! It's better than the films! . . . And the minute it comes out that I've got two convictions, he's the one who is believed! So I killed Captain Fallut! . . . Because I was jealous of him, is that it? . . . What else? . . . Oh yes, didn't I kill the wireless operator too?'

He ran one hand feverishly though his hair, which left it in a mess. It also made him look thinner. His eyes had darker rings under them, his complexion was duller.

'If you're going to arrest me, what are you waiting for?'

'Shut up!' snapped Adèle.

But she too had started to panic, though this did not stop her giving Gaston sceptical looks.

Did she have her suspicions? Or was this some sort of play-acting game?

'If you're going to arrest me, do it now . . . But I demand to confront the man . . . Then we'll see!'

Maigret had pressed an electric bell. The station duty officer showed his face warily round the door.

'I want you to keep the gentleman and the lady here until tomorrow, until we get a ruling from the examining magistrate.'

'You rat!' Adèle yelled at him and she spat on the floor. 'You want to lock me up for telling the truth! . . . Right then, listen to me: every word of what I just told you was made up! . . . I'm not going to sign any statement! . . . That'll put the tin lid on your little scheme! . . . So this is the way . . . '

And turning to Gaston:

'Never mind! . . . They can't touch us! You'll see, when it comes to it it's us who'll have the last laugh . . . Only thing is, a woman who's been on the Vice Squad's books, well, all she's good for is for banging up in the cells . . . Oh by the way, just asking, was it me who killed the captain? . . . '

Maigret left the room without listening to the rest. Outside, he filled his lungs with sea air and knocked the ash out of his pipe. He hadn't gone ten metres when he heard Adèle from inside the police station regaling officers with the choicest items of her vocabulary.

It was now two in the morning. The night was unnaturally calm. It was high tide, and the masts

236

of the fishing boats swayed to and fro above the roofs of the houses.

And over everything the regular murmur, wave after wave, of sea on shingle.

Harsh lights surrounded the *Océan*. It was still being unloaded round the clock, and the dock-hands strained to push the trucks as they filled with cod.

The Grand Banks Café was closed. At the Hôtel de la Plage, the porter, wearing a pair of trousers over his nightshirt, opened the door for the inspector.

The lobby was lit by a single lamp. It was why it took a moment before Maigret made out the figure of a woman in a rattan chair.

It was Marie Léonnec. She was asleep with her head resting on one shoulder.

'I think she's waiting for you,' whispered the porter.

She was pale. And possibly anaemic. There was no colour in her lips, and the dark shadows under her eyes showed just how exhausted she was. She slept with her mouth open, as if she was not getting enough air.

Maigret touched her gently on the shoulder. She gave a start, sat up, looked at him in a daze.

'I must have dropped off . . . Aah!'

'Why aren't you in bed? Didn't my wife see you to your room?'

'Yes. But I came down again. I was very quiet. I wanted to know . . . Tell me . . . '

She was not as pretty as usual because sleep had made her skin clammy. A mosquito bite had left a red spot in the middle of her forehead.

Her dress, which she had probably made herself from hard-wearing serge, was creased.

'Have you found out anything new? No? Listen, I've been thinking a lot. I don't know how to say this . . . Before I see Pierre tomorrow, I want you to talk to him. I want you to say that I know all about that woman, that I don't hate him for it. I'm certain, you see, that he didn't do it. But if I speak to him first, he'll feel awkward. You saw him this morning. He's all on edge, If there was a woman on board, isn't it only natural if he . . . '

But it was too much for her. She burst into tears. She could not stop crying.

'And most of all, nothing must get into the papers. My parents mustn't know. They wouldn't understand. They . . . '

She hiccupped.

'You've got to find the murderer! I think if I could question people . . . I'm sorry, I don't know what I'm saying. You know better than me. Only you don't know Pierre. I'm two years older than him. He's like a little boy really, especially if you accuse him of anything, he is likely to clam up — it's pride — and not say anything. He is very sensitive. He has been humiliated too often.'

Maigret put his hand on her shoulder, slowly, holding back a deep sigh.

Adèle's voice was still going round and round in his head. He saw her again, seductive, desirable in the full bloom of her animal presence, magnificent in her sensuality.

And here was this well-brought-up anaemic

girl, who was trying to hold back her tears and smile brightly.

'When you really know him . . . '

But what she would never really know was the dark cabin around which three men had circled for days, for weeks on end, far away, in the middle of the ocean, while other crewmen in the engine room and in the foredeck dimly sensed that a tragedy was unfolding, kept watch on the sea, discussed changes of course, felt increasingly uneasy and talked of the evil eye and madness.

'I'll talk to Le Clinche tomorrow.'

'Can I too?'

'Perhaps. Probably. But now you must get some rest.'

A little later, Madame Maigret, still half-asleep, murmured:

'She's very sweet! Did you know she's already got her trousseau together? All hand-embroidered . . . Find out anything new? You smell of perfume . . . '

No doubt lingering traces of Adèle's overpowering scent which had clung to him. A scent as common as cheap wine in cheap bistros which had, on board the trawler and for months on end, mingled with the rank smell of cod while men prowled round a cabin, as determined and pugnacious as dogs.

'Sleep well!' he said, pulling the blanket up to his chin.

The kiss he placed on the forehead of his drowsy wife was solemn and sincere.

6

The Three Innocents

The staging was basic: the setting was the same as for most confrontations of witnesses and accused. This one was taking place in a small office in the jail. Chief Inspector Girard, of the Le Havre police, who was in charge of the investigation, sat in the only chair. Maigret stood with his elbows leaning on the mantelpiece of the black granite fireplace. On the wall were graphs, official notices and a lithograph of the President of the French Republic.

Standing in the full glare of the lamp was Gaston Buzier. He was wearing his tan-coloured shoes.

'Let's have the wireless operator in.'

The door opened. Pierre Le Clinche, who had been given no warning, walked in, brow furrowed, like a man in pain who is expecting to get more of the same treatment. He saw Buzier. But he paid him not the slightest attention and looked all round him, wondering which man he should face.

On the other hand, Adèle's lover looked him up and down, a supercilious smile hanging on his lips.

Le Clinche had a crumpled air. His flesh was grey. He did not try to bluster or conceal his dejection. He was as lost as a sick animal.

'Do you recognize this man here?'

He stared at Buzier, as if searching through his memory.

'No. Who is he?'

'Take a good look at him, from head to foot . . . '

Le Clinche obeyed, and the minute his eyes reached the shoes, he straightened up.

'Well?'

'Yes.'

'Yes what?'

'I understand what you're getting at. The tan shoes . . . '

'So that's it!' Gaston Buzier suddenly burst out. He had not said a word until then but his face was now dark with anger. 'Why don't you tell them again that I'm the one who did your captain in? Go on!'

All eyes were on the wireless operator, who looked at the floor and gestured vaguely with one hand.

'Say it!'

'Perhaps those weren't the shoes.'

'Oh yes!' Gaston crowed, already claiming victory. 'So you're backing down . . . '

'You don't recognize the man who murdered Fallut?'

'I don't know . . . No.'

'You are probably aware that this man is the lover of a certain Adèle, who you most certainly do know. He has already admitted that he was near the trawler at the moment the crime was committed. Also that he was wearing tan-coloured shoes.'

All this time, Buzier was facing him down, bristling with impatience and fury.

'That's right! Make him talk! But he'd better be telling the truth or else I swear I'll . . . '

'Hold your tongue! Well, Le Clinche?'

The young man passed his hand over his brow and winced, literally, with pain.

'I don't know! He can go hang for all I care!'

'But you did see a man wearing tan shoes attack Fallut.'

'I forget.'

'That's what you said when you were first interviewed. That wasn't very long ago. Are you sticking to what you said then?'

'No, that is . . . Look, I saw a man wearing tan shoes. That's all I saw, I don't know if he was the murderer.'

The longer the interview went on, the more confident Gaston Buzier, who also looked rather seedy after a night in the cells, became. He was now shifting his weight from one leg to the other, with one hand in his trouser pocket.

'See? He's backing down! He doesn't dare repeat the lies he told you.'

'Answer me this, Le Clinche. Thus far, we know for certain that there were two men near the trawler at the time when the captain was murdered: you were one, and Buzier the other. You say you didn't kill anybody. Now, after pointing the finger at this man, you seem to be withdrawing the accusation. So was there a third person there? If so, then it is impossible you could not have seen him. So who was it?'

Silence. Pierre Le Clinche continued to stare at the ground.

Maigret, still leaning with elbows propped up on the fireplace, had taken no part in the interrogation, happy to leave it to his colleague and content just to observe the two men.

'I repeat the question: was there a third person on the quay?'

'I don't know,' said the prisoner in a crushed voice.

'Is that a yes?'

A shrug of the shoulder which meant: 'As you wish.'

'Who was it?'

'It was dark.'

'In that case tell me why you said the murderer was wearing tan shoes . . . Wasn't it a way of drawing attention away from the real murderer who was someone you knew?'

The young man clutched his head in both hands.

'I can't take any more!' he groaned.

'Answer me!'

'No! You can do what you like . . . '

'Bring in the next witness.'

The moment the door was open, Adèle walked through it with an exaggerated swagger. She swept the room with one glance to get a sense of what had been going on. Her eye lingered in particular on the wireless operator, whom she seemed shocked to see looking so defeated.

'I assume, Le Clinche, that you recognize this woman, whom Captain Fallut hid in his cabin throughout the entire voyage and with whom you were intimate.'

He looked at her coldly. Yet already Adèle's lips were parting and preparing to frame a captivating smile.

'That's her.'

'To cut a long story short, there were three of you on board, who, in plain language, were sniffing around her: the captain, the chief mechanic and you. You went to bed with her at least once. The chief mechanic got nowhere. Was the captain aware that you had deceived him?'

'He never spoke to me about it.'

'He was very jealous, wasn't he? And it was because he was so jealous that he didn't speak to you for three months?'

'No.'

'No? Was there some other reason?'

Now he was red-faced, not knowing which way to look, talking too fast:

'Well it could have been that. I don't know . . .'

'What else was there between you that might have created hatred or suspicion?'

'I . . . There wasn't anything . . . You're right, he was jealous.'

'What feelings did you have that led you to become Adèle's lover?'

A silence.

'Were you in love with her?'

'No,' he sighed in a small dry voice.

But the woman screeched:

'Thanks a million! Always the gentleman, eh? But that didn't stop you hanging round me until the very last day! Isn't that the truth? And it's also true that you probably had another girl waiting for you on shore!'

Gaston Buzier pretended to be whistling under his breath, with his fingers hooked in the arm-holes of his waistcoat.

'Tell me again, Le Clinche, if, when you went on board after witnessing the death of the captain, Adèle was still locked inside her cabin.'

'Locked in, yes!'

'So she couldn't have killed anyone.'

'No! It wasn't her, I swear!'

Le Clinche was getting ruffled. But Chief Inspector Girard went on remorselessly:

'Buzier states that he didn't kill anybody. But, after accusing him, you withdraw the accusation . . . Another way of looking at it is that the pair of you were in it together.'

'Oh very nice, I must say!' cried Buzier in a burst of brutal contempt. 'When I take up crime, it won't be with a . . . a . . . '

'All right! Both of you could have killed because you were jealous. Both of you had been sleeping with Adèle.'

Buzier said with a sneer:

'Me jealous! Jealous of what?'

'Have any of you anything further to add? You first, Le Clinche.'

'No.'

'Buzier?'

'I wish to state that I am innocent and demand to be released immediately.'

'And you?'

Adèle was putting on fresh lipstick.

245

'Me . . .' — a thick stroke of lipstick — ' . . . I . . .'
— a look in her mirror — ' . . . I've nothing to
say, not a thing . . . All men are skunks! You
heard that boy there, the one I'm supposed to
have been prepared to do silly things for . . . It's
no good looking at me like that, Gaston. Now if
you want my opinion, there's things we know
nothing about in this business with the boat. The
minute you found out a woman had been on
board, you thought it explained everything . . . But
what if there was something else?'

'Such as?'

'How should I know? I'm not a detective . . .'

She crammed her hair under her red straw
toque. Maigret saw Pierre Le Clinche look away.

'The two chief inspectors exchanged glances.
Girard said:

'Le Clinche will be returned to his cell. You
two will stay in the waiting room . . . I'll let you
know whether you are free to go or not in a
quarter of an hour.'

The two detectives were left alone. Both
looked worried.

'Are you going to ask the magistrate to let
them go?' asked Maigret.

'Yes. I think it's the best thing. They may be
mixed up in the killing, but there are other things
we may be missing . . .'

'Right.'

'Hello, operator? Get me the law courts at Le
Havre . . . Hello? . . . Yes, public prosecutor's
office please . . .'

A few moments later, while Chief Inspector
Girard was talking to the magistrate, there was

the sound of a disturbance outside. Maigret ran to see what was happening and saw Le Clinche on the ground, struggling with three uniformed officers.

He was terrifyingly out of control. His eyes were bloodshot and looked wild and staring. Spittle drooled from his mouth. But he was being held down now and couldn't move.

'What happened?'

'We hadn't 'cuffed him, seeing as how he was always so quiet . . . Anyway, as we were moving him down the corridor, he made a grab for the gun in my belt . . . He got it . . . was going to use it to kill himself . . . I stopped him firing it.'

Le Clinche lay on the floor, staring at the ceiling. His teeth were digging into the flesh of his lips, reddening his saliva with blood.

But most disturbing were the tears which streamed down his leaden cheeks.

'Maybe get the doctor . . . ?'

'No! Let him go!' barked Maigret.

When the prisoner was alone on his back on the stone floor:

'On your feet! . . . Look sharp now! . . . Get a move on! . . . And no antics . . . otherwise you'll feel the back of my hand across your face, you miserable little brat!'

The wireless operator did what he was told, unresistingly, fearfully. His whole body trembled with the aftershock. In falling he had dirtied his clothes.

'How does your girlfriend fit into that little display?'

Chief Inspector Girard appeared:

247

'He agreed,' he said. 'All three are free to go, but they mustn't leave Fécamp ... What happened here?'

'This moron tried to kill himself! If it's all right with you, I'll look after him.'

★   ★   ★

The two of them were walking along the quays together. Le Clinche had splashed water over his face. It had not washed the crimson blotches away. His eyes were bright, feverish and his lips too red.

He was wearing an off-the-peg suit with three buttons which he'd done up anyhow, not caring about what he looked like. His tie was badly knotted.

Maigret, hands in pockets, walked grimly and kept muttering as if for his own benefit:

'You've got to understand that I haven't got time to tell you what you should and should not do, except for this: your fiancée is here. She's a good kid, got a lot of grit. She dropped everything and came here all the way from Quimper. She's moving heaven and earth ... Maybe it wouldn't be such a good idea to dash her hopes ... '

'Does she know?'

'There's no point in talking to her about that woman.'

Maigret never stopped watching him. They reached the quays. The brightly coloured fishing boats were picked out by the sunshine. The streets nearby were busy.

There were a few moments when Le Clinche seemed to be rediscovering his zest for life, and he looked hopefully at his surroundings with optimism. At others, his eyes hardened, and he glared angrily at people and things.

They had to pass close by the *Océan*, now in the final day of unloading. There were still three trucks parked opposite the trawler.

The inspector spoke casually as he gestured to various points in space.

'You were there . . . Gaston Buzier was here . . . And it was on that spot that the third man strangled the captain.'

Le Clinche breathed deeply, then looked away.

'Only it was dark, and none of you knew who the others were. Anyway, the third man wasn't the chief mechanic or the first mate. They were both with the crew in the Grand Banks Café.'

The Breton, who was outside on deck, spotted the wireless operator, went over to the hatch and leaned his head in. Three sailors came out and looked at Le Clinche.

'Come on,' said Maigret. 'Marie Léonnec is waiting for us.'

'I can't . . . '

'What can't you?'

'Go there! . . . Please, leave me alone! . . . What's it to you if I do kill myself? . . . Anyway, it would be best for all concerned!'

'Is the secret so heavy to bear, Le Clinche?'

No answer.

'And you really can't say anything, is that it? Of course you can. One thing: do you still want Adèle?'

'I hate her!'

'That's not what I asked. I said want, the way you wanted her all the time you were at sea. Just between us men: had you had lots of girls before you met Marie Léonnec?'

'No. Leastways nothing serious.'

'And never deep urges? Wanting a woman so much you could weep?'

'Never!' he sighed and looked away.

'So it started when you were on board ship. There was only one woman, the setting was uncouth, monotonous . . . Fragrant flesh in a trawler that stank of fish . . . You were about to say something?'

'It's nothing.'

'You forgot all about the girl you were engaged to?'

'That's not the same thing . . . '

Maigret looked him in the eye and was astounded by the change that had just come over it. Suddenly the young man had acquired a determined tilt to his head, his gaze was steady, and his mouth bitter. And yet, for all that, there were traces of nostalgia and fond hopes in his expression.

'Marie Léonnec is a pretty girl,' Maigret went on in pursuit of his line of thought.

'Yes.'

'And much more refined than Adèle. Moreover, she loves you. She is ready to make any sacrifice for . . . '

'Why don't you leave it alone!' said the wireless operator angrily. 'You know very well . . . that . . . '

' . . . that it's something else! That Marie Léonnec is a good, well-brought-up girl, that she will make a model wife and a caring mother but . . . but there'll always be something missing? Isn't that so? Something more elemental, something you discovered on board shut away inside the captain's cabin, when fear caught you by the throat, in the arms of Adèle. Something vulgar, brutal . . . The spirit of adventure! . . . And the desire to bite, to burn your bridges, to kill or die . . . '

Le Clinche stared at him in amazement.

'How did you . . . '

'How do I know? Because everyone has had a sight of the same adventure come his way at least once in his life! . . . We cry hot tears, we shout, we rage! Then, a couple of weeks later, you look at Marie Léonnec and you wonder how on earth you could have fallen for someone like Adèle.'

As he walked, the young man had been keeping his eyes firmly on the glinting water of the harbour. In it were reflected the reds, whites and greens that decorated the taffrails of boats.

'The voyage is over. Adèle has gone. Marie Léonnec is here.'

There was a moment of calm. Maigret went on:

'The ending was dramatic. A man is dead because there was passion on that boat and . . . '

But Le Clinche was again in the grip of wild ideas.

'Stop it! Stop it!' he repeated in a brittle voice. 'No! Surely you can see it's not possible . . . '

He was haggard-eyed. He turned to see the

trawler, which, almost empty now, sat high in the water, looming over them.

Then his fears took hold of him once more.

'I swear . . . You've got to let me alone . . . '

'And onboard, throughout the entire voyage, the captain was also stretched to breaking point, wasn't he?'

'What do you mean?'

'And the chief mechanic too?'

'No.'

'It wasn't just the two of you. It was fear, Le Clinche, wasn't it?'

'I don't know . . . Please leave me alone!'

'Adèle was in the cabin. Three men were on the prowl. Yet the captain would not give in to his urges and refused to speak to his woman for days on end. And you, you looked in through the portholes but after just one encounter you never touched her again . . . '

'Stop it!'

'The men down in the bunkers, the crew in the foredeck, they were all talking about the evil eye. The voyage went from bad to worse, lurching from navigational errors to accidents. A ship's boy lost overboard, two men injured, the cod going bad and the mess they made of entering the harbour . . . '

They turned at the end of the quay, and the beach stretched out before them, with its neat breakwater, the hotels, beach-huts and multicoloured chairs dotted over the shingle.

Madame Maigret in a deckchair was picked out by a patch of sunshine. Marie Léonnec, wearing a white hat, was sitting next to her.

Le Clinche followed the direction of Maigret's eyes and stopped suddenly. His temples looked damp.

The inspector went on:

'But it took more than a woman . . . Come on! Your fiancée has seen you.'

And so she had. She stood up, remained motionless for a moment, as if her feelings were too much for her. And then she was running along the breakwater while Madame Maigret put down her needlework and waited.

7

Like a Family

It was one of those situations which crop up spontaneously from which it is difficult to get free. Marie Léonnec, alone in Fécamp, had been placed under the wing of the Maigrets by a friend and had been taking her meals with them.

But now her fiancé was there. All four of them were together on the beach when the hotel bell announced that it was time for lunch.

Pierre Le Clinche hesitated for a moment and looked at the others in embarrassment.

'Come on!' said Maigret, 'we'll get them to lay another place.'

He took his wife's arm as they crossed the breakwater. The young couple followed, not speaking. Or rather, only Marie spoke and did so in a firm voice.

'Any idea what she's telling him?' the inspector asked his wife.

'Yes. She told me a dozen times this morning, to see if I thought it was all right. She's telling him she's not cross with him about anything, *whatever it was that happened*. You see? She's not going to say anything about a woman. She's pretending she doesn't know, but she did say she'd be stressing the words *whatever it was that happened*. Poor girl! She'd go to the ends of the earth for him!'

'Alas!' sighed Maigret.

'What do you mean?'

'Nothing . . . Is this our table?'

Lunch passed off quietly, too quietly. The tables were set very closely together so that speaking in a normal voice was not really possible.

Maigret avoided watching Le Clinche, to put him at his ease, but the wireless operator's attitude gave him cause for concern, and it also worried Marie Léonnec, whose face had a pinched look to it.

Her young man looked grim and depressed. He ate. He drank. He spoke when spoken to. But his thoughts were elsewhere. And more than once, hearing footsteps behind him, he jumped as if he sensed danger.

The bay windows of the dining room were wide open, and through them could be seen the sun-flecked sea. It was hot. Le Clinche had his back to the view and from time to time, with a jerk of the head, would turn round quickly and scour the horizon.

It was left to Madame Maigret to keep the conversation going, mainly by talking to the young woman about nothing in particular, to keep the silence at bay.

Here they were far removed from unpleasant events. The setting was a family hotel. A reassuring clatter of plates and glasses. A half-bottle of Bordeaux on the table next to a bottle of mineral water.

But then the manager made a mistake. He came up as they were finishing dessert and asked:

'Would you like a room to be made up for this gentleman?'

He was looking at Le Clinche: he had spotted a fiancé. And no doubt he took the Maigrets for the girl's parents.

Two or three times the wireless operator made the same gesture as he had that morning during the confrontation. A rapid movement of his hand across his forehead, a very boneless, weary gesture.

'What shall we do now?'

The other guests were getting up and leaving. The group of four were standing on the terrace.

'Shall we sit down for a while?' suggested Madame Maigret.

Their folding chairs were waiting for them, on the shingle. The Maigrets sat down. The two young people remained standing for a moment, uncertain of what they should do.

'I think we'll go for a little walk, shall we?' Marie Léonnec finally brought herself to say with a vague smile meant for Madame Maigret.

The inspector lit his pipe and, once he was alone with his wife, he muttered:

'Tell me: do I really look like the father-in-law!'

'They don't know what to do. Their position is very delicate,' remarked his wife as she watched them go. 'Look at them. They're so awkward. I may be wrong but I think Marie has more backbone than her fiancé.'

He certainly made a sorry sight as he strolled listlessly along, a slight figure who paid no attention to the girl at his side and, you would have sworn even from a distance, did not say anything.

But the girl gave the impression that she was doing her level best, that she was talking as a way of distracting him, that she was even trying to appear as if she was having a good time.

There were other groups of people on the beach. But Le Clinche was the only man not wearing white trousers. He was wearing a dark suit, which made him look even more pitiful.

'How old is he?' asked Madame Maigret.

Her husband, lying back in his deckchair with eyes half-closed, said:

'Nineteen. Just a boy. I'm very afraid that he'll be easy meat for anybody now.'

'Why? Isn't he innocent?'

'He probably never killed anybody. No. I'd stake my life on it. But all the same, I'm afraid he's had it . . . Just look at him! And look at her!'

'Nonsense. Leave the pair of them alone for a moment and they'll be kissing.'

'Perhaps.'

Maigret was pessimistic.

'She isn't much older than him. She really loves him. She is quite ready to become a model little wife.'

'Why do you think . . . '

'That it won't ever happen? Just an impression. Have you ever looked at photos of people who died young? I've always been struck by the fact that those pictures, which were taken when the subjects were fit and healthy, always have something of the graveyard about them. It's as if those who are doomed to be the victims of some

257

awful experience already have a death sentence written on their faces.'

'And do you think that boy . . . '

'He's a sad case. Always was! He was born poor. He suffered from being poor. He worked like a slave, put his head down, like a man swimming upstream. Then he managed to persuade a nice girl from a higher social class than his to say yes . . . But I don't believe it'll happen. Just look at them. They're groping in the dark. They're trying to believe in happy endings. They want to believe in their star . . . '

Maigret spoke quietly, in a half-whisper, as he stared at the two outlines, which stood out against the sparkling sea.

'Who is officially in charge of the investigation?'

'Girard, a chief inspector at Le Havre. You don't know him. An intelligent man.'

'Does he think he's guilty?'

'No. In any case, he's got nothing solid on him, not even any real circumstantial evidence.'

'What do you think?'

Maigret turned round, as if to get a glimpse of the trawler, though it was hidden from him by a row of houses.

'I think that the voyage was, for two men at least, tragic. Tragic enough that Captain Fallut *couldn't go on living any longer* and the wireless operator *couldn't go back to living his old, normal life.*'

'All because of a woman?'

He did not answer the question directly but went on:

'And the rest of them, the men who had no part in events, all of them including the stokers, were, if they did but know it, deeply marked by it too. They came back angry and scared. For three months, two men and a woman raised the tension around the deck-house in the stern. A few black walls with portholes . . . But it was enough.'

'I've hardly ever seen you get so worked up about a case . . . You said three people were involved. What on earth did they do out there in the middle of the ocean?'

'Yes, what did they do exactly? Something which was serious enough to kill Captain Fallut! And also bad enough to leave those two young people not knowing which way to turn. Look at them out there, trying to find what's left of their dreams in the shingle.'

The young people were coming back, arms swinging, uncertain whether courtesy required them to rejoin the Maigrets or whether it would be more tactful to leave them to themselves.

During their walk, Marie Léonnec had lost much of her vivaciousness. She gave Madame Maigret a dejected look. It was as if all her efforts, all her high spirits had run up against a wall of despair or inertia.

★ ★ ★

It was Madame Maigret's custom to take some light refreshment of an afternoon. So at around four o'clock, all four of them sat down on the hotel terrace under the striped umbrellas, which

259

exuded the customary festive air.

Hot chocolate steamed in two cups. Maigret had ordered a beer and Le Clinche a brandy and soda.

They talked about Jorissen, the teacher from Quimper who had written to Maigret on behalf of the wireless operator and had brought Marie Léonnec with him. They said the usual things:

'You won't find a better man anywhere . . . '

They embroidered on this theme, not out of conviction, but because they had to say something. Suddenly, Maigret blinked, then focused on a couple now walking towards them along the breakwater.

It was Adèle and Gaston Buzier. He slouched, hands in pockets, his boater tilted on the back of his head, seemingly unconcerned, while she was as animated and as eye-catching as ever.

'As long as she doesn't spot us . . . ' the inspector thought.

But at that very moment, Adèle's eye caught his. She stopped and said something to her companion, who tried to dissuade her.

Too late! She was already crossing the road. She looked around at all the tables in turn, chose the one nearest to the Maigrets, then sat down so that she was facing Marie Léonnec.

Her boyfriend followed with a shrug, touched the brim of his boater as he passed in front of the inspector and sat astride a chair.

'What are you having?'

'Not hot chocolate, that's for sure. A kümmel.'

What was that if not a declaration of war? When she mentioned chocolate, she was staring at Marie Léonnec's cup. Maigret saw the girl flinch.

She had never seen Adèle. But surely the penny had dropped? She glanced across at Le Clinche, who looked away.

Madame Maigret's foot nudged her husband's twice.

'What say the four of us walk over to the Casino.'

She too had worked it out. But no one answered. Only Adèle at the next table said anything.

'It's so hot!' she sighed. 'Take my jacket, Gaston.'

She removed her suit jacket and was revealed in pink silk, opulently sensual and bare-armed. She did not take her eyes off the girl for an instant.

'Do you like grey? Don't you think they should ban people from wearing miserable colours on the beach?'

It was so obvious. Marie Léonnec was wearing grey. But Adèle was demonstrating her intention to go on the attack, by any means and without wasting any time.

'Waiter! Shift yourself! I can't wait all day.'

Her voice was shrill. And it sounded as if she was deliberately exaggerating its coarseness.

Gaston Buzier scented danger. He knew Adèle of old. He muttered a few words to her. But she replied in a very loud voice:

'So what? They can't stop anyone sitting on this terrace. It's a free country!'

Madame Maigret was the only one with her

261

back to her. Maigret and the wireless operator sat sideways on but Marie Léonnec faced her directly.

'We're all as good as everybody else, isn't that right? Only there's some people who trail round after you when you're too busy to see them and then won't give you the time of day when they're in company.'

And she laughed. Such an unpleasant laugh! She stared at the girl, whose face flushed bright red.

'Waiter! What do I owe you?' asked Buzier, who was anxious to put a stop to this.

'We've got plenty of time! Same again, waiter. And bring me some peanuts.'

'We don't have any.'

'Well go and get some! That's what you're paid for, isn't it?'

There were people at two other tables. They all stared at the new couple, who could not go unnoticed. Maigret began to worry. He wanted of course to put an end to a scene which might turn nasty.

On the other hand, the wireless operator was trapped opposite him: he could see him sit there and sweat.

It was fascinating, like being present at a dissection. Le Clinche did not move a muscle. He was not facing the woman, but he must surely have been able to see her, however vaguely, on his left, at the very least to make out the pink cloud of her blouse.

His eyes, grey and lacklustre, were fixed and staring. One hand lay on the table and was closing slowly, as slowly as the tentacles of some undersea creature.

There was no telling yet how it would all turn out. Would he get up and run away? Would he turn on the woman who talked and talked? Would he . . . ?

No. He did none of those things. What he did was quite different and a hundred times more unnerving. It was not just his hand that was closing, but his whole being. He was shrivelling, shrinking into his shell.

His eyes steadily turned as grey as his face.

He did not move. Was he still breathing? Not a tremor. Not a twitch. But his stillness, which grew more and more complete, was mesmerizing.

' . . . puts me in mind with another of my gentleman friends, married he was, with three kids . . . '

Marie Léonnec, on the other hand, was breathing quickly. She gulped down her chocolate to hide her confusion.

' . . . now he was the most passionate man on the planet. Sometimes, I refused to let him in and he'd stop outside on the landing and sob, until the neighbours worked up a right old head of steam! 'Adèle my sweety pie, my pet, my own . . . ' All the usual lovey-dovey stuff. Anyway, one Sunday I met him out walking with his wife and kiddies. I heard his wife ask him:

' 'Who's that woman?'

'And all pompous, he says to her:

' 'Obviously a floozie. You can tell from the ridiculous way she's dressed.' '

And she laughed, playing to the crowd. She looked at the faces around her to see what effect her behaviour was having.

'Some people are that slow on the uptake you can't get a rise out of them.'

Again Gaston Buzier said something to her quietly in an attempt to shut her up.

'What's the matter? Not turning chicken are you? I pay for my drinks, don't I? I'm not doing anybody any harm! So nobody's got any right to tell me what to do . . . Waiter, where are those peanuts? And bring another kümmel!'

'Maybe we should leave,' said Madame Maigret.

It was too late. Adèle was on the rampage. It was clear that if they tried to leave, she would do anything to cause a scene, whatever the cost.

Marie Léonnec was staring at the table. Her ears were red, her eyes unnaturally bright, and her mouth hung open in distress.

Le Clinche had shut his eyes. And he went on sitting there, unseeing, with a fixed expression on his face. His hand still lay lifelessly on the table.

Maigret had never had an opportunity like this to scrutinize him. His face was both very young and very old, as is often the case with adolescents who have had difficult childhoods.

Le Clinche was tall, taller than average, but his shoulders were not yet those of a man.

His skin, which he had not looked after, was dotted with freckles. He had not shaved that morning, and there were faint blond shadows around his chin and on his cheeks.

He was not handsome. He could not have

laughed very often in his life. On the contrary, he had burned large quantities of midnight oil, reading too much, writing too much, in unheated rooms, in his ocean-tossed cabin, by the light of dim lamps.

'I'll tell you what really makes me sick. It's seeing people putting on airs who're really no better than us.'

Adèle was losing patience. She was ready to try anything to get what she wanted.

'All these proper young ladies, for instance. They pretend to be lily-white hens but they'll run after a man the way no self-respecting trollop would dare to.'

The hotel owner stood by the entrance, surveying his guests as if trying to decide whether or not he should intervene.

Maigret now had eyes only for Le Clinche, in close-up. His head had dropped a little. His eyes had not opened.

But tears squeezed out one by one from under his clamped eyelids, oozed between the eyelashes, hesitated and then snaked down his cheeks.

It wasn't the first time the inspector had seen a man cry. But it was the first time he had been so affected by the sight. Perhaps it was the silence, the stillness of his whole body.

The only signs of life it gave were those rolling, liquid pearls. The rest was dead.

Marie Léonnec had seen nothing of all this. Adèle was still talking.

Then, a split second later, Maigret *knew*. The hand which lay on the table had just

265

imperceptibly opened. The other was out of sight, in a pocket.

The lids rose no more than a millimetre. It was enough to allow an eye-glance to filter through. That glance settled on Marie.

As the inspector was getting to his feet, there was a gunshot. Everyone reacted in a confused pandemonium of screams and overturned chairs.

★ ★ ★

At first, Le Clinche did not move. Then he started to lean imperceptibly to his left. His mouth opened, and from it came a faint groan.

Marie Léonnec, who had difficulty understanding what had happened, since no one had seen a gun, flung herself on him, grabbed him by the knees and his right hand and turned in panic:

'Inspector! . . . What . . . ?'

Only Maigret had worked out what had happened. Le Clinche had had a revolver in his pocket, a weapon he had found God knows where, for he hadn't had one that morning when he was released from his cell. And he'd fired from his pocket. He'd been gripping the butt all the interminable time Adèle had been talking, while he kept his eyes shut and waited and maybe hesitated.

The bullet had caught him in the abdomen or the side. His jacket was scorched, cut to ribbons at hip level.

'Get a doctor! Ring for the police!' someone somewhere was shouting.

A doctor appeared. He was wearing swimming trunks. He'd been on the beach hardly a hundred metres from the hotel.

Hands had reached out and held Le Clinche up just as he began to fall. He was carried into the hotel dining room. Marie, utterly distraught, followed the stretcher inside.

Maigret had not had time to worry about Adèle or her boyfriend. As he entered the bar, he suddenly saw her. She looked deathly pale and was emptying a large glass, which rattled against her teeth.

She had helped herself. The bottle was still in her hand. She filled the glass a second time.

The inspector paid her no further attention, but retained the image of that white face above the pink blouse and particularly the sound of her teeth chattering against the glass.

He could not see Gaston Buzier anywhere. The dining-room door was about to be closed.

'Move along, please,' the hotel-owner was telling guests. 'Keep calm! The doctor has asked us to keep the noise down.'

Maigret pushed the door open. He found the doctor kneeling and Madame Maigret restraining the frantic Marie, who was trying desperately to rush to the wounded man's side.

'Police!' the inspector muttered to the doctor.

'Can't you get those women out of here? I'm going to have to undress him and . . . '

'Right.'

'I'll need a couple of men to help me. I assume someone has already phoned for an ambulance?'

He was still wearing his trunks.

'Is it serious?'

'I can't tell you anything until I've probed the wound. You do of course understand . . . '

Yes! Maigret understood all too well when he saw the appalling, lacerated mess, a coalescence of flesh and fabric.

The tables had been laid for dinner. Madame Maigret took Marie Léonnec outside. A young man in white trousers asked shyly:

'If you'll allow me, I could help . . . I'm studying pharmacy.'

A burst of fierce red sunlight slanted through a window and was so blindingly bright that Maigret closed the Venetian blind.

'Will you take his legs?'

He recalled the words he had said to his wife that afternoon as he lounged in his folding chair watching the gangling figure move across the beach with the smaller and livelier outline of Marie Léonnec at his side:

'Easy meat.'

Captain Fallut had died as soon as he had docked. Pierre Le Clinche had fought long and hard, perhaps had even still been fighting as he sat eyes closed, one hand on the table, the other in his pocket, while Adèle went on talking, endlessly talking and playing to the gallery.

8

The Drunken Sailor

It was a little before midnight when Maigret left the hospital. He had waited to see the stretcher being wheeled out of the operating theatre. On it lay the prone figure of a tall man swathed in white.

The surgeon was washing his hands. A nurse was putting the instruments away.

'We'll do our best to save him,' he said in reply to the inspector. 'His intestine is perforated in seven places. You could say it's a very, very nasty wound. But we've tidied him up.'

He gestured to receptacles full of blood, cotton-wool and disinfectant.

'Believe me, it took a lot of damned hard work!'

They were all in high good humour, surgeons, assistant-surgeons and theatre nurses. They had been brought a patient as near to death's door as he could be, bloodstained, abdomen not only gaping but scorched too, with scraps of clothing embedded in his flesh.

And now an ultra-clean body had just been carried out on a trolley. And the abdomen had been carefully stitched up.

The rest would be for later. Maybe Le Clinche would regain consciousness, maybe not. The hospital did not even try to find out who he was.

'Does he really have a chance of pulling through?'

'Why not? We used to see worse than that during the War.'

Maigret had phoned the Hôtel de la Plage at once, to set Marie Léonnec's mind at rest. Now he set out to walk back by himself. The doors of the hospital closed behind him with the smooth sound of well-oiled hinges. It was dark. The street of small middle-class houses was deserted.

He had only gone a few metres when a figure stepped away from the wall and the light of a street lamp illuminated the face of Adèle. In a mean voice she asked:

'Is he dead?'

She must have been waiting for hours. Her features were drawn, and the kiss-curls at her temples had lost their shape.

'Not yet,' replied Maigret in the same tone of voice.

'Will he die?'

'Maybe, maybe not.'

'Do you think I did it on purpose?'

'I don't think anything.'

'Because it's not true!'

The inspector continued on his way. She followed him and to do so she had to walk very quickly.

'Basically, it was his own fault, you must see that.'

Maigret pretended he wasn't even listening. But she was stubborn and persisted:

'You know very well what I mean. On board he nearly got to the point of asking me to marry him. Then once we'd docked . . . '

She would not give up. She seemed driven by an over-mastering need to talk.

'If you think I'm a bad woman, it's because you don't know me. Only, there are times . . . Look, inspector, you've got to tell me the truth. I know what a bullet can do, especially in the belly from point-blank range. They performed a laparotomy on him, right?'

She gave the impression that she was no stranger to hospitals, that she had heard how doctors talked and knew people who'd been shot more than once.

'Was the operation a success? . . . I believe it depends on what the patient has been eating before . . . '

Her distress was not acute. More a raw, stubborn refusal to take no for an answer.

'Aren't you going to say? But there, you know, don't you, why I sounded off like that this afternoon. Gaston is a cheap crook. I never loved him. But the other one . . . '

'He may live,' said Maigret carefully, looking the girl straight in the eyes. 'But if what happened on the *Océan* is not cleared up, it won't do him much good.'

He paused, expecting her to say something, to have a reaction. She dropped her eyes.

'Of course, you think that I know everything . . . From the moment both men were my lovers . . . But I swear . . . No, you don't know what sort of man Captain Fallut was, so you'll never understand . . . He was in love with me, it's true. He used to come to Le Havre to see me. And

271

falling, I mean really falling, for a woman at his age turned his brain . . . But that did not stop him being pernickety about everything, very controlled, very faddy about wanting everything just so . . . I still can't work out why he ever agreed to let me hide on board . . . But what I do know is the minute we were out on the open sea he regretted it and because he regretted it he began to hate me . . . His character changed just like that.'

'But the wireless operator hadn't spotted you yet?'

'No. That didn't happen until the fourth night, like I told you . . . '

'Are you quite sure that Fallut was already in a strange mood before then?'

'Maybe not quite as strange. But afterwards there were days when it all got weird, and I wondered if he wasn't actually mad.'

'And you had no idea about what the reason for the change might have been?'

'No. I thought about it. Sometimes I told myself there had to be some funny business going on between him and the wireless operator. I even thought they were involved in smuggling . . . Ah, you won't ever get me to go anywhere near a fishing boat again! Can you believe that it went on for three months? And then for it to end like that! One is murdered as soon as he steps ashore and the other who . . . It is true, isn't it, that he's not dead?'

They had reached the quays, and the young woman seemed reluctant to go any further.

'Where is Gaston Buzier?'

'Back at the hotel. He knows it's not the moment to rub me up the wrong way, that I'd dump him if he says one word out of place.'

'Are you going back to him now?'

She gave a shrug, a gesture which signified: 'Why not?'

And then there was a glimpse of her flirtatious self. Just as she was taking her leave of Maigret, she murmured with an awkward smile:

'Thank you so much, inspector. You've been ever so kind . . . I . . . '

But she didn't dare say the rest. It was an invitation. A promise.

'All right, all right!' he growled and walked on.

He pushed open the door of the Grand Banks Café.

⋆   ⋆   ⋆

Just as he reached for the latch, he clearly heard a hubbub coming from inside the bar, like a dozen men's voices all talking at once. The moment the door opened, complete silence fell with brutal abruptness. Yet there were more than ten men there, in two or three groups, who must have been calling to each other from one table to the next.

The landlord stepped forward to meet Maigret and shook his hand, though not without a certain unease of manner.

'Is it true what they're saying? That Le Clinche shot himself?'

His customers toyed with their drinks in a show of indifference. Present were Louis, the

273

black sailor, the chief mechanic from the trawler and a few others besides whom Maigret had finally got to know by sight.

'Quite true,' he said.

He observed that the chief mechanic, looking suddenly very shifty, kept fidgeting on the oil-cloth of the bench seat.

'Some voyage!' muttered someone in a corner in a pronounced Norman accent.

The words probably were a fair expression of the general opinion, for many heads dropped, a fist was brought down on a marble tabletop while one voice echoed the sentiment:

'Yes! A voyage of the damned!'

But Léon gave a cough to remind his customers to watch what they said and with a nod to them motioned towards a sailor in a red jerkin, who was drinking alone in a corner.

Maigret sat down near the counter and ordered a brandy and soda.

No one was talking now. Every man there was trying to look calm and unruffled. Léon, a practised master of ceremonies, called out to the group sitting around the largest table:

'Want me to bring the dominoes?'

It was a way of breaking the silence, of occupying hands. The black-backed dominoes were shuffled on the marble tabletop. The landlord sat down next to the inspector.

'I shut them up,' he said quietly, 'because the fellow in the far corner, to your left, by the window, is the father of the boy . . . You know who I mean?'

'What boy?'

274

'The ship's boy, Jean-Marie, the one who fell overboard on their third day out.'

The man had his head on one side and was listening. If he hadn't heard the words, he had certainly understood that they concerned him. He called to the serving girl to refill his glass and downed it in one, with a shudder of disgust.

He was already drunk. He had bulging light-blue eyes which were now more sea-green. A quid of tobacco raised a lump in his cheek.

'Does he go out on the Grand Banks boats too?'

'He used to. But now that he's got seven kids, he goes out after herring in winter, because the periods away are shorter: a month to start with and then for increasingly shorter spells as the fish go south.'

'And in summer?'

'He fishes for himself, lays dragnets, lobster pots . . . '

The man was sitting on the same bench-seat as Maigret, at the far end of it. But the inspector had a good view of him in a mirror.

He was short, with wide shoulders. He was a typical northern sailor, squat, fleshy, with no neck, pink skin and fair hair. Like most fishermen, his hands were covered with scars of old ulcers.

'Does he usually drink this much?'

'They're all hard drinkers. But he's been really knocking it back since his boy died. Seeing the Océan again hit him hard.'

The man was now staring at them, openly insolent.

275

'What you after, then?' he spluttered at Maigret.

'Nothing at all.'

All the mariners followed the scene without interrupting their game of dominoes.

'Because you'd better out with it . . . A man's not entitled to have a drink, is that it?'

'Not at all!'

'Go on, say it, say I'm not entitled to have a sup or two,' he repeated with the obstinacy of a drunk.

The inspector's eye picked out the black armband he wore on one sleeve of his red jerkin.

'So what you up to, then, sneaking around here, the pair of you, talking about me?'

Léon shook his head, advising Maigret not to reply, and went over to his customer.

'Easy now! Don't go kicking up a fuss, Canut. The inspector's not talking about you but about the lad who shot himself.'

'Serve him right! Is he dead?'

'No. Maybe they can save him.'

'Too bad! I wish they'd all die!'

The words had an immediate impact. All heads turned to stare at Canut, who felt the urge to shout it ever louder:

'That's right! The whole lot of you!'

Léon was worried. He looked imploringly at everyone there, adding a gesture of helplessness in Maigret's direction.

'Go home. Go to bed. Your wife will be waiting up . . . '

'Don't give a damn!'

'In the morning, you won't feel like going out to clear your nets.'

The drunk sniggered. Louis took the opportunity to call to Julie:

'How much does it come to?'

'Both rounds?'

'Yes. Put it on the slate. Tomorrow I'll get my advance pay before I sail.'

He got to his feet. The Breton automatically followed his lead, as if he were his shadow. He tipped his cap. Then he did it again for Maigret's particular benefit.

'Bunch of chicken-hearts!' muttered the drunk as the two men walked past him. 'Cowards, the whole lot of them!'

The Breton clenched his fists and was about to say something. But Louis dragged him away.

'Go home to bed,' Léon repeated. 'Anyway, it's closing time.'

'I'll go when everybody else goes. My money's as good as the next man's, right?'

He looked around for Maigret. It was as if he was ready to start an argument.

'It's like the big fella there . . . What's he trying to ferret out?'

He was referring to the inspector. Léon was on tenterhooks. The last customers lingered, sure that something was about to happen.

'Second thoughts, I think I'd rather go home. What do I owe you?'

He fumbled beneath his jerkin and produced a leather wallet, threw a few greasy notes on the table, stood up, swayed and staggered to the door, which he had difficulty opening.

He kept muttering indistinctly what might have been insults or threats. Once outside, he pressed his face to the window for a last look at Maigret, flattening his nose against the steamed-up glass.

'It hit him real hard,' sighed Léon, returning to his seat. 'He had just the one son. All his other kids are girls. Which is to say they don't count.'

'What are they saying here?' asked Maigret.

'About the wireless operator? They don't know anything. So they make things up. Fanciful tales . . . '

'Such as?'

'Oh, I don't know. They're always on about the *evil eye* . . . '

Maigret sensed that there was a keen eye watching him. It belonged to the chief mechanic, who was sitting at the table opposite.

'Has your wife stopped being jealous?' the inspector asked.

'Given that we sail in the morning, I'd like to see her try to keep me stuck in Yport!'

'Is the *Océan* leaving tomorrow?'

'With the tide, yes. If you think the owners intend to let her fester in the harbour . . . '

'Have they found a new captain?'

'Some retired master or other who hasn't been at sea for eight years. And on top of that, he was then skipper of a three-masted barque! It'll be no fun!'

'And the wireless operator?'

'Some kid they've got straight out of college . . . Some big technical school, they said it was.'

'And is the first mate coming back?'

'They recalled him. Sent him a cable. He'll be here in the morning.'

'And the crew?'

'The usual story. They take whatever's hanging around the docks. It always works, doesn't it?'

'Have they found a ship's boy?'

The chief mechanic looked at him sharply.

'Yes,' he said curtly.

'Glad to be off?'

No reply. The chief mechanic ordered another grog. Léon, keeping his voice low, said:

'We've just had news of the *Pacific*, which was due back this week. She's a sister ship of the *Océan*. She sank in less than three minutes after splitting her seams on a rock. All hands lost. I've got the first mate's wife staying upstairs. She came from Rouen to meet her husband. She spends every day down by the harbour mouth. She doesn't know yet. The Company is waiting for confirmation before breaking the news.'

'It's the design of those boats,' growled the chief mechanic, who had overheard.

The black sailor yawned and rubbed his eyes but was not thinking of leaving just yet. The abandoned dominoes formed a complicated pattern on the grey rectangle of the tabletop.

'So in a word,' Maigret said slowly, 'no one has any idea why the wireless operator tried to kill himself?'

His words met with an obstinate silence. Did all the men there know why? Was this the freemasonry of seamen taken to an extreme, closing ranks against landlubbers who poked their noses into their business?

'What do I owe you, Julie?' asked Maigret.

He stood up, paid, headed wearily to the door. Ten pairs of eyes followed him. He turned but saw only faces that were blank or resentful. Even Léon, for all his barkeeper's chumminess, stood shoulder to shoulder with his customers.

It was low tide. All that could be seen of the trawler was the funnel and the derricks. The trucks had all gone. The quay was deserted.

A fishing boat, with its white light swinging at the end of its mast, was slowly moving away towards the jetties, and the sound of two men talking could be heard.

Maigret filled one last pipe, looked across the town and the towers of the Palais de la Bénédictine, at the foot of which were walls which were part of the hospital.

The windows of the Grand Banks Café punctuated the quay with two rectangles of light.

The sea was calm. There was a faint murmur of water lapping the shingle and the wooden piles of the jetties.

The inspector stood on the edge of the quay. Thick hawsers, the ones holding the *Océan* fast, were coiled round bronze bollards.

He leaned over. Men were battening down the hatches over the holds in which salt had been stowed earlier that day. One of them was very young, younger than Le Clinche. He was wearing a suit and, leaning against the wireless room, was watching the sailors as they worked.

It could only be the replacement for the wireless operator who not long since had put a bullet in his own belly. He was smoking a cigarette, taking shallow, nervous pulls on it.

He'd come straight from Paris, fresh out of the National Technical School. He was apprehensive. Perhaps he dreamed of adventure.

Maigret could not tear himself away. He was rooted there by a feeling that the mystery was close, within his grasp, that he had to make just one last effort.

Suddenly, he turned, sensing a strange presence behind him. In the dark, he made out a red jerkin and a black armband.

The man had not seen him, or at least was not paying him any attention. He was walking along the lip of the quayside, and it was a miracle that in the state he was in that he did not go over the edge.

The inspector now had only a rear view of him. He had a feeling that the drunk, overcome by dizziness, was about to fall down on to the deck of the trawler.

But no. He was talking to himself. He laughed derisively. He brandished a fist.

Then he spat, once, twice, three times on the boat below. He spat to express his total and utter disgust.

After which, doubtless having relieved his feelings, he wandered off, not in the direction of his house, which was in the fishermen's quarter, but towards the lower end of town, where there was a bar still with its lights on.

9

Two Men on Deck

From the cliff side of the town came a silvery chime: it was the clock of the Palais de la Bénédictine, striking one.

Maigret, his hands clasped behind him, was walking back to the Hôtel de la Plage. But the further he went the slower he walked until he finally came to a complete stop halfway along the quay.

In front of him was his hotel, his room and his bed, a welcoming, comforting combination.

Behind him . . . He turned his head. He saw the trawler's funnel, from which smoke was gently rising, for the boilers had just been lit. Fécamp was asleep. There was a wide splash of moonlight in the middle of the harbour. The wind was rising, blowing in off the sea, raw and almost freezing, like the breath of the ocean itself.

Maigret turned back wearily, reluctantly. Again he stepped over the hawsers coiled round the bollards, then stood on the side of the quay, staring down at the *Océan*.

His eyes were small, his mouth threatening, his hands were bunched into fists deep in his pockets.

Here was Maigret in solitary mood, disgruntled, withdrawn, when he digs his heels in defiantly and is not afraid of making a fool of himself.

It was low tide. The deck of the trawler was four or five metres below the level of the quay. But a plank had been laid between the quayside and the bridge. It was thin and narrow.

The sound of the surf was growing louder. The tide must be on the turn. Pallid waves ate imperceptibly into the shingle of the beach.

Maigret stepped on to the plank, which bent into the arc of a circle when he reached the middle. His soles squealed when he reached the iron bridge. But he did not go any further. He sat down on the seat of the officer of the watch, behind the wheel and the compass, from which dangled Captain Fallut's thick sea mittens.

Maigret settled in the way grim dogs crouch stubbornly by the mouth of a burrow where they have got a scent of something.

Jorissen's letter, his friendship with Le Clinche, all the steps taken by Marie Léonnec were no longer the issue. It was now personal.

He had formed a picture of Captain Fallut. He had met the wireless operator, Adèle and the chief mechanic. He had gone to considerable lengths to get a sense of the whole way of life on board the trawler.

But it was not enough. Something was eluding him. He felt he understood everything except, crucially, what was at the heart of the case.

Fécamp was asleep. On board, the sailors were in their bunks. The inspector slumped heavily in the seat of the officer of the watch, round-shouldered, legs slightly apart, his elbows on his knees.

His eye settled on random details: the gloves, for instance, huge, misshapen, which Fallut would have worn during his spells on the bridge and had left hanging there.

And half turning, he looked back over the afterdeck. Ahead were the full sweep of the deck, the foredeck and, very near, the wireless room.

The sound of water lapping. A barely perceptible surge as the steam began to stir. Now that the furnace had been lit and water filled the boilers, the boat felt more alive than it had in the last few days.

And wasn't Louis asleep below, next to the bunkers full of coal?

To the right was the lighthouse. At the end of one jetty, a green light; a red light at the head of the next.

And the sea: a great black hole emitting a strong, heavy smell.

There was no conscious effort of the mind involved, not in the strict sense. Maigret let his eye roam slowly, sluggishly, seeking to bring his surroundings to life, to acquire a feel for them. Gradually he slipped into something akin to a state of trance.

'It was a night like this, but colder, because spring had scarcely begun . . . '

The trawler, tied up at the same berth. A thin spiral of smoke rising from the funnel.

A few sleeping men.

Pierre Le Clinche, who had dined at Quimper in his fiancée's house. Family atmosphere. Marie

284

Léonnec had doubtless shown him to the door, so that they could kiss unobserved.

And he had travelled all night, third class. He would return in three months. He would see her again. Then another voyage and after that, when it was winter, around Christmas time, they would marry.

He had not slept. His sea-chest was on the rack. It contained provisions made for him by his mother.

At the same time, Captain Fallut was leaving the small house in Rue d'Étretat, where Madame Bernard was asleep.

Captain Fallut was probably uneasy and very troubled, racked in advance by guilt. Was it not tacitly agreed that one day he would marry his landlady?

Yet all winter he had been going to Le Havre, sometimes three times a week, to see a woman. A woman he dared not show his face with in Fécamp. A woman he was keeping as his mistress. A woman who was young, attractive, desirable, but whose vulgarity gave her an aura of danger.

A respectable man, of regular, fastidious habits. A model of probity, held up as an example by his employers, whose sea-logs were masterpieces of detailed record-keeping.

And now he was making his way through the sleeping streets to the station where Adèle was due to arrive.

Perhaps he was still hesitating?

But three months! Would he find her waiting for him when he got back? Wasn't she too alive, too eager for life not to deceive him?

She was a very different kind of woman from Madame Bernard. She did not spend her time keeping her house tidy, polishing brasses and floors, making plans for the future.

Absolutely not! She was a woman, a woman whose image was fixed on his retina in ways that brought a flush to his cheek and quickened his breath.

Then she was there! She laughed with that tantalizing laugh which was almost as sensual as her inviting body. She thought it would be fun to sail away, to be hidden on board, to have a great adventure!

But should he not tell her that the adventure would not be much fun? That being at sea cooped up in a locked cabin would be an ordeal?

He vowed that he would. But he didn't dare. When she was there, when her breasts heaved as she laughed, he was incapable of saying anything sensible.

'Are you going to smuggle me on board tonight?'

They walked on. In the bars and the Grand Banks Café, members of the crew went on the spree with the advance on their wages they'd been paid that afternoon.

And Captain Fallut, short, smartly turned out, grew paler the nearer he got to the harbour, to his boat. Now he could see the funnel. His throat was dry. Perhaps there was still time?

But Adèle was hanging on his arm. He could feel her leaning against him, warm and trembling with excitement.

★   ★   ★

Maigret, facing the quayside which was now deserted, imagined the two of them.

'Is that your ship? It smells bad. Have we got to go across on this plank?'

They walked over the gangway. Captain Fallut was nervous and told her to not to make a noise.

'Is this the wheel for driving the ship?'

'Sh!'

They went down the iron ladder. They were on the deck. They went into the captain's cabin. The door closed behind them.

'Yes! That's how it was!' muttered Maigret. 'There they are now, the pair of them. It's the first night on board . . . '

He wished he could fling back the curtain of night, reveal the pallid sky of first light and make out the figures of the crew staggering, slowed by alcohol, as they made their way back to the boat.

The chief mechanic arrived from Yport by the first morning train. The first mate was on the way from Paris and Le Clinche from Quimper.

The men tumbled on to the deck, argued in the foredeck about bunks, laughed, changed their clothes and reemerged stiffly in oilskins.

There was a boy, Jean-Marie, the ship's boy. His father had brought him, leading him by the hand. The sailors jostled him, made fun of his boots, which were too big, and of the tears already welling in his eyes.

The captain was still in his cabin. Finally, he opened the door. He closed it carefully behind

287

him. He was curt, very pale, and his features were drawn.

'Are you the wireless operator? . . . Right. I'll give you your orders in a little while. Meanwhile, take a look round the wireless room.'

Hours passed. Now the boat's owner stood on the quay. Women and mothers were still arriving with parcels for the men who were about to sail.

Fallut shook, fearful for his cabin, whose door was not to be opened at any price, because Adèle, dishevelled, mouth half open, was sprawled sideways, fast asleep, across the bed.

A touch of the early-morning nausea, which was felt not only by Fallut but by all the men who had toured the bars of the town or travelled there overnight by train.

One by one, they drifted away to the Grand Banks Café, where they drank coffee laced with spirits.

'See you soon! . . . if we come back!'

A loud blast of the ship's horn. Then two more. The women and children, after one last hug, rushing towards the end of the breakwater. The ship's owner shaking Fallut's hand.

The hawsers were cast off. The trawler slid forward, moved clear of the quay. Then Jean-Marie, the ship's boy, choking with fright, stamped his feet in desperation and thought of making a bid to get back to dry land.

Fallut had been sitting where Maigret was sitting now.

'Half ahead! . . . One five-oh turns! . . . Full steam ahead!'

Was Adèle still asleep? Would she be woken up

by the first swell and be nervous?

Fallut did not move from the seat which had been his for so many years. Ahead of him was the sea, the Atlantic.

His nerves were taut, for he now realized what a stupid thing he had done. It had not seemed so serious when he was ashore.

'Two points port!'

And then there were shouts, and the group on the breakwater rushed forward. A man, who had clambered up the derrick to wave goodbye to his family, had fallen on to the deck!

'Stop engine! . . . Astern engine! . . . Stop engine!'

There was no sign of life from the cabin. Wasn't there still time to put the woman ashore?

Rowing boats approached the vessel, which was now stationary between the jetties. A fishing boat was asking for right of way.

But the man was injured. He would have to be left behind. He was lowered into a dinghy.

The women were demoralized. They were deeply superstitious.

On top of which the ship's boy had to be restrained from jumping into the water because he was so terrified of leaving!

'Ahead steam! . . . Half! . . . Full! . . . '

Le Clinche was settling into his workplace, headphones on head, testing the instruments. And there, in his domain, he was writing:

My Darling Girl,
    It's eight in the morning! We're off. Already we can't see the town and . . .

289

Maigret lit a fresh pipe and got to his feet so that he would have a better view of his surroundings.

He was in full possession of the characters in the case and, in a sense, was now able to move them around like counters on the boat which lay spread out before him.

'First meal in the narrow officers' mess: Fallut, the first mate, the chief mechanic and the wireless operator. The captain announces that henceforth he will be taking all his meals in his cabin, alone.'

They have never heard the like of it! Such an outlandish idea! They all try in vain to come up with a reason for it.

Maigret, clasping his hand to his forehead, muttered:

'It's the ship's boy's job to take the captain his food. The captain opens the door only part of the way or else hides Adèle under the bed, which he has propped up.'

The two of them have to make do with a meal for one. The first time, the woman laughs. And no doubt Fallut leaves nearly all his share to her.

He is too solemn. She makes fun of him. She is nice to him. He unbends. He smiles.

And up in the foredeck are they not already muttering about the evil eye? Aren't they talking about the captain's decision to eat by himself? And moreover, who ever saw a captain walking around with the key to his cabin in his pocket!

The twin screws turn. The trawler has acquired the sense of unease which will continue to fill it for three months.

Below deck, men like Louis shovel coal into

the maw of the furnaces for eight or ten hours a day or keep a drowsy eye on the oil-pressure gauge.

Three days. That's the general view. It has taken just three days to create an atmosphere of anxiety. And it was at that point that the crew began wondering if Fallut was mad.

Why? Was it jealousy? But Adèle stated that she didn't see Le Clinche until about day four.

Until then, he is too busy with his new equipment. He tunes in and listens, for his personal satisfaction. He makes trial transmissions. And with his headphones constantly on his head, he writes page after page as if the postman was standing by to whisk his letters away and deliver them to his fiancée.

Three days. Hardly time to get to know one another. Perhaps the chief mechanic, peering through portholes, has caught sight of the young woman? But he never mentioned it.

The atmosphere on board builds only gradually as the crew are drawn together through shared adventures. But as yet there are no adventures to share. They have not yet even started to fish. For that they must wait until they reach the Grand Banks, yonder, off Newfoundland, on the other side of the Atlantic, where they will not be for another ten days yet, at the earliest.

★　★　★

Maigret was standing on the bridge, and any man waking then and seeing him would have wondered what he was doing there, an imposing, solitary figure calmly surveying his surroundings.

And what was he doing? He was trying to understand! All the characters were in position, each with a particular outlook and all with their own preoccupations.

But after this point, there was no way of guessing the rest. There was a large gap. The inspector had only witnesses to rely upon.

'It was on about the third day out that Captain Fallut and the wireless operator started thinking of each other as enemies. Each had a revolver in his pocket. They seemed afraid of each other.'

Yet Le Clinche was not yet Adèle's lover!

'But from that moment, the captain behaved as if he was mad.'

They are now in the middle of the Atlantic. They have left the regular lanes used by the great liners. Now they hardly ever sight even other trawlers, English or German, as they steam towards their fishing grounds.

Does Adèle start to grumble and complain about being cooped up?

. . . *wondered if he wasn't actually mad* . . .

Everyone agrees that mad is the right word. And it seems unlikely that Adèle alone is responsible for bringing about such an astonishing change in a well-adjusted man who has always made a religion of order.

She has not deceived him yet! He has allowed her two or three turns around the deck, at night, provided she takes multiple precautions.

So why is he behaving as if he is *actually mad*?

Here the evidence of witnesses begins to mount up:

'He gives the order to anchor the trawler in a position where for as long as anyone can remember no one ever caught a single cod . . . '

He is not an excitable man or a fool, nor does he lose his temper easily! He is a steady, upstanding citizen of careful habits who for a time dreamed of sharing his life with his landlady, Madame Bernard, and of ending his days in the house full of embroidery in Rue d'Etretat.

'There's one accident after another. When we finally get on to the Banks and start catching fish, it gets salted in such a way that it's going bad by the time we get back.'

Fallut is no novice! He's about to retire. Until now, no one has ever had reason to question his competence.

He takes all his meals in his cabin.

'He doesn't talk to me,' Adèle will say. 'He goes for days, weeks sometimes, without saying a word to me. And then suddenly it comes over him again . . . '

A sudden wave of sensuality! She's there! In his cabin! He shares her bed! And for weeks on end he manages to stay at arm's length until the temptation proves too strong!

Would he behave this way if his only grievance was jealousy?

The chief mechanic prowls round the cabin, licking his lips. But he doesn't have the nerve to force the lock.

And finally, the Epilogue. The *Océan* is on the

293

way home to France, laden with badly salted cod.

Is it during the voyage back that the captain draws up what is virtually his will in which he says no one should be accused of causing his death?

If so, he clearly wants to die. He intends to kill himself. No one on board, except him, is capable of taking a ship's bearings, and he has enough of the seafaring spirit to bring his boat back to port first.

Kill himself because he has infringed regulations by taking a woman to sea with him?

Kill himself because insufficient salt was used on the fish, which will sell for a few francs below the market rate?

Kill himself because the crew, bewildered by his odd conduct, believe that he is a lunatic?

The captain, the most cool-headed, the most scrupulously careful master in all Fécamp? The same man whose log books are held up as models?

The man who for so long has been living in the peaceful house of Madame Bernard?

The steam vessel docks. The members of the crew rush on shore and make a bee-line for the Grand Banks Café, where they can at last get a proper drink.

And every man jack of them is stamped with the mark of mystery! On certain questions they all remain silent. They are all on edge.

Is it because a captain has behaved in ways that no one understands?

Fallut goes on shore alone. He will have to

wait until the quays are deserted before he can disembark Adèle.

He takes a few steps forwards. Two men are hiding: the wireless operator and Gaston Buzier, the girl's lover.

But the captain is jumped by a third man, who strangles him and drops his body into the harbour.

★ ★ ★

And all this happened at the very spot where the *Océan* is now gently rocking on the black water. The body had got tangled in the anchor chain.

Maigret was smoking. He scowled.

'Even at the first interview, Le Clinche lies when he talks about a man wearing tan-coloured shoes who killed Fallut. Now the man with the tan-coloured shoes is Buzier. When he is brought face to face with him, Le Clinche retracts his statement.'

Why would he lie about this if not to protect a third person, in other words the murderer? And why wouldn't Le Clinche name him?

He does no such thing. He even lets himself be put behind bars instead of him. He makes little effort to defend himself, even though there is every likelihood that he will go down for murder.

He is grim, like a man riddled with guilt. He does not dare look either his fiancée or Maigret in the eye.

One small detail. Before returning to the trawler, he headed back to the Grand Banks

Café. He went up to his room. He burned a number of papers.

When he gets out of jail, he isn't happy, even though Marie Léonnec is there, encouraging him to look on the bright side. And somehow he manages to get hold of a revolver.

He is afraid. He hesitates. For a long time he just sits there, eyes closed, finger on the trigger.

And then he fires.

★　★　★

As the night wore on, it turned cooler, and the smell of seaweed and iodine weighed more strongly on the breeze.

The trawler had risen by several metres. The deck was now level with the quayside, and the push and drag of the tide caused the boat to buck sideways and made the gangway creak.

Maigret had forgotten how tired he was. The hardest time was over. It would soon be dawn.

He summarized:

Captain Fallut, who had been retrieved dead from the anchor chain.

Adèle and Gaston Buzier, who argued all the time, reached the stage where they could not stand each other and yet had no one else to turn to.

Le Clinche, who had been wheeled out on a trolley, swathed in white, from the operating theatre.

And Marie Léonnec . . .

Not forgetting the men in the Grand Banks

Café, who, even when drunk, seemed haunted by painful memories . . .

'The third day!' Maigret said aloud. 'That's where I need to look!'

Something much worse than jealousy . . . *But something which flowed directly from the presence of Adèle on board the boat.*

The effort took it out of him. The effect of the strain on all his mental faculties. The boat rocked gently. A light came on in the foredeck, where the sailors were about to get up.

'The third day . . . '

His throat contracted. He looked down on the afterdeck and then along the quay, where, hours before, a man had leaned over and brandished a fist.

Maybe it was partly the effect of the cold and maybe not. But either way he suddenly shivered.

'The third day . . . The ship's boy, Jean-Marie, who kicked up a fuss because he did not want to go to sea, was swept overboard by a wave, at night . . . '

Maigret's eye ran round the whole deck, as if trying to determine where the accident had happened.

'There were only two witnesses, Captain Fallut and the wireless operator, Pierre Le Clinche. The next day or the day after that, Le Clinche became Adèle's lover!'

It was a turning point! Maigret did not loiter for another second. Someone was stirring in the foredeck. No one saw him stride across the plank connecting the boat to dry land.

With his hands in his pockets, his nose blue

297

with the cold, unsmiling, he returned to the Hôtel de la Plage.

It was not yet light. Yet it was no longer night because, out at sea, the crests of waves were picked out in crude white. And gulls were light flecks against the sky.

A train whistled in the station. An old woman set out for the rocks, a basket on her back and a hook in her hand, to look for crabs.

10

What Happened on the Third Day

When Maigret left his room and came downstairs at around eight that morning, his head felt empty and his chest woolly, the way a man feels when he has drunk too much.

'Aren't things going the way you'd like?' asked his wife.

He had given a shrug, and she had not insisted. But there on the terrace of the hotel, facing a frothing, sly-green sea, he found Marie Léonnec. And she was not alone. There was a man sitting at her table. She stood up quickly and stammered to the inspector:

'May I introduce my father? He's just got here.'

The wind was cool, the sky overcast. The gulls skimmed the tops of the water.

'An honour to meet you, sir. Deeply honoured and most happy . . . '

Maigret looked at him without enthusiasm. He was short and would not have been any more ridiculous to look at than the next man but for his nose, which was disproportionately large, being the size of three normal noses and, furthermore, was stippled, like a strawberry.

It wasn't his fault. But it was a physical affliction. And it was all anyone saw. When he spoke it was the only thing people looked at, so that it was impossible to feel any sympathy for him.

'You must join us in a little . . . ?'

'Thank you, no. I've just had breakfast.'

'Perhaps a small glass of something, to warm the cockles?'

'No, really.'

He was insistent. Is it not a form of politeness to make people drink when they don't want to?

Maigret observed him and observed his daughter, who, apart from that nose, bore him a strong resemblance. By looking at her in this light, he was able to get a picture of what she would be like in a dozen years, when the bloom of youth had faded.

'I'll come straight to the point, inspector. That's my motto, and I've travelled all night to do just that. When Jorissen came to me and said that he would accompany my daughter, I gave him my permission. So I don't think anyone could say that I am at all narrow-minded.'

Unfortunately Maigret was anxious to be elsewhere. Then there was the nose. And also the pompous tone of the middle-class worthy who likes the sound of his own voice.

'Even so, it's my duty as a father to keep myself fully informed, don't you agree? Which is why I'm asking you to tell me, in your heart and conscience, if you think this young man is innocent.'

Marie Léonnec did not know where to look. She must have known deep down that her father's initiative was unlikely to help arrange matters.

As long as she had been by herself, rushing to the aid of her fiancé, she had seemed rather admirable. Or at any rate she made a touching figure.

But now, inside the family, it was another matter. There was more than a whiff here of the shop back in Quimper, the discussions which had preceded her departure, the tittle-tattle of the neighbours.

'Are you asking me if he killed Captain Fallut?'

'Yes. You must understand that it is essential that . . . '

Maigret stared straight in front of him in his most detached manner.

'Well . . . '

He noticed the girl's hands, which were shaking.

'No, he didn't kill him. Now, if you'll excuse me, there's something I really must attend to. I shall doubtless have the pleasure of meeting up with you later . . . '

Then he turned tail! He fled so fast that he knocked over a chair on the terrace. He assumed that father and daughter were startled but did not turn round to find out.

Once on the quay, he followed the paved walkway. The *Océan* was some distance away. Even so, he noticed that a number of men had arrived with their sailor's kitbags slung over their shoulders and were getting their first sight of the boat. A cart was unloading bags of potatoes. The company's man was there with his polished boots and his pencil behind his ear.

There was a great deal of noise coming from the Grand Banks Café. Its doors were open, and Maigret could just make out Louis holding forth in the middle of a circle of the 'new' men.

He did not stop. Though he saw the landlord making a sign to him, he hurried on his way. Five minutes later he was ringing the bell of the hospital.

★   ★   ★

The registrar was very young. Visible under his white coat were a suit in the latest fashion and an elegant tie.

'The wireless operator? It was I who took his temperature and pulse this morning. He's doing as well as can be expected.'

'Has he come round?'

'Oh yes! He hasn't spoken to me, but his eyes followed me around all the time.'

'Is it all right if I talk to him about important matters?'

The registrar waved a hand vaguely, an indifferent gesture.

'Don't see why not. If the operation has been a success and he hasn't got a temperature, then . . . You want to see him?'

Pierre Le Clinche was by himself in a small room with distempered walls. The air was hot and humid. He watched Maigret coming towards him. His eyes were bright, and there was not a trace of anxiety in them.

'As you see, he's making excellent progress. He'll be on his feet in a week. On the other

302

hand, there's a chance that he'll be left with a limp, for a tendon in his hip was severed. And he'll have to take care. Would you prefer it if I leave you alone with him?'

It was really quite disconcerting. The previous evening, a bleeding, unwholesome mess had been brought which could not possibly, it seemed, have harboured the faintest breath of life.

And now Maigret found a white bed, a face that was slightly drawn and a little pale which was more tranquil now than he had ever seen it. And there was what looked like serenity in those eyes.

That is perhaps why he hesitated. He paced up and down the room, leaned his head for a moment against the double window, from which he could see the port and the trawler, where men in red jerkins were busily moving about.

'Do you feel strong enough to talk to me?' he growled, firing the question without warning as he turned to face the bed.

Le Clinche assented with a faint nod of his head.

'You are aware that I am not officially involved in this case? My friend Jorissen asked me to prove your innocence. It is done. You are not the killer of Captain Fallut.'

He sighed deeply. Then, to get it over with, he put his head down and charged:

'Tell me the truth about what happened on the third day out, I mean about the death of Jean-Marie.'

He avoided looking directly at the patient. He

filled a pipe as a way of appearing casual and when the silence went on and on, he murmured:

'It was evening. There were only Captain Fallut and you on deck. Were you standing together?'

'No!'

'The captain was walking near the afterdeck?'

'Yes. I'd just left my cabin. He didn't see me. I watched him because I felt there was something odd about the way he was behaving.'

'You didn't know at that point that there was a woman on board?'

'No! I thought that if he was being so careful about keeping his door locked, it was because he was storing smuggled goods inside.'

The voice was weary. And yet, it became suddenly more emphatic for he said distinctly:

'It was the most terrible thing I ever saw, inspector! Who talked? Tell me!'

And he closed his eyes, exactly as he had as he sat waiting for the moment when he would fire a bullet through his pocket into his belly.

'Nobody. The captain was strolling on deck, feeling apprehensive no doubt, just as he had ever since he'd left port. Was there anybody at the wheel?'

'A helmsman. He couldn't see us because it was dark.'

'The ship's boy showed up . . . '

Le Clinche interrupted him by heaving himself half up, both hands gripping the rope hanging from the ceiling which enabled him to change his position.

'Where's Marie?'

'At the hotel. Her father has just come.'

'To take her back! Fair enough. He should take her home. But whatever happens, she mustn't come here!'

He was getting worked up. His voice was flatter and its flow more broken.

Maigret could sense that his temperature was climbing. His eyes were becoming unnaturally bright.

'I don't know who has been talking to you. But it's time I told you everything.'

His agitation had reached such a pitch, and was so vehement, that he looked and sounded as if he was almost raving.

'It was awful! You never saw the kid. Skinny's not the word. Wore clothes made from an old cut-down canvas suit of his father's . . . On the first day, he'd been scared and he blubbed. How can I explain . . . Afterwards he got his own back by playing nasty tricks on people. What do you expect at his age? Do you know what *a little brat* is? Well, that was him. Twice I caught him reading the letters I wrote to my fiancée. He'd just look me brazenly in the eye and say:

' 'Writing to your bit of fluff?'

'That evening . . . I think the captain was walking up and down because he was too jumpy to sleep. There was quite a swell on. From time to time, a green sea would wash over the foredeck rail and flood across the metal plates of the deck. But it wasn't a storm.

'I was maybe ten metres from them. I only heard a few words but I could see their shapes. The kid was on his high horse, he was laughing.

And the captain stood there, his neck sunk in his jerkin and his hands in his pockets . . .

'Jean-Marie had talked about my 'bit of fluff' and he must have been taking the same sort of rise out of Fallut. He had a piercing voice. I remember catching a couple of words:

' 'And if I ever told everybody how . . . '

'I didn't understand until later . . . He'd found out that the captain was hiding a woman in his cabin. He was full of himself. There was a swagger about him. He wasn't aware of how vindictive he was being.

'Then this is what happened. The captain raised one hand to give him a cuff over the ear. The kid was very nimble and ducked. Then he shouted something, probably another threat about telling what he knew.

'Fallut's hand struck a rigging stay. It must have hurt like the devil. He saw red.

'It was the fable of the lion and the gnat all over again. Forgetting he was a ship's master, he started chasing the kid. At first, the boy ran off laughing. The captain started to panic.

'A chance remark and anyone who heard it would know everything. Fallut was out of his mind with fear.

'I saw him reach out to catch Jean-Marie by the shoulders, but instead of grabbing hold of him he pushed him over, head first . . .

'That's it. Fatalities occur. His head collided with a capstan. I heard the sound, it was awful, a dull thud. *His skull . . .* '

★   ★   ★

He held both hands up to his face. He was deathly pale. Sweat streamed down his forehead.

'A big wave swept over the deck at that moment. So it was a waterlogged body that the captain bent down to examine. At the same time, he caught sight of me. I don't think it crossed my mind to hide. I started walking towards him. I got there just in time to see the boy's body clench and then stiffen in a reflex that I'll never forget.

'Dead! It was so senseless! The two of us looked at each other, not taking it in, unable to understand what an appalling thing had happened.

'No one else had seen or heard anything. Fallut didn't dare touch the boy. It was me who felt his chest, his hands and that crumpled skull. There was no blood. No wound. Just the skull, which had cracked.

'We stayed there for maybe a quarter of an hour, not knowing what to do, grim, shoulders frozen, while at intervals the spray lashed our faces.

'The captain was not the same man. It was as if something inside him had been broken too.

'When he spoke, his voice was sharp, without warmth.

' 'The crew mustn't learn the truth! Bad for ship's discipline.'

'And while I looked on, he himself picked the boy up. Then just one more effort. Though . . . though I do remember that with his thumb he made the sign of the cross on the boy's forehead.

'The body, which had been snatched by the sea, was swept back twice against the hull. Both of us were still standing in the dark. We did not dare look at each other. We didn't dare speak.'

Maigret had just lit his pipe, clamping his teeth hard on the stem.

A nurse came in. Both men watched her with eyes that seemed so vacant that she was disconcerted and stammered:

'Time to take your temperature.'

'Come back later!'

When the door closed behind her, the inspector asked:

'Was it then that he told you about the woman?'

'From then on, he was never the same again. He probably wasn't certifiably mad. But there was definitely something unhinged about him. He put one hand on my shoulder and murmured:

'"And all because of a woman, young man!"

'I was cold. I was not thinking straight. I couldn't take my eyes off the sea on the side where the body had been carried away.

'Did they tell you about the captain? A short, lean man with a face full of energy. He usually spoke in terse, unfinished phrases.

'That was it! Fifty-five years old. Coming up to retirement. Solid reputation. A little put by in the bank. All over! Finished! In one minute! Less than a minute. On account of a kid who . . . No, on account of a woman . . .

'And then and there, in the darkness, in a quiet, angry voice, he told me the whole story, bit by bit. A woman from Le Havre. A woman who couldn't have been up to much, he was well aware of that. But he couldn't live without her . . .

'He'd brought her with him. And the moment he did, he had a sudden feeling that her presence on board would mean trouble.

'She was there. Asleep.'

The wireless operator began to fidget restlessly.

'I can't remember everything he told me. For he had this need to talk about her, which he did with a mixture of loathing and passion.'

' "A captain is never justified in causing a scandal likely to undermine his authority."

'I can still hear those words. It was my first time out on a boat and I now thought of the sea as a monster which would swallow us all up.

'Fallut quoted examples. In such a year such and such a captain, who had brought his mistress along with him . . . There were so many fights on board that three men never came back.

'The wind was strengthening. The spray kept coming at us. From time to time, a wave would lick at our feet which kept sliding on the slippery metal deck.

'He wasn't mad, oh no! But he wasn't Fallut any more either.

' "See this trip through and then we'll see!"

'I didn't understand what he meant. He struck me as being both sensible and freakish, a man still clinging to his sense of duty.

' "No one must know! A captain can never be in the wrong!"

'My nerves were so strung out I was ill with it. I couldn't think any more. My thoughts were all jumbled up in my head, and by the finish it felt as if I was living through a waking nightmare.

'That woman in the cabin, the woman a man like the captain could not live without, the woman whose very name made him catch his breath.

'And there was me writing reams and reams to my fiancée, who I wouldn't be seeing again for three months, and I never felt obsessed, possessed like that! And when he said words like her *flesh* or her *body* I felt my cheeks go hot without knowing why.'

Maigret put the question slowly:

'And no one, apart from the two of you, knew the truth about the death of Jean-Marie?'

'No one!'

'And was it the captain who, in the customary way, read out the prayers for the dead?'

'At first light. The weather had got thick. We were steaming through icy grey mist.'

'Didn't the crew say anything?'

'There were funny looks and some whispering. But Fallut was more authoritarian than ever, and his voice had acquired a new cutting edge. He would not tolerate any answering back. He got angry with anyone who looked at him in a way he didn't like. He spied on the men, as if he was trying to detect any suspicions they might be getting.'

'What about you?'

Le Clinche didn't answer. He stretched out one arm for a glass of water on his bedside table and drank from it greedily.

'So you began prowling round the cabin more often, didn't you? You wanted to see this woman who had got so far under the captain's skin? Did you start the following night?'

'Yes. I ran into her, just for a moment. Then the next night . . . I'd noticed that the key to the wireless room was the same as the key of the cabin. It was the captain's watch. I crept in, like a thief.'

'You went to bed with her?'

The wireless operator's face hardened.

'I swear you won't understand, you can't! The whole atmosphere was nothing like anything that happens in the real world. The kid . . . the previous day's ceremony . . . But whenever I thought about it, the same picture kept surfacing in my mind, the image of a woman unlike any other, a woman whose body, whose flesh could turn a man into something that he was not.'

'She led you on?'

'She was in bed, half-dressed . . . '

He turned bright scarlet. He looked away.

'How long did you stay in the cabin?'

'Maybe a couple of hours, I don't remember. When I left with the blood still pounding in my ears, the captain was there, just outside the door. He didn't say a word. He watched me walk past. I almost went down on my knees so I could say it wasn't my fault and that I was sorry. But he remained stony-faced. I walked on. I returned to my post.

'I was scared. After that, I always went around with my loaded revolver in my pocket because I was convinced he was going to kill me.

'He never spoke to me again, except for ship's business. And even then, most of the time he sent me his orders in writing.

'I wish I could explain it better, but I can't. Each day it got worse. I had a feeling that everybody knew about the terrible thing that happened.

'The chief mechanic went sniffing around the cabin too. The captain stayed inside it for hours and hours.

'The men started giving us inquisitive, anxious looks. They guessed that something was going on. How many times did I hear talk of the evil eye?

'But there was only one thing I wanted . . . '

'Of course there was,' grunted Maigret.

There was a silence. Le Clinche stared at the inspector with eyes full of resentment.

'We ran into bad weather, ten days on the trot. I was seasick. But I kept thinking about her. She was . . . fragrant! She . . . I can't explain. It was like a pain. That's it! A desire capable of inflicting pain, of making me weep tears of rage! Especially when I saw the captain go into his cabin. Because now, I could imagine . . . You see, she'd called me her *big boy*! In a special voice, sort of breathy. I kept saying those two words over and over to torture myself. I stopped writing to Marie. I built impossible dreams: I'd run away with that woman the moment we got back to Fécamp.'

'What about the captain?'

'He got even more stony-faced and brusque.

312

Maybe there was a touch of madness about him after all, I don't know. He gave orders that we were to fish at some location or other, and all the old hands claimed no one had ever seen a fish in those waters. He refused to have his orders questioned. He was afraid of me. Did he know I had a gun? He had one too. Whenever we met, he kept his hand near his pocket. I kept trying to see Adèle again. But he was always around, with bags under his eyes and his lips drawn back. And the stink of cod. The men who were salting the fish down in the hold . . . There was one accident after another.

'And the chief mechanic was also on the prowl. It got so that none of us spoke freely any more. We were like three lunatics. There were nights when I believe I could have killed somebody to get to her. Can you understand that? Nights when I tore my handkerchief to shreds with my teeth while I repeated over and over, in the same voice that she had used:

"*My big boy! That's my big fool!*'

'How long it seemed! Each night was followed by a new day! And then more days! And with nothing but grey water around us, freezing fogs, fish-scales and cod guts everywhere!

'A taste of pickling brine in the back of the throat that made your stomach heave . . .

'Just that once! I believe that if I could have gone to her one more time I'd have been cured! But it was impossible. *He* was there. He was always there, more hollow-eyed all the time.

'The constant pitching and tossing, with

313

nothing as far as the eye could see. And then we saw cliffs!

'Can you grasp the fact that it had been like that for three months? Well, instead of being cured, I was even sicker. It's only now that I'm beginning to realize that it was a sickness.

'I hated the captain who was always in my way. I detested that man who was already old and kept a woman like Adèle under lock and key.

'I was afraid of returning to port. I was afraid of losing her for ever.

'By the finish, I was as scared of him as of the devil himself! Yes, as if he were some kind of evil genie who was keeping the woman all to himself!

'As we got in, there were a few navigation errors. Then the men jumped ashore, relieved to be back, and headed straight for the bars. But I knew the captain was only waiting for the cover of night to get Adèle off the boat.

'I went back to my room over Léon's bar. There were old letters, photos of my fiancée and the like, and I don't know why but I got into a vile temper and I burned the whole lot.

'Then I went back out. I wanted her! I'll say it again: I wanted her! Hadn't she told me that when we got back Fallut would marry her?

'I bumped into a man . . . '

He let himself slump back on to his pillow, and on his tortured features appeared an expression of agonized torment.

'Because you know . . . ' he gasped.

'Yes. Jean-Marie's father. The trawler was berthed. Only the captain and Adèle were still on board. He was about to bring her out. And then . . . '

'Please, no more!'

'And then you told the man who had come to look at the boat on which his boy had died that his son had been murdered. True? And you followed him. You were hiding behind a truck when he went up to the captain . . . '

'Stop!'

'The murder happened there, while you watched.'

'Please stop!'

'No! You were there when it happened. Then you went on board and let the woman out.'

'I didn't want her any more!'

From outside came a long blast of a hooter. Le Clinche's lips trembled as he stammered:

'The *Océan* . . . '

'That's right. She sails at high tide.'

Neither of them spoke. They could hear all the sounds made in the hospital, down to the muffled swish of a patient's trolley being wheeled to the operating theatre.

'I didn't want her any more!' the wireless operator repeated wildly.

'But it was too late!'

There was another silence. Then Le Clinche's voice came again:

'And yet . . . now . . . I want so much to . . . '

He did not dare pronounce the word that stuck to his tongue.

'Live?'

Then he went on:

'Don't you understand? I was mad. I don't

understand it myself. It all happened elsewhere, in another world . . . Then we got back here, and I realized what had been happening. Listen. There was that dark cabin and men prowling round, and nothing else existed. I felt as if that was my whole life! I longed to hear those words again, *my big boy!* I couldn't even begin to say how it all happened. I opened the door. She slipped out. There was a man in tan-coloured shoes waiting for her, and they started hugging each other on the side of the quay.

'And I woke up — it's the only word for it. And ever since all I've wanted is not to die. Marie Léonnec came with you to see me. Adèle came too, with that other man.'

'What do you want me to say?'

'It's too late now, isn't it? I was let out of jail. I went on board and got my revolver. Marie was waiting for me by the boat. She didn't know . . .

'And that same afternoon, that woman was there, talking. And the man in the tan-coloured shoes . . .

'Who could possibly make sense of it all? I pulled the trigger. It took me an age to bring myself to do it, on account of Marie Léonnec, who was there!

'And now . . . '

He sobbed. Then he literally screamed:

'All the same, I've got to die! And I don't want to die! I'm afraid of dying! I . . . I . . . '

His body was racked by such spasms that Maigret called a nurse, who quietly and unfussily subdued him with an economical ease born of long professional experience.

316

The trawler gave a second harrowing summons on its hooter, and the women hurried down to line the jetty.

11

The *Océan* Sails

Maigret reached the quay just as the new captain was about to give the order to cast off the hawsers. He caught sight of the chief mechanic, who was saying goodbye to his wife. He went up to him and took him to one side.

'Something I need to know. It was you, wasn't it, who found the captain's will and dropped it into the police station letterbox?'

The man looked worried and hesitated.

'You've nothing to worry about. You suspected Le Clinche. You thought that it was a way of saving his neck. Even though you both had had your eye on the same woman.'

The hooter, peremptory now, barked at the latecomers, and hugging couples on the quayside peeled away from each other.

'Don't bring all that up again, do you mind? Is it true that he's going to die?'

'Unless we can save him. Where was the will?'

'Among the captain's papers.'

'What exactly were you looking for?'

'I was hoping to find a photo,' the man said, lowering his eyes. 'Look, let me go, I've got to . . . '

The hawser fell into the water. The gangway was being raised. The chief mechanic jumped on to the deck, gave his wife a last wave and cast a final look at Maigret.

Then the trawler headed slowly towards the harbour entrance. A sailor lifted the ship's boy, who was barely fifteen, on to his shoulders. The boy had got hold of the man's pipe and was proudly clenching it between his teeth.

On the land, women were weeping.

By walking quickly, they could follow the vessel, which did not pick up speed until it was clear of the jetties. Some voices were shouting out reminders:

'If you come across the *Atlantique*, don't forget to tell Dugodet that his wife . . . '

The sky was still low and threatening. The wind pressed down on the water, ruckling its surface and raising small white-crested waves, which made an angry washing sound.

A Parisian in whites was taking photos of the departing trawler. He had two little girls in white dresses in tow. They were laughing.

Maigret collided with a woman, almost knocking her over. She clutched his arm and asked:

'Well? Is he better?'

It was Adèle, who hadn't powdered her nose since at least that morning, and the skin of her face was shiny.

'Where's Buzier?' asked the inspector.

'He said he'd rather go back to Le Havre. He doesn't want any trouble. Anyway, I said I was finishing with him. But what about that boy, Le Clinche?'

'Don't know.'

'Go on, you can tell me!'

319

Absolutely not. He turned and left her standing there. He'd picked out a group on the jetty: Marie Léonnec, her father and Madame Maigret. All three were facing in the direction of the trawler which for a moment drew level with them. Marie Léonnec was saying fervently:

'That's *his* boat!'

Maigret slowly walked towards them, in a surly mood. His wife was the first to spot him among the crowd which had gathered to see the trawler set off for the Grand Banks.

'Did he pull through?'

Monsieur Léonnec, looking anxious, turned his misshapen nose in his direction.

'Ah! I'm so glad to see you. Where are you with your inquiries, inspector?'

'Nowhere.'

'Meaning?'

'Nothing . . . I don't know.'

Marie opened her eyes wide.

'But Pierre?'

'The operation was a success. It seems he'll be all right.'

'He's innocent, isn't he? Oh please! Tell my father he didn't do it!'

She put her whole heart into the words. Contemplating her, he saw how she would be in ten years' time, with the same look as her father, a somewhat overbearing manner ideally suited to dealing with customers in the shop.

'He didn't kill the captain.'

Turning to his wife:

'I've just had a telegram calling me back to Paris.'

'So soon? I'd promised to go swimming tomorrow with . . . '

She caught his eye and understood.

'If you'll excuse us.'

'We'll walk back to the hotel with you.'

Maigret saw Jean-Marie's father, dead drunk, still brandishing his fist at the trawler, and looked away.

'Don't put yourselves out, please.'

'Tell me,' said Monsieur Léonnec, 'do you think I could arrange for him to be transferred to Quimper? People are bound to talk.'

Marie looked pleadingly at him. She was very pale. She said in a faltering voice:

'After all, he is innocent.'

'I don't know. You are better placed . . . '

'But at least you must allow me to offer you something? A bottle of champagne?'

'No thanks.'

'Just a glass of something? Benedictine, for example, since we're in the town where . . . '

'A beer, then.'

Upstairs, Madame Maigret was shutting their cases.

'So you share my opinion, then. He's a fine boy who . . . '

She still had that little-girl look about her! The look that pleaded with him to say yes!

'I think he'll make a good husband.'

'And be a good hand at business!' said her father, going one better. 'Because I won't have him sailing the high seas for months on end. When a man's married, he has a responsibility to . . . '

321

'Goes without saying.'

'Especially since I have no son. Surely you can understand that!'

'Of course.'

Maigret was keeping an eye on the stairs. Eventually, his wife appeared.

'The luggage is all ready. They say there's not a train until . . . '

'Doesn't matter. We'll hire a car.'

It was a getaway!

'If ever you have occasion to be in Quimper . . . '

'Yes, yes . . . '

And the way the girl looked at him! She seemed to have understood that things were not all as straightforward as they seemed, but her eyes pleaded with Maigret not to say any more.

She wanted her fiancé.

The inspector shook hands all round, paid the bill and finished his beer.

'Thank you so much Detective Chief Inspector Maigret.'

'There really is no need.'

The car which had been hired by phone arrived.

so unless you have come up with something which I have missed, I shall sign off with a recommendation that the case be closed.

This was a passage from a letter sent by Chief Inspector Grenier, of the Le Havre Police, to Maigret, who replied by telegraph:

Agreed.

Six months later, he was sent a card through the post, which said:

Madame Le Clinche has great pleasure in announcing the wedding of her son, Pierre, and Mademoiselle Marie Léonnec, which . . .

And shortly afterwards, when in connection with another inquiry he was looking round a certain kind of establishment in Rue Pasquier, he thought he recognized a young woman who looked quickly away.

Adèle!

And that was all. Or not quite. Five years later, Maigret was on a short visit to Quimper. He saw the proprietor of a chandler's shop, standing in his doorway. He was still a young man, very tall with the beginnings of a paunch.

He walked with a slight limp. He called to a toddler of three, who was playing with his top on the pavement.

'Come in now, Pierrot. Your mother will be cross!'

The man, too preoccupied with his offspring, did not recognize Maigret, who in any case quickened his step, looked away and pulled a wry face.